Praise for
Juliet Landon

A Scandalous Mistress
"…sensual and emotion-filled read…"
—*RT Book Reviews*

Dishonour and Desire
"…lush and fervid descriptions…her deep knowledge
of the era and willingness to deal with social issues
without taking the focus off the romance makes
this an enjoyable novel."
—*RT Book Reviews*

The Rake's Unconventional Mistress
"Landon's understanding of the social mores and
language of the era flow through the pages."
—*RT Book Reviews*

His Duty, Her Destiny
"Landon has written a titillating and entertaining
battle of the sexes…"
—*RT Book Reviews*

The Bought Bride
"Landon carefully creates the atmosphere of the eleventh
century, incorporating intriguing historical details…"
—*RT Book Reviews*

Juliet LANDON

Scandalous Innocent

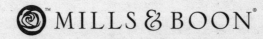

MILLS & BOON

First published in Great Britain 2010
Harlequin Mills & Boon Limited,
Eton House, 18-24 Paradise Road, Richmond, Surrey TW9 1SR

© Juliet Landon 2010

ISBN: 978 0 263 88764 8

027-0610

Harlequin Mills & Boon policy is to use papers that are
natural, renewable and recyclable products and made from
wood grown in sustainable forests. The logging and
manufacturing processes conform to the legal environmental regulations
of the country of origin.

Printed in Great Britain
by Clays Ltd, St Ives plc

*Novels by **Juliet Landon**:*

MARRYING THE MISTRESS
THE RAKE'S UNCONVENTIONAL MISTRESS ★
DISHONOUR AND DESIRE ★
A SCANDALOUS MISTRESS ★
THE WARLORD'S MISTRESS
HIS DUTY, HER DESTINY
THE BOUGHT BRIDE
THE WIDOW'S BARGAIN
ONE NIGHT IN PARADISE

★ *Ladies of Paradise Road* trilogy

Author Note

The name Tollemache is the family name of the Earls and Countesses of Dysart that originated in 1649 when Elizabeth Murray married Sir Lionel Tollemache, a country gentleman with ancestors dating back to the Norman Conquest. Ham House was the Murray family home where Elizabeth (the Duchess of our story) was brought up.

Ham House was built in the year 1610 beside the River Thames, only one-and-a-half miles from Richmond in the county of Surrey. The beautiful Jacobean mansion might have suffered severe damage during the Civil War if the mistress of the house, Catherine Murray, and her daughter Elizabeth Tollemache (who became Countess of Dysart after her father's death in 1655), had not shown friendship to Oliver Cromwell, although they and their relatives were staunch Royalists. Elizabeth knew John Maitland, second Earl of Lauderdale, at this time, but it was not until her husband and the Earl's wife died that they married. In 1672, the Earl was created Duke of Lauderdale, after which began a programme of extensions, renovations and costly refurbishings at Ham House in order to tempt the King, Charles II, and his wife Catherine of Braganza, to stay there. The Duke was an important member of the King's inner cabinet, High Commissioner for Scotland, and Secretary of State. The Duchess was a very ambitious and clever woman, but her excessive spending was to be the cause of much anguish in later years.

So much is true. Where the facts begin to merge into fiction is shown in the episodes in Part I of my story, where the Duchess and her family play a part in the relationship between the fictional Sir Leo Hawkynne and Mistress Phoebe Laker. The place names, Richmond, Ham and Mortlake, are factual, but the houses of the fictional characters do not exist.

Ham House was inherited by Wilbraham, sixth Earl of Dysart in 1799. Apparently, he was as I have described him, kind, generous, cultured, a patron of the arts and well loved.

I hope that by including real characters in a fictional setting I have kept, broadly speaking, within the confines of their characters although, by the sound of things, the Duke and Duchess of Lauderdale were even more extrovert in every way than I have made them. Not for one moment do I think it would have been beyond them to interfere atrociously in the affairs of other people. In fact, one could easily write a book devoted entirely to these two alone, fact often being stranger than fiction.

Acknowledgements

I would like to thank the National Trust staff at Ham House for their generous help during my visits, particularly Gary Calland, the Property Manager, and the on-duty room guides whose expertise never once wavered under my deluge of seemingly abstruse questions. Their knowledge was put to good use.

My son-in-law, Brian Evans, helped me to negotiate the rooms, levels and gardens via ramps, lifts and circuitous routes with great enthusiasm and patience, and to him I owe my thanks for entering into the spirit of the venture so wholeheartedly.

Last, but by no means least, my thanks go to my wonderful editor, Linda Fildew, who proposed the Ham House project and steered me safely through every critical phase of publication. Her support and approval have always been the mainstay of my work with Mills & Boon, and *Scandalous Innocent* is truly a collaborative effort.

FAMILY TREE

CONFIDO CONQUIESCO
I trust and am content

Owners of Ham
are shown in CAPITALS
Asterisk denotes a portrait
in the house

WILLIAM MURRAY, 1st EARL OF DYSART* = Katherine Bruce*
(c.1600–55) | (d.1649) of Clackmannan

ELIZABETH MURRAY = (1) Sir Lionel Tollemache, 3rd Bt*
COUNTESS OF DYSART later COUNTESS | (1624–69)
and DUCHESS OF LAUDERDALE* | (2) John Maitland, 2nd Earl and 1st Duke
(1626–98) | of Lauderdale* (1616–1682)

MARGARET
LADY
MAYNARD*
(c.1638–82)

ANNE
(d.1679)

KATHERINE
(d.1666/70)

LIONEL TOLLEMACHE = Grace
3rd EARL OF DYSART* | Wilbraham
(1649–1727) | (d.1740)

Gen. Thomas*
(c.1651–94)

Capt. William
(d.1694)

Elizabeth, Lady Lorne,
later Duchess of Argyll*
(d.1735)

Katherine, Viscountess Doune,
later Countess of Sutherland
(1661–1703)

Lionel Tollemache (1682–1712) = Henrietta Cavendish*
Viscount Huntingtower | (d.1717/18)

LIONEL TOLLEMACHE = Lady Grace Carteret*
4th EARL OF DYSART* (1708–70) | (1713–55)

LIONEL = (1) Charlotte Walpole*
TOLLEMACHE | (1738–89)
5th EARL OF DYSART* | (2) Magdalena Lewis
(1734–99) | (d.1823)

Frances*
(1738–
1807)

WILBRAHAM = Anna Maria
TOLLEMACHE | Lewis
6th EARL OF DYSART* | (1745–1804)
(1739–1821)

John* = Lady
(1744–77) | Bridget
| Lane
| Fox

Lionel Robert* (1775–93)

LOUISA = John
COUNTESS OF | Manners
DYSART* | (1730–92)
(1745–1840)

Jane = (1) John
(1750– | Halliday
1802) | (2) George
| Ferry

Admiral John (Halliday) Tollemache* = Lady Elizabeth Stratford
(1772–1837) | (d.1861)

Sir William Tollemache, Viscount Huntingtower (1766–1833) = Catherine Gray
cr. Bt 1793, assumed name and arms of Tollemache 1821 | (1766–1852)

Hugh = Matilda Hume
(1802–90) | (d.1873)

John, cr. Baron Tollemache = Georgina Best
of Helmingham | (d.1846)
(1805–90)

LIONEL TOLLEMACHE = Elizabeth Toone
8th EARL OF DYSART* | (d.1869)
(1794–1878)

Felix = Sarah Gray
(1796–1843) | (d.1831)

Wilbraham = (1) Lady Emma Stuart (d.1869)
2nd Baron Tollemache | (2) Hon. Mary Hamilton
(1832–1904) | (d.1939)

Hamilton = Mabel
(1853–93) | Hanbury
| (d.1941)

William Tollemache = Katherine
Viscount Huntingtower | Burke
(1820–72) | (1822–96)

Ralph = Caroline Tollemache
(1826–95) | (1828–67)

Hon. Lyonel = Lady
(1860–1902) | Blanche
| King

Edward = Violet
(1885– | Ridgeway
1947) | (d.1970)

Caroline
(d.1867)

Agnes = Charles
(1853– | Scott
1912) | (1853–1938)

Sir Lyonel Tollemache, = Hersilia
4th Bt (1854–1952) | Collingwood
jointly gave Ham to NT 1948 | (d.1953)

Bentley = Wynford
3rd Baron Tollemache | Kemball
(1883–1955) | (d.1926)

John, 4th Baron = Dinah
Tollemache | Jamison
(1910–75)

WILLIAM TOLLEMACHE = Cecilia
9th EARL OF DYSART* | Onslow Newton
(1859–1935) | (d.1917)

Sir Cecil Lyonel = Nora
Tollemache, 5th Bt | Taylor
(1886–1969) | m.1926

Sir Humphry = Dinah
6th Bt
(1897–1990)

Sir Lyonel, 7th Bt = Mary Whitbread
(b.1931) | m.1960

Timothy, 5th Baron = Alexandra
Tollemache (b.1939) | Meynell

Wynefrede = Owain Greaves
(1882–1941)
(1889–1972) | m.1913

Katherine, Countess of Dysart = John Peter Grant
(b.1918) m.1941 | of Rothiemurchus (d.1987)

Rosamund, Countess of Dysart
(1914–2003)

© National Trust 2009

PART ONE 1676

CHAPTER ONE

'SO, I'M TO SEE the wee lass for myself at last, am I?' the Duke of Lauderdale asked his Duchess, supporting her as they took the first step down the grand staircase. Automatically, his Scottish parsimony showed as his heavy-lidded eyes caught the lavish gilding over the carved wooden panels. 'How much did you say this cost?'

'Gilding doesn't come cheap, my lord. Even as a girl, I longed for these shields and helmets and things to be painted. Plain wood can be so dull. As for Phoebe, you must not think I've been keeping her from meeting you, you know. No such thing. But if I told her you'd be here, she'd turn round and go straight back to Mortlake like a hare with a pack of hounds on its tail. Thing is, I think it's time something was done about it after three years.'

'About what? Leo? You matchmaking again, Duchess? If so, I think you might be wasting your time. They canna stand the sight of each other.'

'They're both still unmarried, John. That tells me something.'

They had reached an angle in the staircase just out of sight from above or below when John Maitland, Duke of Lauderdale, caught his wife round her stiffly boned waist, as she knew he would, and pulled her against him with all the vigour of a man thirty years younger. He was, in fact, fifty-nine years old. The Duchess was forty-nine, both of them more enamoured by their second spouses than ever they'd been by their first, despite the eleven pregnancies she'd endured as the wife of Sir Lionel Tollemache.

'Elizabeth,' he growled in the Scottish brogue that had steadfastly spurned the polish of the English court, 'gimme a kiss, woman, and stop yer scheming a while. Leo's never been short of women, you know that.'

'It's not your Leo I care about, my dear,' she tried to say before her reply was stopped by a smothering kiss that tasted of porridge, smoked bacon and everything breakfasty. She didn't mind the taste at all. In four years of marriage, it was John's enforced absences at court and in Scotland that she disliked most. As Secretary of State for Scotland, he was often obliged to be away for weeks, hence his need to make up for the time he'd lost out of her arms. Yes, she could tolerate his healthy appetites as well as he could tolerate hers, even her appetite for ostentation.

'Four years, and I'm still like a green lad with you, lass.'

Elizabeth smiled against his warm cheek. 'Oh, I wouldn't say that, my lord. There was nothing of the green lad about you last night, was there? Will you be around when Mistress Laker arrives?'

'Aye, if you wish it. Or shall we let Leo meet her alone?'

She held him away, carefully removing a pale red hair from his shoulder that obviously did not belong to his periwig. 'Don't be provoking, dreadful man. Of course we shall not. You and I will be there together, and Leo can appear later on. She knows *he*'ll be here, if you are.'

Sir Leo Hawkynne, personal assistant and secretary to the Duke of Lauderdale, was as Scottish as his master although, being thirty years his junior, had become more flexible and receptive to all the courtesies that oiled diplomatic wheels and soothed sensitive egos. There had been times in the past, however, when his natural northern tendency for blunt speaking had earned him enemies, which concerned him more than the Duke's notorious tactlessness. One such occasion had been three years ago when a chance remark had tripped thoughtlessly off Leo's tongue in relation to Mistress Phoebe Laker which she, understandably, had taken exception to as soon as she'd heard it from green-eyed gossips. There had been little love lost between them even before this incident, and less so afterwards, but the repercussions had been tragic, to say the least, since when Phoebe had only visited Elizabeth at Ham House when she knew the Duke and his faithful secretary would not be in residence. To Phoebe's mind, Scotland was not too far away for them.

'As you wish. There's some paperwork for him to do in my library.' The Duke took her hand again, leading her down to the great hall where a large billiard table occupied the centre of the black-and-white marble floor. A fire burned in the iron fireplace on the largest wall, even though it was June, and on the mantelshelf stood two large plaster figures in Graeco-Roman helmets, their scanty drapes defying gravity. Mars and Minerva, Elizabeth had explained to her husband's initial and not altogether polite astonishment, based on her own mother and father, the first Earl and Countess of Dysart. As the eldest daughter, Elizabeth was now a Countess in her own right, since the Scottish title was allowed to pass into the female line, but the higher-ranking title of Duchess was the one by which she had been known these last four years.

'Good,' she said. 'Then keep him there till I give the word. Phoebe has not seen all the latest additions yet.'

'No more have I,' said the Duke. 'Whose idea was the billiard table?'

Elizabeth could see the expenses adding up inside his head, and was quick to forestall the inevitable questions. 'It was mine, John. It's for you. Oh, dear, you're not going to chide me for overspending, are you? It *has* to look right, dear, after all the rebuilding. It's no use hoping the royals will stay, is it, if we don't offer them the very best?'

'Och, lassie! I've never chided you on that, have I? The place badly needed more rooms and a wee lick o' paint, I know, and you had to replace the plate that was melted doon for the last King's war. Is that why you've invited your friends over, so they can take a peek at all your newest gee-gaws?'

Patting her bunched red-gold ringlets, Elizabeth frowned at a footman who appeared at the outer door. 'No, not entirely. I asked Phoebe again because her mama and I were good friends, and because I promised her I'd keep an eye on Phoebe if anything should happen. Well, it did, didn't it? So I've kept my promise. What is it, man?' she snapped at the hovering footman who had opened and closed the door several times while she was talking. 'You can see…*what?* Oh, my lord!'

Through the wobbly green-glass squares of the hall

windows, the dark shape of a coach and two horses had appeared as if from nowhere, though the drive leading from the road was clearly visible all the way down to the river. Guessing that his orders were about to change, the footman threw open the heavy doors just in time for her Grace's voluminous green-brocade skirts to squeeze through the gap and for her to sweep down the first shallow flight of steps before halting uncertainly.

Hesitation was not one of Elizabeth's besetting sins, yet the events she was sure she'd timed to perfection had not taken account of Mistress Laker's enthusiasm and now, instead of the two antogonists being kept apart until the precise moment their hostess decreed, they were there, facing each other like two cats in a stand-off, bristling with surprise.

Yet it was Elizabeth's appearance that redirected Mistress Laker's attention from the uncomfortable situation in which neither she nor Sir Leo had offered a single word of greeting. Having arrived on the scene too late to make himself useful, Sir Leo bowed as she emerged like a beautiful butterfly from the low-slung coach, the floating blue-and-silver tissue that trailed from one silk-clad shoulder adding to the illusion. Her neat ankles disappeared beneath the hem of the deep blue silk skirt, her feet encased in shoes of matching blue satin with silver buckles. Froths of white lace spilled out of her sleeves, and a sapphire winked from somewhere as it caught the sun. She was, he thought, even lovelier than he remembered her and probably even more prickly with three extra years of practice since they had last met. Fashions had evolved at the pace of King Charles II's mistresses, the latest one from France, and Mistress Phoebe Laker had kept up with them with very little effort. Her abundant black ringlets needed neither curl-papers nor extra hair to bulk them out, as others did. They bounced as she walked, framing the perfect oval of her face with coiled wisps like watch-springs, and the delicate arch of her eyebrows lifted a fraction as she ran towards her friend. There were twenty-six years between them, but they embraced like sisters.

'Dearest Phoebe…*what* a delight!'

'My dear lady, I know I'm early but I couldn't wait. I made Sam Coachman hurry the horses, poor things. Do forgive me.'

'Forgive you indeed! We're all on tenterhooks, my dear. Sir Leo could hardly wait for you to arrive.'

'Really? How *sweet*.' Phoebe laughed, glancing over one shoulder at the athletic figure sending the coachman and her lady's maid round to the side. 'But if I'd known he'd…'

'Yes, dear,' Elizabeth cut short the protest, 'but it's been four years since our wedding and you *still* have not met my Duke. See, here he is. Allow me to present you. My lord?' she said, beckoning to her husband who ambled down the steps. 'Mistress Phoebe Laker, my favourite neighbour.' The wedding had been a very private affair conducted only two months after the death of the first duchess. There had been talk, of course.

'Aboot time too, lass!' the Duke bellowed, bowing.

Phoebe's curtsy was appropriately low and graceful as she took stock of the great man who was a member of King Charles's inner circle of ministers, an active, scholarly and energetic man for all his size, typically hard-living, respected but not universally adored. His large loose features were crowded by a long mouse-brown periwig that flapped upon his shoulders as he came to stand erect. But there was nothing of the sloven about him: his Duchess had seen to that.

The hooded eyes took in everything about her at one glance, and Phoebe knew he would have been made aware of her antipathy towards his secretary for, as she came up from her curtsy, she saw that the two men's eyes had met over the top of her head. 'Your Grace,' she murmured, deciding against offering her cheek for him to kiss until she could be more sure of him.

The Duke was not one to mince his words. 'A fine bonny lass,' he said. 'I can see now why my Duchess has kept ye out of my sight for sae long. Welcome to Ham Hoose, Mistress Laker. Sir Leo, come ye here, man, and make your courtesies as if ye meant it.'

Smiling ruefully at the command, Sir Leo came forwards. 'Mistress Laker and I met some years ago, my lord. Your servant, ma'am.' Whether tinged with cynicism or not, none of them could tell, but his bow was lower than his master's and made with an extravagant sweep of his arm, with an ostrich-plumed hat to make it even more so. He rose only a second later than Phoebe from her shallow curtsy, his deep brown eyes holding hers, allowing them to reveal the clear memory of what had passed between them to cause her such appalling heartache. It had not been her doing but his, and clearly she had not forgiven him. Her cold eyes told him so, but she could not, as a guest, impose this upon her hosts.

Nevertheless, she could renew her own memory of his heart-stopping good looks in one dismissive glance. As usual, he scorned to wear a wig, his own dark glossy thatch being swept back from a high intelligent forehead in deep waves that overlapped the tops of his ears, gathered at the nape of his neck by a dark ribbon. Ribbon bunches fluttered from shoulders, neck and boots, red against the long charcoal-grey vest, coat and breeches with gold buttons by the yard on deep braided pockets, deep cuffs above the elbows, puffs of white linen shirt below, and a fall of fine lace over his knuckles, a leather sword-belt slung across his chest. Instead of plain hose and buckled shoes, he wore brown leather bucket-top boots with red heels, and Phoebe could just see the lace tops to his hose nestling inside them. His well-paid position permitted him to adopt the latest styles, but he was more than capable of setting his own for others to follow. The spurs on his boots suggested that he intended to ride.

'If you were about to ride out, Sir Leo, please don't let my arrival detain you,' Phoebe said, knowing that her tone was betraying her.

The Duke was soothing. 'Whisht, lass,' he said. 'Dinna send him off sae soon, not before he's—'

'Yes, dear,' interrupted the Duchess, catching his drift, 'but first Mistress Laker will wish to take a little refreshment after her journey.' She took Phoebe by the hand. 'Come, my dear. Did you not bring Mrs Overshott with you this time? Or did she go round with your luggage?'

'No, my lady, a slight indisposition, that's all, so I told her I could manage well enough with you to chaperon me, this time. She sends her regards, and her apologies. She would like to have seen the newest alterations. You've had the gardens restyled too, have you not?' Her glance round from the top of the steps at the green lawns and flower-beds happened to collide with Sir Leo's which, far from being subdued by her icy manner, was regarding her with a directness that made her blink and turn away in some confusion. *You will not dismiss me as easily as that,* it said. *If you don't like my being here, you'll have to get used to it.*

'Indeed I have,' said the Duchess, giving her skirts a shake. 'Even the Duke has not seen the latest changes. He and Sir Leo arrived only last night.'

'Oh, I see. Then…?'

Just behind her shoulder, Sir Leo gave a huff of laughter as he answered. 'No, mistress, we shall not be going anywhere. Not for a wee while. Did you hope we would?'

'Of course she didn't, Leo. Don't be so provoking. Now, which of you gallant gentlemen is going to open the door? What in *heaven's* name is the matter with the footmen today? Thank you.'

Sweeping through into the great hall, the sudden change of light sent a cold shiver down Phoebe's arms, and the event to which she had looked forward with such eagerness now took on all the aspects of a burden to which, yet again, she would have to bring all her reserves of light-heartedness in order to convince those around her that she was carefree.

To her credit, Elizabeth, Duchess of Lauderdale, took her friendships very seriously. She and Phoebe's mother had formed an affection twenty years ago while Phoebe and her elder brother Timothy were still in their infancy. Master Adolphus Laker had been an exceedingly prosperous banker and goldsmith with enough wealth to forge connections in society and clients in Court circles. Elizabeth and her first husband had purchased gold and silver plate from the Laker premises at the Royal Exchange in London, neither of them being too high and mighty to include merchants amongst their friends.

It was the Great Plague of 1665 that had put a grisly end to it when Master Laker and his wife became victims within days of each other. They had been exemplary parents, and the shock to Phoebe and her brother was severe. Although still young, Timothy had set about buying a new house for him and his sister in the country further up the Thames at Mortlake where they could live well away from such terrors. At the same time, he had revived his father's business after so great a decline in the population. Compared to some, the brother and sister had counted themselves fortunate, living together with a distant relative named Mrs Overshott who had nursed their parents through that terrible time.

Then, as had happened to so many others, disaster struck again in the September of the following year when the Great Fire destroyed so much of the city of London, including the Royal Exchange where the Lakers' business was. Only fate could have dealt Phoebe such a cruel blow, for after Timothy had removed all the valuable contents of the shop and transported them to Mortlake for safe keeping, he had returned to London to collect the paperwork on which the business depended: order books and receipts, stock and pattern books, tools and correspondence.

But he had left it too late, for the building was already ablaze and unsafe when he arrived, and he and his manager were trapped in the the Exchange as it crashed. Phoebe never recovered his remains. She was virtually alone without a family. Wealthy and safe, but alone and without a single grave to mark her losses.

The usual procedure for a young lady in her position would have been to go and live with her nearest relative, but wild horses could not have dragged her up to Manchester to live with an aged widowed aunt who had made no contact in all Phoebe's thirteen years. So she remained in the care of Mrs Overshott who, while being distant in relationship terms, was devoted to her, and sensible of her privileged position. And although the house at Mortlake was too large for them, Phoebe clung to it as to a life raft, being the one place where the spirit of her beloved brother still remained. The people of Mortlake gave her their support in every way possible, but there was only so much they could do to ease her grief.

Predictably, those traumatic events left their mark on her, not least of which was a feeling of guilt at being the only one left in the family, as if she had somehow been marked out for special treatment. Why her? Why had she been left the wealth that they had worked so hard to acquire? And what had her brother meant when he had told her he had to get something for her? Was

it her fault he had died? No one, it seemed, could provide an acceptable answer to that, or to the dark trou-
bles that haunted her adolescent years. She grew into
the kind of beauty that brought her instant attention,
and friends, and power to sail through the teething
pains of youth at too fast a pace, taking whatever was
offered before it could be snatched away from her
again.

The one person to whom life had also dealt some
unkindness, the one Phoebe would talk to about herself, was Elizabeth, then the Countess of Dysart. She
too had had a stormy upbringing during the violent
Commonwealth of Oliver Cromwell when her father
had had to escape danger and leave her mother to hold
Ham House against possession by soldiers, alone with
four daughters, three of whom had disabilities. Elizabeth,
the only healthy one, had married Sir Lionel
Tollemache, but had lost all but five of her eleven children. Yet she had always had time for Phoebe whenever Phoebe could find time for her.

Elizabeth wished it had been oftener, especially
after hearing how the blossoming young beauty had
attracted the attentions of young blades on the lookout for wealthy wives, particularly innocent and helpless ones with no parents to get in the way. No
warnings could slow Phoebe down. Her reputation as
a wild beauty reached the Royal Court. No event was
complete without her. Elizabeth had heard how Mis-

tress Phoebe Laker was living life as if, without any warning, it might all come to a violent end before she could sample its gifts, and not even Elizabeth could make her understand that life's gifts have a price, and that some of them are more expensive than others. It was only Mrs Overshott's gentle restraint that saved Phoebe from acquiring more than a reputation for wildness.

Moving through to the new south side of the house, Phoebe was impressed by the size, the opulence, the vivid colour schemes that were the Duchess's hallmark. 'We've doubled the size,' the Duchess said, proudly. 'Come through to the new dining room. I think you'll like it.'

The Duke and Sir Leo followed. 'You'd better say you do, lass,' the Duke mumbled, 'or there'll be nothing but bread and water for your dinner.'

'Nonsense!' his wife chided him, simpering a little. 'How could she not like it? This is the smaller of the two, Phoebe. The larger one is above the hall. Well, one cannot entertain royalty in a room of *this* size, can one? And the hall is really not convenient any more,' she said to the Duke's shaking head.

Privately, Phoebe thought that the continuation of the black-and-white chequered floor might have been better changed to polished wood. But the Duchess's conspicuous display of wealth was, she supposed, a reaction to those early years of childbearing when the

Civil War had prevented any thoughts of spending except on essentials. Now, it was as if she was wading
knee-deep in the brilliance of her new position, for all
the rooms into which she led them, while pointing out
the newest acquisitions, blazed with gilt and shone
with marble. There were polished wood and crimson
curtains, fringed cushions and fat tassels everywhere
hanging from ropes of satin, cherubs, cornucopia, lacquered cabinets, obscene caryatids holding up ornate
tables, gilded mirrors, picture frames and portraits by
the score, flowery plasterwork ceilings, heavily patterned curtains hiding painted gold-knobbed shutters,
knobs, scrolls, barley-sugar legs and velvet seats with
yet more braid. She must have bought the stuff by the
mile, Phoebe thought, imagining the poor upholster-
ers buried under mountains of it, crying out for air and
plain surfaces.

The Duke and Duchess were examining the inside
of a cabinet when a whisper at Phoebe's shoulder reminded her, 'You must say you like it, you know. It
gets worse…er…better.'

Quickly, she turned to find the voice that had spoken her thoughts out loud, stopping the answering
smile before it could show in her eyes, before he could
think he was to be rewarded by even the smallest
token. The chill in her voice was already there. 'Don't
waste your precious time talking to me, sir,' she remarked sharply under her breath. 'If I'd known you'd

be here, I would have stayed at home to tend my gentlewoman.' She would like to have rejoined her hosts as they strolled away into the hall, but Sir Leo was in the way and, as her eyes signalled her intention, he moved aside to stop her.

'What, and miss all this?' he whispered, unsmiling. 'You may not wish to see me here, Mistress Laker, but after three years I think it's time to put matters straight between us, don't you?'

Her eyes blazed with dark fury. 'I don't wish to see you anywhere, sir, and matters are as straight as they'll ever be. Disapproval and dislike on your part, pure hatred on mine. There. What could be straighter than that?'

'It cannot continue, even if it were true that I dislike you. As it happens, I don't.'

'Sir Leo, I really do not care in the slightest whether you do or not. All I know is that I do not wish to be reminded of what happened, when I've spent the last three years trying to forget. The duel you fought was not to defend *my* honour but your own, and the result of that débâcle was the loss of a good man's life, directly or indirectly, depending on whose side you're on. If you think three years is enough to erase the memory of that tragedy, then you know less about women than you claim to.'

'Then it's up to me to convince you, isn't it?'

Like quicksilver, she dodged round him, arching her

body to evade his arm, running to the doorway through which voices floated. Her silk skirts crackled angrily. 'Find something more rewarding to do,' she said, 'and leave me alone.'

He let her go. 'That, Mistress Phoebe Laker, is something I shall not be doing, whatever your wishes,' he murmured, sauntering after her.

It was not quite so difficult for Phoebe to admire her beautiful yellow bedroom upstairs on the first floor when the sun had begun to slant across the satin-covered walls, flooding the yellow-curtained bed with light. Conveniently placed at the top of the staircase, two smaller rooms snuggled next to hers in the angle of the south front where her maid Constance had been given a small bed, to be near her mistress.

'Now this is completely new,' said the Duchess, sliding a heavily ringed hand over the marquetry lid of a writing desk. 'And the tapestries came originally from the Mortlake factory when it was still in full production, but I may move them yet. A good price they were, too.'

Fortunately, Phoebe was not obliged to comment, for the Duchess had seen from the window that more coaches were rolling down the long drive, and she was quite suddenly abandoned. The last time she had seen Ham House was when it was surrounded by scaffolding, workmen's huts and piles of bricks and wood. The hammering had been constant, the dust and mud on every surface, Elizabeth constantly interfering and scolding.

From the window, she watched the green brocade figure emerge from the door below on the south side to lean over the stone balustrade at the top of the double steps before tripping down to meet her guests. Footmen ran to catch at door handles before the coaches stopped. No one, Phoebe thought, could fault the Duchess of Lauderdale as a hostess.

Much further up the drive where it passed through the trees of the Wilderness, she noticed a lone rider on a dapple-grey horse turn to watch as the coaches reached the house. The horse pranced restively, eager to go on. A red plume in the rider's hat fluttered in the breeze, and Phoebe saw the white flash of lace against the grey coat, and she knew instantly by the lurch of her disobedient heart who it was. His head lifted towards the upper window where she stood and, instead of scuffling back out of sight, she remained there defiantly, exchanging looks with him until he lifted his hat and swung it to one side in acknowledgement before replacing it. Then he turned and rode away. After their harsh words, anyone might have supposed he was leaving, but Phoebe knew otherwise. He was not that kind of man.

It was not the first time she had watched him ride away, although on previous occasions he had always been in the grand company of his master, whose business took him from the Royal Court in a retinue to rival that of any other minister of state. The Duke was a powerful man in every sense. His men reflected this, and none more so than Sir Leo, able, intelligent, honest and with enough influence for his opinions to be heeded. A man in his position could not afford liaisons with any but the best-bred and best-regarded women, of whom Phoebe could not count herself one. The daughter of a goldsmith, given to bouts of imprudent behaviour, the subject of gossip and innuendo, beautiful, wealthy and under no man's protection and therefore open to any kind of verbal criticism, whether deserved or not. No, she could never have won the approval of a man like him.

For her part, Phoebe had been no more immune to Sir Leo's attractions than any other woman visiting the Royal Court but, unlike them, she had taken care never to let him know how he affected her, how she longed for a man like him to be her guardian, her lover, her powerful keeper. His reputation was linked to more mature women with faultless pedigrees, women of the Queen's household whose lives were as peripatetic as his, who were unconcerned by his frequent departures to Scotland for months at a time. Even if she had not been so in awe of him, and afraid of her unreciprocated feelings for him, his long absences would have made it difficult for her to form any kind of relationship and, in any case, he had never shown any real interest in her or her friends.

Occasionally, she had seen him looking her way, mostly during those embarrassing moments when the loud laughter of her group or a silly prank had made her long to be a hundred miles away. Naturally, he would believe her to be an unsuitable addition to his circle of friends, and she would not give him the satisfaction of trying to convince him otherwise. The man had enough pride already. His disapproval showed in his curt bows when she passed by, in his glances and in his silence whenever they met in a stately dance. Their hands touched, but although she would have responded to any invitation to linger, she was never the one with whom he stayed to talk.

It had been at times like that when she had most resented the clinging company of Sir Piers Kelloway, a possessive young man with an overdeveloped sense of chivalry, almost medieval in its intensity, whose insistence in being wherever *she* was had at first been endearing, and then annoying. He had written her love poems, sung his verses to her, dogged her footsteps, took her part in arguments as if she could not do that herself; when a chance remark had come to his ears, he had passed it on to Phoebe with childlike innocence, then immediately had challenged the one who had made it—Sir Leo Hawkynne—to take back the remark and apologise, or to fight a duel of honour.

Deaf to all Phoebe's pleading, the self-styled protector had been determined to play the part to the hilt,
though he was well aware of Sir Leo's reputation as
one of England's best swordsmen. Prepared to die for
her, Sir Piers would not listen to reason, not to
Phoebe's, or his friends', or to Sir Leo himself, who
had declared he didn't know what all the fuss was
about since he'd only been stating an opinion that had
nothing to do with anyone except himself and Mistress
Laker, who must surely have heard such a thing before. Sir Piers was no friend of his, but neither was he
an enemy, but there was nothing he could say to dis-
suade him except the apology he would not make. If
the fool wanted to make an exhibition of himself, Sir
Leo had said, then let him.

The Duchess's information regarding Phoebe's wild
behaviour was out of date, since they had not met for
at least two years, in spite of the few miles between
them. The Duchess had been fully occupied in her new
role as wife of one of England's most senior ministers,
in London at her Whitehall Palace apartment, or on her
other estates and dealing with her massive building
projects. Two years had sped past with little opportunity to exchange news. Had they seen each other oftener in a social context instead of all the near-misses
of coming and going, Elizabeth would probably have
noticed how Phoebe's manner had swung so much in

the opposite direction, since the scandal that had shocked their friends. Now, far from revolving in a wide circle of fawners and flatterers, she had gained a different reputation for being unattainable, bordering on aloofness. The scandal involving Sir Leo Hawkynne and Sir Piers Kelloway had affected her deeply and, without parents to advise her and the Duchess too often unavailable, Phoebe had reacted in the only way she knew, by *over*reacting.

It was only when the Duchess's guests began to assemble at around two o'clock for the main meal of the day that she saw a side of her beloved Phoebe that was unfamiliar to her. She had warned her husband to expect a certain amount of playful teasing and some coquetry. His first bluff greeting had offered Phoebe a chance to respond flirtatiously, but she had not responded. 'Is she not weel?' he said to his wife in a loud whisper. 'I thought there'd be some fluttering o' those lashes, at least.'

'Oh, she'll come round,' said the Duchess. 'I've placed her between Sir Geoffrey and Lord Salisport. She knows them both. She'll warm up with them.' But she was wrong. Phoebe did not warm up to anything like the degree her hostess had expected, for which she did not know whether to be relieved or disappointed.

On the other hand, Sir Leo had heard rumours of Phoebe's sea-change and was curious to discover whether her aversion was to the male sex in general or only towards himself. Seated opposite her at the dining table, he noticed how seldom she smiled, how she responded to her companions very soberly, refusing their flirtations and not playing one off against the other as she would once have done. Nor had there been any fluttering of eyelashes. So, he thought, his information had not been wrong. From once being anybody's, she was determined to be nobody's, and if that sounded too much like overstating the case, blame it on his northern education that thrived on such masculine absurdities.

She had, in fact, never been anybody's, for the only man to whom she would once have given herself, if she'd been asked, was the one whose insult had hurt her more than if all her friends combined had delivered it. He was the man who sat opposite her at the table, the one who would ever speak his mind in a roomful of sycophants, the one she would gladly run through with a sword, given half a chance. The strange thing was that, until today, she had barely exchanged a word with him.

Without the unsettling presence of Sir Leo close at hand, Phoebe would have stood a better chance of enjoying the rest of the afternoon and evening; being acquainted with most of the company, she found it easy to get to know the others. The Duchess's two young daughters were there, Elizabeth and Katherine

Tollemache, old enough at seventeen and fifteen to take their place amongst the guests, but not old enough to disguise their infatuation with Sir Leo. Wherever he went, whoever he spoke to, their eyes followed him like spaniels'.

After dinner they all strolled out into the sunny gardens to admire the parterres, the fragrant orangery and aviary, the fountain-garden and the statues that surrounded the great house on all sides. The north avenue led to the river where the Duke's barge was moored ready for journeys to London, with steps down to the water's edge where swans reached for the scraps they had taken. Then on through the meadow they strolled, splitting off into twos and threes towards the viewing platforms at either end of the Melancholy Walk, and the banqueting house where they were to partake of the sweets and delicacies that completed the meal.

Lord Salisport, a young gallant who appeared to sprout bunches of fluttering ribbons and bows from every seam like a tree in blossom, had known Phoebe for several years, on and off, but could not be called one of nature's more perceptive individuals except in the latest modes, of which he missed nothing that would add to his personal finery. Supposing that her unresponsiveness was no more than an affectation, he threw a knowing wink at his friend, Sir Geoffrey

Mawes, a like-minded fop who, although a pleasant enough fellow, would have accepted anyone's offer of entertainment at the drop of a hat. Especially when he too felt that Mistress Laker was not as flirtatious as he remembered her being some years ago.

At ease in their undemanding company, Phoebe thought nothing of climbing up to the new viewing platform behind Lord Salisport, wishing to see along the river as much as he apparently did. But when she found herself enclosed by both men with none of the other ladies to accompany them, she became first impatient and then angered by the men's familiar hands on her waist, their expressions disturbingly impertinent. She turned to go, but could find no way round them.

'C'mon, Phoebe,' whispered Lord Salisport, touching the end of one dark ringlet. 'It's not like you to be so standoffish. Is it because Hawkynne is here? Eh?'

Pushing hard against his lace-covered coat, Phoebe frowned and tried to lean away from his leering face, but she was held rigid by the boned stays inside her bodice, and with Sir Geoffrey close behind her she was trapped between them, their closeness both oppressive and dangerous. She tried to twist away from pawing hands, jabbing hard with her elbows. 'Stop…stop!' she shouted. 'This is insulting behaviour. This is *not* what I came here for.'

The small viewing platform was suddenly crowded

with yet another body that cut out the light from the
doorway, and although she was not prone to hyster-
ics, the sense of imminent threat and loss of control
sent messages to every part of her body, making her
lash out wildly in all directions. Frantic and swamped
with fear, she kicked like a mule at everything she
could reach and, for a few brief seconds, there was
pandemonium when her fingers managed to reach one
of the men's wigs.

'His Grace the Duke and his Duchess are on their
way here, my lords.'

The deep voice was coloured by a soft Scottish lilt
that made the announcement sound more like a reprim-
and than an invitation to leave, and all at once the attentions of the two men were redirected to themselves,
to the straightening of wigs and the adjusting of lace
cravats. Fending off Phoebe's fists, their hands
dropped away, prinking and pulling at coats, and then
without a word they disappeared through the door and
down the wooden steps.

Phoebe felt her face go into a kind of spasm as she
tried to regain control, her gasps saying more than
words about the distress she was suffering. She realised Sir Leo was watching her and, once again,
found herself caring what he must be thinking, and
hating herself for caring. Of all people, why must it
be him?

He glanced towards the two departing figures, then

back at her, but came no closer. 'Did they harm ye?' he said, softly.

Placing a hand to her forehead, she felt the dampness there. 'No,' she said.

'The Duchess is not here yet. There's no great hurry.'

She wiped her nose with the back of her hand and sniffed. 'Oh, my cuff!' she whispered. 'The lace… 'tis torn. Oh!'

'Here, let me see. Lift your arm. Hold still.'

Obediently, she held her arm up while he tucked the loose piece between two pins. Her arms were mottled with an angry pink and her breathing would not settle. 'I suppose you think I asked for it, don't you?' she said, firing up at his silence. 'Well, I didn't. I came up here to see…to look…oh, why should I care *what* you think? You'll think the worst, won't you? You always did.'

'You'd hardly be so upset if you'd asked for it, would you? I'm not blind, lass. I can see what happened. I was following.'

'Why?'

'Why? Huh! Those two are as daft as balm-cakes, that's why. I could see how hard they tried over dinner, and they don't take women anywhere to look at the view.'

'So I suppose I should have known that,' she replied sharply.

'Hush, lass. Calm down. Do you want to put your lace collar straight before we go? It might be best.'

Glancing from shoulder to shoulder, she tried, but without a mirror could not be sure it was level. 'Is that it?' she said. 'I can't see.'

He smiled, and without asking permission reached out to hitch up one side by a fraction and then, as if he'd done this kind of thing a dozen times, tied the ribbon that held her sleeve to her bodice at the shoulder. 'I don't know how you managed to clout either of them with your arms pinioned to your sides by this lot,' he said. 'It's a wonder you didn't burst a seam. There. Ready now?'

She nodded. 'Thank you.'

'No charge,' he said with a smile.

He went first, helping her down the steps and strolling with her by his side along the river bank, neither of them speaking. But nor did he have the slightest notion that Phoebe could still feel the warm touch of his fingers upon her shoulder where he'd adjusted her collar. And he had called her *lass,* as if he didn't care whether she hated him or not.

CHAPTER TWO

THEIR UNHURRIED WALK gave Phoebe time to notice that they both wore green, the colour of hope. How inappropriate, she thought. Sir Leo's green was that of pine forests with patterns of acanthus leaves woven into the brocade. It must have cost him a fortune, with its clusters of satin ribbons and gold buttons. She noticed also that he did not wear the long vest that was the latest fashion, but a short jacket that showed a lot of white linen shirt around his middle, and more shirt showed where his buttons were undone, still more below the short jacket sleeves. Her eyes were drawn to one hand showing beneath the lace cuff, its thumb idly hooked into the gold-and-green sword-sash slung across him. No man would be correctly attired without his sword.

She had heard of his prowess with the rapier long before she saw him for the first time. Such men were a breed apart and confident to the point of arrogance, especially a Scot whose arrogance would have been fed to him with his mother's milk. Soon after his notorioius duel with Sir Piers Kelloway and the events that followed, Phoebe had started taking daily lessons from one of England's best fencing masters, an Italian by birth, Signor Luigi Verdi. Not that she expected to use her new skills in combat, but one never knew these days; anyway, she was by no means the only woman to enjoy the art for its own sake. A recent mode was for younger women to dress up in men's clothing occasionally, and Phoebe found it both gratifying and liberating to adopt a masculine persona for an hour each morning with only her fencing master to see. They had laughed at the suggestion that now she would be able to fight her own duels but rather that, she thought, than waste someone else's life. Too many lives had been lost for no good reason.

Her own gown was of sea-green silk shot with turquoise, the neckline, full sleeves and tight bodice bound with braids of pink and gold that accentuated her peachy skin and glossy black curls. The silk swished seductively as she moved and, as she paused to lift the hem of her skirt higher, so too did he wait politely until she had gathered it, though he did not offer her his arm.

* * *

For the rest of the afternoon he stayed close by her, and others noticed that she made no objections. 'D'ye see that then, Duchess?' said the Duke of Lauderdale. 'He's sticking to her like a leech and she's nae making too much fuss aboot it.'

'Yes John, I do see. Could he have been annoyed that I put her between Salisport and Mawes at the table, I wonder?'

'Ach, I think he's keener on her than she is on him, mind.'

The Duchess smiled. 'I would not be too sure about that, John.'

'Wishful thinking,' he said, walking away. 'He's got some ground to make up if he wants to get anywhere with your Mistress Laker.'

But Phoebe was unexpectedly relieved to have the unsolicited guardianship of Sir Leo after what had happened earlier, for it had not pleased her at all to be fumbled and pawed over like a common street-walker. It brought home to her quite forcibly that perhaps they were not the only ones to so regard her. And while she could still feel humiliated that it was Sir Leo who had found her in that situation, she realised that if he had believed she was enjoying herself, presumably he would not have interfered. She was also relieved that he had not reported the incident to the Duke, who would certainly have asked the men to leave, spoiling the party.

The dainty repast in the small two-storey banqueting house by the river passed pleasantly in nibbling and drinking, in word-games and singing after which they strolled back to the bowling green for a game until suppertime. Phoebe made an effort to encourage the two young daughters of her hostess and to make them her partners in the games, knowing only too well the inexplicable pain of a love that will come to nothing. The Duchess's plans for her daughters would not include her husband's secretary.

Except for Phoebe, the guests departed in a fleet of coaches lit by the torches of the running link-men, leaving Ham House to unloose its stays and relax into the peace of the night. Phoebe's yellow bedroom became a haven where her last thoughts were of the excuses she could use to make an early return home. Mrs Overshott's condition had worsened? That would be the most plausible, except that she had nothing more than a head cold, and no one had come from Mortlake with such a message.

By morning, her decisions were veering like a weather-vane in a gale between staying in the same house as a man she had made a point of hating for the past three years and galloping off home on an excuse that was as transparent as the June sky. It was, after all, the first time she had spent so long in his company, and her first impressions bore little resemblance to these more recent ones when he appeared to be less objectionable and more at ease. She decided to give it another day. For the Duchess's sake, she told herself.

They went riding round the estate after breakfast, even the Duchess who would usually have kept to her rooms until mid-day. For much of the time, Phoebe was content to maintain a noticeable reserve towards Sir Leo while Elizabeth and Katherine accompanied him and, to her relief, he seemed content to have it so, leaving her to converse with the Duke and Duchess, her ladies, the chaplain and the estate steward. Showing the two young ladies some basic *haute école* moves, Sir Leo made them more in love with him than ever. But Phoebe refused to join in the laughing lessons, penalising herself, wondering whether this self-inflicted emptiness was the reason why hate had found a secure place in her heart. Perhaps, as he'd said, it *was* time matters were put straight between them, just for the record. The weather-vane veered again. No, she would find an excuse to leave early. She did not want a confrontation that would surely bring back all those grievous memories. She did not want another dose of this man's scorn, even though he'd said he didn't dislike her. To dislike, he would have to think deeply about the reasons, and, judging by his laughter with Elizabeth and her sister, she herself was not deeply in his thoughts. She would have to go. To spend more time in his company would be unbearable.

She watched how he rode his massive dapple-grey

Andalusian stallion so effortlessly, straight-backed and graceful, his hands light on the reins, his signals imperceptible. She saw how his hand stroked softly down the curve of the horse's neck and she turned her head away, her mouth dry, her heart behaving very strangely. Yes, she would have to return home.

Dinner with the Lauderdales was taken at two o'clock, and although the exercise had given them appetites, Phoebe could eat only sparingly while her emotions were so unsettled. Her forced attempts at lightness were difficult to maintain with Sir Leo sitting opposite. It was a family affair, taken in the new dining room with the Duchess's sister joining them for once—a dear lady in her forties who was usually unwell and kept to her rooms. Fortunately, due to the gossip that surrounded all the King's ministers, Phoebe had heard about the Duke's unorthodox table manners, which, while not disturbing his wife in any way, caused some restrained amusement elsewhere, especially amongst his stepdaughters. The two-pronged fork with the ivory handle, which the Duchess had introduced to Ham House, he used to scratch his head—through his wig— and for picking his teeth rather than for eating. The Duke's knowledge of etiquette might not be of the best, Phoebe thought, but his devoted manner towards his second wife was something she herself would not have grumbled at from the man she loved. The Duke was also a brilliant scholar, with one of the sharpest minds at Court, fluent in several languages, some of them ancient.

She was too well bred to exclude Sir Leo entirely from her contributions to the conversation, but the experience still left her feeling hypocritcal and annoyed by her own inability to move on.

After the meal, she went to her room to rest, but soon exchanged that bolt-hole for a different one in the garden where no one would find her. Passing through a doorway in the mellow brick wall, she came to the vegetable garden, a huge walled place filled with green textures, earthy aromas and the zesty tang of oranges from the open doors of the Orangery behind her. The long room was lit and warmed by a row of windows, the space almost filled by regiments of square boxes from which sprouted the slender stems of orange and lemon trees and not a weed could be seen. A seat had been set at the far end, a perfect place for her to sit and reflect upon her intentions.

A gardener entered, doffed his hat, and went out again. Every now and then, one of them would pass the windows and disappear, so when another man entered, she kept her eyes closed to breathe in the warm moist perfume and to savour the peace. A slight sound close at hand made her open them, to be confronted by the very person she'd hoped to avoid, Sir Leo

Hawkynne, perched on the edge of an orange box with his long booted legs stretched out across the only escape route.

The problem, she thought, with those wide-brimmed hats was that the wearer's eyes were in shadow and, although Sir Leo had one side saucily cocked and plumed, his shaded face was difficult for her to read. 'No,' she said, as if the word had been waiting on the tip of her tongue. 'Go away. I don't want to talk.'

'That's too bad, mistress, because you're going to have to. It's the only way.'

'The only way to what? I owe you no explanation, Sir Leo.'

'I think you do.'

Swinging her feet down to the stone slabs, she stood up to go. 'If you will kindly move your legs, sir?'

'Mistress Laker,' he said, not moving an inch, 'it's been three long years now. D'ye really want to carry your hate around for so long? It's weighing you down.'

'What does it matter to you?' she argued, looking through the bleary glass of the window. 'Please move.'

'No, I'm not moving. Sit down again, if you please.'

'I warn you, I shall scream.'

'Then I'd better give you something to scream about.'

'Is that a threat? If so…'

'An offer to assist you, that's all. Like my offer to

confront these demons of yours. It cannot go on, lass.'
He still had not moved, but now he lifted his head to
look at her, showing her the steely determination
etched upon every line of his face, his eyes like two
dark splinters, watching her. She stood no chance of
evading him.

The talk of hate and demons, however, immediately
triggered a hot spring of emotion within her, bringing
it from its deep well to tighten her throat and lungs,
tearing her apart with conflicts she was unable to
name. 'It *will* go on!' she cried. 'It will. What's done
cannot be undone. Even *you* cannot unsay that insult.
Even you cannot bring a man back to life.'

'I'm not talking about bringing him back to life, but
you cannot lay Sir Piers's death at my door, mistress.
He took his own life for reasons that had more to do
with you than with me. He's not the first man to die
of love and he'll not be the last. 'Tis a powerful thing.'

'There was no love on my part,' she replied, rounding on him like a wildcat. 'There was *nothing* between us. Nothing whatever. What he did was as a
result of the duel. The shame of it.'

'Rubbish! You know better than that. A wee cut on
the arm is no great shame. Not worth taking your life
for.'

'But losing a duel is, sir, as you well know.' She sat
down on the bench amidst a susurration of silk, her
back posing an inflexible barrier, the emotions she

had tried so hard to suppress surging forwards again, as raw now as they had been at the time. What Sir Piers had done was *not* a direct result of the duel, and well she knew it. It was a direct result of his own impetuosity, his sureness of the medieval code where a lady accepted the love of the man who had put his life at her disposal. Except that she had never wanted him to, had tried to stop him, had not promised him anything. His wound had stopped the fight. Sir Piers lost face, but believed Phoebe would take pity on him, tend his wound, act the mother-lover-wife that he desired.

For her, however, the growing scandal had been too much. When a friend had offered her a hiding place near Canterbury, she had taken it and stayed there for the rest of the summer, thinking that Sirs Piers had been fortunate to remain alive while her name was still as tarnished as before. If only, she had thought, it had been Sir Leo Hawkynne who'd leapt to her defence instead of silly Sir Piers. If only matters had been reversed.

But Sir Piers had been nothing if not totally dedicated to his cause, and the fever that ensued as a result of his wound had gone to his brain, they said. Friends found him hanging from a beam in his room, and the scandal had continued to burn brightly.

'Ach, lassie! Will you stop deceiving yourself a wee while?' Sir Leo said.

'I'm *not!*'

'Yes, you are. Listen to me, and let's get this bit straight, shall we? Losing a duel is a daily event. Every man loses at least one.'

'Have you?'

'Not yet, but that's not the point. He was the one to challenge me over something I said that he disliked, something that had nothing to do with him personally. The fact that he was not your lover confirms that. I had little option but to accept the challenge or back down, which I was not inclined to do, but it was a risk he preferred to take. And he lost. Which he must have known he would. If he expected you to accept him as a result of his defence of you, well…that's something no one can explain. But you preferred to…'

'I didn't *prefer* anything, Sir Leo,' she returned over her shoulder. 'I went away for three months to escape the gossip that *you* were the cause of, initially. Had you not voiced your so-righteous opinions, none of it would have happened and Sir Piers would still be alive. Unfortunately, your opinions seem to be valued more than they're worth.'

'And he'd still be alive to pester you, presumably,' he murmured, callously.

'Your remarks are unnecessary and mischievous. He was gallant. He wished only to protect my good name.'

His voice hardened. 'While you were doing your

best to drag your good name through the mire, lass. Weren't you? He had his work cut out.'

'How *dare* you?' Phoebe was on her feet again and, this time, Sir Leo stood to confront her, watching her eyes like a hawk for the attack she intended, but which did not come. 'I was doing no more than living my life in the best way I knew how, with genuine love and friendship to all. And when you—' her voice choked and faltered as the painful memories came back to shake her '—and when *you* have lost *your* entire family…and not seen them buried…and have no place to go to mourn them, then perhaps you will be in a better position to criticise the actions of those who have. I kept open house then, Sir Leo, to ease my grief. Yes, I heard the gossip and I didn't care, until…' Her tone deepened with emotion, her lungs gasping at the air.

'Until I happened to remark—'

'That I was too easy for *you,* and that you'd not be showing up at my door because you like a chase, not a sitting duck. Have I got it right, Sir Leo? Were those not your words? Well, my fine cavalier, let me tell you something. I'd not invite *you* to my door if you were the last man on this earth.' On a cry of distress, her breath ran out as she swerved round him and ran to the door towards the sunshine and the open space of the garden.

His voice followed her, close behind. 'And that's why you changed tack then, mistress. Well, if it took my remark to do that…'

In a flash and a swish of silk, Phoebe whirled round to face him, her eyes blazing like black coals. 'You great…oaf!' she said. 'It was not your impertinence that caused the change, but Sir Piers's suicide and the scandal it caused. I was being blamed for it, though heaven only knows why. After the duel, I went away to let things die down, but instead it got worse. What was I supposed to do on my return, pray? Dance on the poor man's grave and carry on as before?' Shaking with fury, she strode on along the path, past the intrigued gardeners and through the doorway in the wall, through the Fountain Garden and on towards the house, stopping only once to prise a stone out of her shoe, pointedly refusing the offer of Sir Leo's hand. 'Leave me alone! I should never have come here.'

'What will ye do then, lass? Run away again?'

'Mind your own damned business.'

'You *are* my business,' he answered, under his breath. Cursing himself for a fool for leaving matters so long to fester and intensify, he followed her out of the Orangery. He could have sorted things out before this, he told himself, if he'd not been dragged hither and thither by the demands of his office, though other men had managed their affairs of the heart better than he. Yes, he'd made her aware of his disdain, always believing that there would be a moment when he would catch her alone, away from the garrulous friends with whom she surrounded herself. He had watched her from a respectable distance, angrily, jealously, impotently. Then, out of sheer frustration, he had muttered his jaundiced opinion too loudly, not expecting that Kelloway would pick it up and use it to fuel his own fantasies. It had been true that he'd not be presenting himself at her door, but that had not represented the end of his interest. On the contrary, he'd been interested since she had first appeared, but had believed that the usual manner of introductions would not do for her. For one thing, she was young and vulnerable; for another, she was clearly afraid of him. His waiting game had proved disastrous, and he had no one to blame but himself.

Blindly, forgetting her way through the new additions, she ran all the way round to the door on the north side with Sir Leo following, his long stride matching three of hers. At the end of the great hall where the family had met by coincidence in a rare gathering, the Duke's loud bellow of laughter was cut short by the crash of the door being thrown back on its hinges and the whirlwind entrance of Mistress Phoebe Laker, with Sir Leo close behind. Still bickering in mid-quarrel, still refusing to concede the smallest point, she was, as they entered, somewhat irrelevantly pointing out that he himself had a reputation for loose living, if the truth be told, and who was he to sit in judgement upon others?

The family turned in surprise, not at the storm itself

but at the physical intensity of it that felt as if an avalanche was about to sweep them away. Mistress Laker's lovely face was flushed, her eyes sparkling with angry tears, her whole body tense with indignation.

Sir Leo closed the door quietly, getting the last word in as he did so. 'Well, nobody else seemed willing to say what they thought, did they? What did I have tae lose by it?'

'Oh, I was the one to lose out, Sir Leo. You made sure of *that.*' It was then, as she turned, that Phoebe became aware of the brightly coloured group on the chequered floor, staring first at her and then at each other, prompting her towards some kind of explanation. 'I'm…er…sorry, your Grace. Er…I wonder if I might impose on you to lend me a coach. I've decided…well…I think it's best for me to leave. My gentlewoman…' Brushing a tear away with the heel of her hand, she looked around her, helplessly, like a child.

The Duchess hurried forwards, with arms outstretched. 'Dear me, Phoebe love. What is all this about? Of course you can't leave. Not yet. Isn't there something we can do to help?' She tried to enclose her guest in a motherly embrace, but Phoebe was too agitated to accept it.

'No, nothing at all, thank you, my lady. I can't stay, that's all.'

The Duke, rising as usual to the diplomatic challenge and making no concessions to his two young stepdaughters, called across to his secretary, 'What ha' you been up to then, Leo? Had your hands where they're not wanted, eh?'

Sir Leo was used to his master's crudity. 'Mistress Laker and I are having a discussion, that's all, my lord, and I'm winning. That's why she's so annoyed.'

'We are *not* having a discussion, my lord,' Phoebe said, loudly. 'And he is *not* winning. And I am *not* annoyed. I simply wish to leave, unless you can find an *extremely* long document for him to transcribe into medieval Latin that will keep him occupied for the next few days, after which he'll retire with a *blinding* headache from which he'll—'

'Whisht…lass!' said the Duke, coming forwards. 'What's amiss here? I knew ye did nae like him much, but ye canna wish the man dead, can ye?'

'Yes, easily, my lord.' She brushed her hands crisply over the skirts of her gown as if to dust him off. 'And to be buried in the Outer Hebrides.'

The Duke whistled through his teeth and looked again at Sir Leo. 'Man, she means it, too. It's as bad as that, is it? I thought—'

'Yes,' said his wife, 'we know what you thought, dear, but we have to try to find a solution to this problem, and running away is not one of them. Come, Phoebe love, can you not accept an apology from Sir Leo for…?'

'Sir Leo has offered me no apology, my lady.'

'Nor is Sir Leo likely to,' said the man himself, resting on the edge of the billiard table and taking up one of the ivory-tipped cues to examine it.

'Nor would I accept it if he did,' Phoebe retorted, tossing her bouncy ringlets.

'Stalemate,' said the Duke, philosophically.

'I believe you're right, my lord,' said Phoebe, looking round for the best way to make an escape. 'It *is* stalemate. I do not accept a word of Sir Leo's explanation, such as it is, and he doesn't accept mine.'

'Such as it is,' he murmured, chalking the cue.

'Sir Leo!' The Duchess's reprimand cracked across the hall like a whip. 'Put that cue down and try to take this seriously, if you will. Mistress Laker is a guest at Ham House and we have a duty to make her visit memorable for all the *right* reasons. And playing a game of billiards by yourself will do nothing to help matters. Think of something useful, will you?'

Promptly, Sir Leo obeyed. 'I beg your pardon, my lady, I meant no disrespect. I've been trying to think of something that would help Mistress Laker since she arrived. Indeed, I told her so at our first meeting, but she has her reasons for not wanting to listen.'

'Then something must be done,' said the Duchess.

'A coach would be best,' said Phoebe. 'Or I could walk. It's not far.'

Young Katherine, eager to help but bursting with

curiosity, felt that things were moving too fast. 'What did Sir Leo say to make Mistress Laker so very angry? Was it about this morning?'

Her elder sister nudged her with a frown. 'Hush, Katherine. They've been over that ground, and Mama is asking for suggestions. What about a sword contest?' she said, innocently.

'Oh, don't be ridiculous, Betty dear,' the Duchess said. 'That's about as helpful as Sir Leo playing billiards.'

'With respect, Mama,' Elizabeth persevered, 'it's not ridiculous at all. I happen to know that Mistress Laker has this last three years been taking fencing lessons from Signor Luigi Verdi. Isn't that so, mistress?'

Horrified by the revelation of her secret, Phoebe's tightly strung nerves sharpened her voice like a butcher's knife. 'That's nobody's business but mine. Where did you hear that?'

The Duke came to the rescue. 'Never mind where she heerd it. Is it true?'

Phoebe had no alternative but to give him the truth. 'Yes, my lord, but—'

'Well, then, why not put it to the test? A good old-fashioned bout or two wi' the tuckes has settled many a dispute.'

'That's really not a very clever idea,' said the Duchess, unconvincingly, which suggested that she thought it was.

Sir Leo took no persuading. His answer came fast and decisive. 'I'm game, but the lady would not—'

'Yes, she *would!*' Phoebe retorted. 'It's time somebody took that clever smile off your face. I could do it.'

'Yes!' cried Elizabeth, clinging to her sister's hand, and already ahead of everyone in her imaginings. 'And if Sir Leo wins, he gets to marry Mistress Laker, and if—'

'And if I win,' said Phoebe, lifting her chin, 'I get to kill him!'

For a few stunned moments the room fell utterly silent except for the sonorous ticking of a clock somewhere while the girls' minds ran riot through mixed fantasies of love and hate, revenge, submission, conquest, mastery and sweet defeat, their own as well as Phoebe's. In effect, what Elizabeth at seventeen was proposing for her rival in love was what she wanted for herself, with the exception of the death scene which would make the whole exercise pointless.

In her case, however, these fantasies had become even more distorted since the recent discussions about her own future, a future that would never involve the man she adored above all others, who would never be allowed to sue for her hand, even if he'd wanted to. Loving him one moment and hating him the next, wanting his happiness yet wishing to punish him for being unattainable, Elizabeth saw this as a chance to put herself in Mistress Laker's shoes and to fight him, physically, to feel the emotion of being conquered and won, as she would never be. Mistress Laker was the perfect go-between, angry like herself, and with just enough skill—according to Signor Verdi—not to disgrace herself over a few bouts. But not enough to win. Sir Leo would claim Mistress Laker's hand and, despite their antagonism, it would end as all the best romances did with the two opponents accepting their fate, whatever it was. She, Elizabeth, would feel it. It was the nearest she would ever come to being pursued by her heart's desire. By proxy.

Even so, she knew that her heart would break when the fantasy was played out and the fiction became fact. Helping it along was more for her own benefit than for theirs, for the nature of that kind of dream was in delusion.

'That's all very well,' said the Duke, 'but there's a penalty for that kind o' thing, mistress. Did you know that? Besides, I'd not be too happy for my best man to be killed just now. He's got letters to write. And if I were you, I'd not be so hell-bent on a fight to the death wi' a man like him. He'd cut you into collops before you could blink.'

'I really don't care, my lord, whether he does or not. He's already damaged my name. Why not the rest of me?'

The bleakness of her reply shocked them all, even the

ones who understood it better than the rest. 'Phoebe dear, don't say that,' the Duchess whispered. 'This is a silly idea. Shall we forget it and try to find another way?'

'No, my lady, thank you. The chance of making him sweat with fear the way his last opponent did is too good to miss. Whoever wins, it will have been worth it.'

'Then let's not forget,' Sir Leo said, sauntering towards her, 'that the stakes are high, Mistress Laker. I get you for a wife when I score two hits.'

'It's academic,' Phoebe replied, glaring at him. 'But I accept. And when I score *my* second hit, I'll make sure you die with as little dignity as he did.'

'Whisht!' said the Duke, on a long slow breath. 'What on *earth* did he say to cause such scorn, lassie? Wouldn't his disappearance do just as well?'

Phoebe chose to answer that with some questions of her own. 'So am I to take it, my lord, that in the unlikely event of a win for Sir Leo, he gets *his* prize, but when I win, all I get is his disappearance for a while? I've had the pleasure of not seeing him for three whole years, you see, and three more is not *quite* the same as eternity, is it? That's what happens to those who fly too close to my flame—my parents, my brother and Sir Piers. They die. What's so special about *him* that he should be spared? If I deserve any reputation at all, let it be for bestowing the kiss of death where I will.

And I think you would be unwise, my lord, to under-estimate my skills with a rapier. I've three years of hard practice behind me.'

'And Sir Leo has had twenty,' the Duke replied, throwing up his hands, 'but if you're still wanting to settle matters this way, go ahead. I doubt it'll take long. I'll go and find the foils.' He was not impressed by Phoebe's dramatic speech.

'Not foils, my lord. Rapiers. I'll have no guards on the points.'

'Oh, dear,' said the Duchess, trying again to take Phoebe's hands. 'Are you sure about this? I know how it pains us when our loved ones die so suddenly and violently, and then Sir Piers, which I *know* was not your fault. But it should not be like this, love. I had no idea… I didn't mean it to… Oh, what have I started? You mustn't *kill* him, love. Really, you mustn't. It can be settled peacefully, can't it? None of us wants blood-shed.'

'But you do realise, don't you,' said Sir Leo, 'that I'd have to fall on my sword anyway, if I lost to a *woman?* Think of my disgrace.'

'I'm glad to see you're not taking this too seriously, Sir Leo,' Phoebe said, walking towards the staircase. 'The fall will be even more rewarding.'

But she was jerked back unexpectedly hard by his hand beneath her arm, swinging her round, off-bal-ance, to face him, pressing her bodice close against his ruffled shirt. 'Oh, I'm taking it seriously all right, mistress, believe me. And you had better do the same because I warn you now—there'll be no concessions for a maid in contest with a man. You have agreed the terms before witnesses, and I'll not have you default on your word, once the contest is won. You have this last chance to back out now, or go through with it. Choose.'

She had waited a long time for revenge, yet it would have been so much easier to fall quietly upon his breast, to say nothing, to let him win without a fight and sort out the consequences, whatever they were. Their heated quarrel in the Orangery, however, had brought back the raw nagging ache to her wounds; the sight and nearness of him seared her heart and demanded some recompense for both the past and the empty future. He had been the only man she had ever wanted, the only one who had not, apparently, wanted her, and she could not forgive him for telling the world of it.

Until this moment, when he demanded that she choose, once and for all, whether to go ahead with this contest or back out, it had been sheer force of temper that had carried her through, blindly riding upon Elizabeth's ridiculous solution of physical combat. The Duke himself had not thought it such a bad idea, but Phoebe's boast about her three years' training had not impressed him and she knew in her heart that she stood no chance whatever of a victory, even before Sir Leo's assurance that he was not about to hand it to her for any chivalrous reason. There was too much at stake for that.

What, then? What was in it for her, after she lost? An ill-fated marriage to a man who had offered her no comfort except to keep uncouth guests at bay? Marriage to a man who'd shown her only coolness and disapproval and a heart made of stone? Well, she could make him fall in love with her. Yes, she could do that. She could make him feel the same despair she'd felt for years, the same yearning. With one taste of her loving, one small taste, she could bring him to her, begging for her warmth, a kind word, a soft touch, a gentle look. She could turn the experience to her advantage, and he would hunger for her the way she hungered for him. No, she had no illusions about winning this contest, for in marriage to him, she could make his life hell. And she would.

Twisting, she freed herself, hoping he would be cowed by the fire in her eyes. 'I *have* chosen,' she said, hoarsely. 'Go and say your prayers, sir.'

But it was admiration, not fear, that she saw in his expression. 'That's my lass,' he whispered so that only she could hear. 'You'll be a tigress of a mother for our bairns.'

She might have asked herself why Sir Leo was so eager to accept the unusual terms that Elizabeth had so blithely suggested in her excitement, but there was little need. She was wealthy, and there were few men on the lookout for a wife who would refuse a chance to get their hands on her inheritance for so little effort. In that, she told herself, Sir Leo would be no different from the rest.

The Duchess touched her hand. 'Go and change then, dear, if you really must do this, while we move the billiard table out of the way. The long gallery is much too dark for this kind of thing, and there's rush matting on the floor.'

Phoebe glanced at the two sisters, still wondering how Elizabeth had discovered about her fencing lessons, and bitterly disappointed that Signor Verdi had betrayed her confidence. Court life was full of such juicy revelations, and these two young ladies had nothing else to do but lap them up and pass them on, having no concerns about the consequences.

They stood close together, clinging anxiously, gazing first at their mother and then at Sir Leo, wide-eyed, perturbed by the change in the man who had laughed with them that morning, courteously teasing. This was an aspect of him they could not have foreseen, showing a physical masculine intensity towards a woman that allowed him to grab her by the arm and pull her to him, to speak to her with blunt authority, to dominate her with his eyes, both angry and applauding. Disturbed, excited and fearful, they saw Mistress Laker pick up her skirts and run towards the staircase, disappearing round the bend, and when at last they drew the gaze of Sir Leo, expecting the usual charming smile, his look passed through them as if they were not there. Then they knew that this was not the stuff of romantic dreams, but the brutal and dark side of the kind of passion already lurking in their own unconsciousness.

CHAPTER THREE

AT THIS POINT, the Duchess might have proposed what any other mother would certainly have done and sent her daughters off in pursuit of something more profitable than to witness such an unusual contest. The lady's only command, however, was to go and sit in that corner and not to move, and certainly not to cry out. She then recalled something and, whispering into Elizabeth's ear, sent her off on an errand, urging her to be quick about it.

The family were assembled and waiting by the time Phoebe descended the great staircase and, if they were too discreet to gasp, there was not one of them prepared for what they saw. Her slender and exquisitely graceful figure was clad in white shirt and brown doeskin knee-length breeches below which were white stockings, muffling her entrance and adding to the air of silent unreality in the hall. Over her shirt, she wore a black velvet sleeveless vest with gold buttons, its neckline touched by her mop of shining ringlets, and although such an unorthodox outfit might in some women have disguised their femininity, in Phoebe it did the opposite.

Restraining, for once, the bawdy remark that sprang unhelpfully to his lips, the Duke came to lead her towards the footman who held an open case of rapiers across his arms. With hands spread over hips, Sir Leo stood next to him, stripped down to his shirt and breeches, shoeless, like her. Watching him closely, the two sisters saw his eyes narrow as he appeared to pull himself up by an extra half-inch.

'Sir Leo and Mistress Laker, understand this,' said the Duke, scowling at them, 'that this is to be a contest, not a duel. There will be no dealing of death blows, whatever you may wish, mistress. I have to keep his Majesty's respect, and duelling in my house is something I cannot permit. A contest of skill is different, so I shall declare the first one to score two hits to be the winner.' He placed the flat of his hand horizontally across Sir Leo's chin. 'Here,' he said, 'and here,' moving it down to his waist, 'is where your hits should be aimed, including the arms, and nowhere else. Now, I need your assurance that there is nothing concealed about your persons that may cause any additional damage. Mistress Laker?'

'Nothing, your Grace,' said Phoebe.

'Nothing, your Grace,' said Sir Leo.

'Then choose your weapons and begin.'

The rapiers were long narrow things of tempered steel, burnished and deadly, with quillons and counterguards lightly curved, the points unprotected. Phoebe took the one nearest her and turned away quickly to weigh it in her hand, to make it her friend. She felt the cool smooth floor through her silken hose, remembering how Signor Luigi had made her wear heavy shoes, at first, to strengthen her legs and teach her to be nimble, and now there were times when she would give him a good run for his money.

Yet having been repeatedly cautioned to keep her anger under control, the rage that had been building up inside her since her arrival at Ham House, which had exploded scarce an hour ago, still seethed and churned, coupled with the fear of losing and a desperation to win. This man was amongst the best in the country and would not allow her the smallest error when his reputation was at stake. Her heart hammered into her throat as she tried in vain to subdue the furies that had ranted and roared since their row in the Orangery, the pain as she had spoken of her losses, and the wound to her pride that still lingered after his well-publicized criticism of her. Well, she would show him just how easy she was. She would make him work harder than he'd ever worked in his life if he wanted her money to pay for those fancy buttons and bows, the prancing stallions, the brocade suits and golden spurs. She turned to face him. Yes, she would make him eat his words, whatever it cost her.

Sir Leo was courteous and in no particular hurry, but too soon, *much* too soon, Phoebe launched herself at her opponent, partly hoping to take him off guard and partly because her anger was not as under control as she would have liked. Sir Leo easily parried her first wild *imbroccata,* his steel wrist warding her off while recognising the temper that lay behind the charging blow. He pushed her back, hard. 'Steady!' he told her, quietly. 'Calm down.'

Taking a deep breath, she began again, body upright, feet dancing, sword arm extended like an antenna, feeling, touching, every move focused, every muscle disciplined, her wrist and arm shocked by his inflexible parries. High, low and wide, he was there before her every time, testing her with an unexpected thrust followed by a quick riposte in which she was forced backwards to the staircase end of the hall. She knew the shallow step of the dais would trip her if she did not take care, so she took it in her stride, glorying in the few extra inches of height until, circling, she pushed him back towards the fireplace in a whirling, flickering, shimmer of steel too fast for the onlookers to see. Her arm began to ache with the jarring of clashing blades, and after only a few minutes she could feel the shirt sticking to her with sweat. Signor Luigi would have allowed her to take a rest, to sip water, to wipe her forehead after a short bout, but this man was not even breathing hard and would see no reason to let her recover.

Then he did something that infuriated her for, after a follow-through in a lightning-quick exchange, the point of his rapier cut the top button of her vest free and sent it flying through the air like a golden coin. She ought not to have allowed it to disturb her, she knew, but the insolence of his action only served to remind her of his dazzling superiority, as if she needed it, and the Duke's warning that this man could cut her into collops began to take on a new meaning.

'A hit!' The Duke's voice echoed round the room. 'First to Sir Leo.'

As if this clever trick had been intended to concentrate her energies into working harder, Phoebe beat fast on his blade time after time, pushing it aside and pressing it down to open a way for a lunge that would reach his shirt, as his had reached hers. Finally, she was rewarded with a prick to his arm with the tip of her blade. 'A hit,' called the Duke, 'first to Mistress Laker. Are you hurt, Sir Leo?'

'No, my lord, but the lady will now have at least one shirt to mend.'

'Then carry on.'

Breathing became more painful, and Sir Leo gave her a moment to wipe her forehead with the back of her hand and then, defiantly, to unbutton her vest and fling it into a corner while reflecting that, with one more hit like the last, his esteem would be tainted for ever. Meanwhile, she would taunt him by showing him a little more of what he would never truly own.

Summoning all her strength, feet sliding and dancing in and out of their combined sword-length, blades clicking and squealing, rarely apart, Phoebe used every trick she had learnt both to defend herself from his relentless attacks and to make some impression on his phenomenal stamina. Recoiling, feeling the waves of exhaustion ready to overwhelm her, she heard her rasping breaths being forced out in gasps, betraying her sheer desperation. Reminded of what she stood to lose and win, she fought on with grim resolution. From the corner of her eye she could see portraits of the Dysart ancestors looking down on their descendants, whose hands covered their mouths, the black-and-white chequered floor blurring into grey, the impassive expression of her opponent, remorseless in his pursuit of victory, sparing her nothing. His lithe body was like a taut bow, perfectly toned and balanced, smooth and agile, trained to fight since he was nine years old. She knew he could continue to fence for hours, and that she could not.

Without mercy, his next attack drove her across the room, allowing her to do the same to him on purpose to tire her, to jolt and jar her arm still more until the pain almost blinded her. Confusion returned as her three years of training began to slip away, her beautiful balletic sword-play to coarsen into clumsiness, her rapier weighing as heavy as a pole-axe. Her legs trembled and sweat dripped into her eyes as his charge beat her back, sliding and slithering until, unable to hold her rapier up to him a moment longer, she was stopped by the discarded billiard table at her back.

'Drop your sword,' he commanded.

Shapes swam before her eyes, her lungs sucked at the air, noisily, stinging her with the effort. 'No,' she croaked.

'D'ye want me to mark ye, then?' he snapped. 'I said *drop* it!'

She felt the prick of his sword under her chin, and it occurred to her then that she had better obey him. But there was still another raging voice that denied what was obvious to everyone else, a voice that came through the years of seeking revenge. As her fingers relaxed their grip on the pommel, the clatter of steel on the floor accompanied her breathless howls of fury and despair. 'No…no… no! I will *not!*'

Holding his rapier to one side to prevent anyone's approach, Sir Leo circled her waist with his free arm, pushing her head on to his shoulder with his own while effectively silencing her cries that filtered through the whispers of the crowd.

'The contest is awarded to Sir Leo Hawkynne,' called the Duke, though neither of the contestants heard him. Nor did they need to. For Phoebe, defeat was in Sir Leo's hard possessive kiss, his arm across her aching shoulders, the heat of him through the fine linen of her shirt, the firm pressure of his thighs against her body. Defeat was in her arms hanging like lead weights and her legs, numbed and boneless. Defeat was in her capture before the shocked I-told-you-so audience, and the sudden lift into his arms as he scooped her useless feet off the floor and carried her through the hall to the stairs.

Helpless with exhaustion, Phoebe kept her eyes closed, vaguely aware of each turn of the staircase and of the scent of Sir Leo's exertions, and she knew with increasing humiliation that if ever he were to tell her how difficult the contest had been for him, he would be lying to lessen her pain. But she would bring his pride crashing down, she would force that apology from him, and she would cost him dear in misery before she would give herself willingly. Of kisses like that, he might be able to count on one hand, if he were lucky. Nevertheless, she was bound to acknowledge a twinge of regret in the process, for that kiss had been as memorable as his swordsmanship, and she'd had enough experience to know how to compare. Even in her fatigue, a nagging curiosity had been satisfied about what it would be like to be held in his arms, while another more unforgiving voice warned her to keep herself aloof from it. She could not. It was not the kind of experience one could keep aloof from. It was the beginning of an addiction, and that kiss was enough to take hold of her, to change all her intentions, and to make of her a walking contradiction. It had happened in the space of a few moments, while she was still at her weakest.

Once inside her sunny bedroom, Sir Leo seemed intent on reinforcing that token of mastery with another more potent one, more private and unforgettable which she, in a daze of half-expectations, took to be an attempted preamble to his victory celebrations, whatever form they might take. No sooner had he shouldered the door closed and tipped her on to her feet, than his supporting arm pulled her close into the hard bend of his body and, even before she could guess what he was about, began a kiss that for sheer skill excelled even the previous one.

With one smooth, stealthy hand he explored the soft contours of her body over the thin damp shirt and doeskin breeches, lifting her arm to his shoulder while sliding the caress downwards, missing nothing, capturing her breast before moving on over her hips and the mounds of her buttocks, tantalising, shocking, venturing where no other man had dared. She could have stopped it, but pretended a shameful, shameless lack of ability, and the craving was fed, turning her resolutions upside-down. She would have done anything for it to continue. Anything.

It was Sir Leo himself who brought her down to earth by taking her arm from his shoulder and, with the last touch of his lips on hers, held her firmly by the waist, easing her backwards until the yellow silk counterpane buckled her legs and made her sit, suddenly, still intoxicated by his audacity and the urgency of her responses. It was too late for her to pretend otherwise.

But the pause in his lovemaking, which had offered her the chance to pull herself together, did exactly the opposite. What he was about to do now, she told herself, was inevitable. She would blame him later for losing control of his desires and for taking advantage of an exhausted, helpless woman. With a moan, she lay back upon the bed and closed her eyes to wait for the warmth of him to cover her, still hardly able to believe her own treacherous change of heart.

'I'll send for your maid,' he said, from a distance.

Phoebe opened her eyes. 'What?' she said, sleepily.

Relaxed, he was leaning against the bed-curtain, shaking the fat tassel like a bell, watching her in open admiration. 'Your maid?' he repeated. 'Well, you know how they'll be jumping to conclusions if we don't appear after half an hour, fully washed and changed. We don't want that, do we? Unless, of course, you want to keep your lad's clothes on, just for effect. Oh, and by the way, mistress, you're quite free now.'

Slowly, struggling to understand him like a sleep-walker awakening, Phoebe sat up. 'Free of what?'

'Free of me. Of the conditions. Marriage. Well, it does seem a mite unfair, doesn't it? You were not allowed to run me through, which I'm *sure* you would have done, so I cannot in all fairness stake my claim to you, can I? Besides, there was all that hootin' and hollerin' down there about not wanting it, and protests by the mile. No man in his senses would inflict himself on a woman who's in *that* frame of mind. You have to admit, it's hardly the way to begin married life, is it? Nay, dinna look at me like that, lass. Is this not to your liking, after all?'

Like a rush of blood returning painfully to numbed fingers, the truth bore in upon her, leaving a gaping void where her plans had been a few moments before. Not content with winning the contest, he had seen her game and was refusing to play it. 'So what was the meaning of *that?*' she whispered, nodding to the space where they'd just been. 'To prove to yourself how easy I am? Easy to make love to when I'm utterly exhausted? Easy to beat at fencing? Easy to accept the stupid suggestion of a moon-struck seventeen-year-old? It's a wonder you bother to get out of bed in a morning, Sir Leo, with life so well laid out for you.' With a leap that totally belied her fatigue, she was halfway across the room before his laconic reply reached her, maddening her still more.

'Aye….well, some days are easier than others, that's true, mistress.'

'And I suppose this must have been one of them. So what do you propose to tell the Duke and Duchess about your decision? That you really didn't want the prize, in spite of that convincing little lecture you gave me beforehand? That you've gone back on the agreement because you're really not up to it these days?'

He rolled himself round to face her from the other side of the curtain, one hand reaching up almost to the tester, his face showing a mild surprise at her bitter tone, which she knew to be feigned. 'I shall remind them, if they're in any doubt, that you were the one to make such a fuss about it with your very noisy refusal to accept the result. Why, even the dairymaid must have heard it out there, let alone those in the hall. No-body will be too surprised after that, Mistress Laker, and I'll not have it said that I was obliged to take a woman to wife who hates my guts enough to want to run a sword through them. The woman I marry will worship the ground I walk on, or I'll do without.'

'You knew how I felt beforehand,' Phoebe retorted, 'yet you agreed to the contest *and* the terms.'

'And you accepted them too, lass. Then you refused. When you'd lost.'

'You *knew* I would lose.'

'Yes. So did you. Well, let this be a lesson to you not to place me in your clever schemes and fanciful talk of flames and kisses of death and suchlike, for I'll have none of it. I don't believe in such airy nonsense. Life may once have roughed you up, as it does to most of us, but you're a lot better off than some poor devils, and to go seeking personal reasons for deaths you had no control over is unworthy of a woman like you. It's childish—'

'How *can* you say that when—'

'Childish and pitiful it is, to load yourself with that kind of guilt. Perhaps it's your way of excusing the wild behaviour I was honest enough to comment on. Now you've turned your wildness in my direction as if harming me would somehow heal your wounds and bring back what you've lost. Well, it wouldn't, would it? Nothing can. You have to *replace* it, woman, not whine about it and carry it about like a trophy. We've *all* suffered losses. There's been a Civil War, a plague and then a fire when wives, mothers and daughters *all* lost their men. Yes, you'd have married me, I know, for your own warped reasons. But I'm two steps ahead of ye, and my second name is not Martyr.'

'And those…kisses?' she whispered, while silent tears slipped across her lips. 'Meant to humble me, were they?'

'Is that what they tasted of?'

'No, Sir Leo, they tasted of curiosity, that's all. Simple male curiosity.'

'Then there's something wrong with your sense of taste, lass. Too much ginger, perhaps. Wipe your tears. You're free. You should be thankful.' Giving her no time to reply, he opened the door and slipped through, leaving her to stare at his disappearance through a sea of tears, almost willing it to change and wipe out the mortification she'd just endured.

After all the schemes for retribution, after all the visions of an abject Sir Leo begging for her favour, and a heart healed and empowered, the terrible emptiness of reality overwhelmed her with a force for which she was quite unprepared. He would tell his friends of his conquest, and she would become a laughing stock, the centre of another scandal. The two Tollemache girls, the Duchess's daughters, would recount every detail to their friends at Court. The Duke would laugh heartily at his secretary's refusal to be cozened by a woman on the lookout for a scapegoat, which is how he'd see it, and the Duchess would agree that Sir Leo was acting honourably by not taking adavantage of terms that, in hindsight, were so objectionable to both participants.

And those intimate, outrageous, forbidden caresses? What of them? Why in heaven's name had she allowed it? Worse still, why had he led her on only to stop and tell her that she was not for him? She had suffered enough—these were questions which she dared not try to answer.

There was yet another enigma that she believed would never now be explained, the one he'd whispered to her before the contest about being a tigress fierce enough to fight for their bairns. *Their* bairns. Had he really changed his mind after that, or had he never meant it in the first place?

To give in to despair, to throw herself face down on the bed and howl herself senseless, to refuse food and then stamp off home would, in the circumstances, have been a perfectly normal thing to do. But Phoebe had never lacked spirit, even when she aimed it in the wrong direction, nor was she so blinkered in her clumsy efforts to solve her problems that she couldn't see when she should re-think her strategies, particularly when her mistakes had been spelled out in such a ruthless fashion. So while Constance undressed her mistress and washed her, laying out her prettiest rose-pink gown with the huge gathered sleeves, Phoebe had time to recall what had been said and done, comparing it to previous calamities in her life when she'd had no one's help but Mrs Overshott's. Then, the advice had always been to pick herself up, to dress in her most becoming gown, put on a brave face and get on with life so as not to attract more attention or, in this case, not to upset her hostess. Far from giving the impression that none of this mattered to her, it was meant to demonstrate courage in the face of adversity. More than that, it would show that smug, holier-than-thou, superior, worship-at-my-feet layabout that she didn't care a damn what he thought of her and that his presence in the house would not affect her at all, after that débâcle. She would leave when she was ready, not before the appointed time. It was a sham, of course, but that was the principle.

To the Duchess's relief and delight, her volatile guest appeared to be no worse for her ordeal, rigged out and radiant in rose-pink silk and white lace, with tiny ribbon-roses in her shining curls. Showing no sign of tears, her eyes were clear and enquiring, looking forward with confidence towards the rest of the evening. It was a polished performance that commended her to the Duke, after he'd recovered from the surprise of her transformation, and not even he could doubt Phoebe's professed relief that his secretary had not insisted on his pound of flesh. It was, she told him with a convincing candour, a close encounter she had no wish to repeat. Nor would she ever in future accept the brilliant suggestions offered by seventeen-year-old ladies, however well meant.

Sympathetic and solicitous, the Duchess was too wily to be quite convinced by this courageous display, though she did everything possible to gloss over any potential awkwardness and to make Phoebe's last evening at Ham House pleasant enough to repeat. All in all, Phoebe managed the situation well, strolling down to the river after supper to feed the swans and to watch the last bargemen haul their loads downriver towards Richmond. The two girls were bewildered by the outcome of the contest that had not followed the usual formula of happy ever after, nor did Mistress Laker appear to be as distressed as she ought. It became obvious that their good intentions had been intrinsically flawed from the start.

Later, in the cool peace of her bed after the strain of her emotional deception, Phoebe fought back the tears of another kind of heartache that lamented the loss of something she had never had—Sir Leo Hawkynne.

Her return to Mortlake came as a relief after two days of the high-powered Lauderdales who, although perfect hosts, left her with a feeling of being overfed on flamboyance and flourish, as if there was a competition for the most staggering show of assets. Phoebe was no Puritan, and she could appreciate beauty wherever it showed, but walking into Ham House since the Duchess's refurbishments was an experience to be taken in small doses. 'I would not be in the least surprised,' she told Mrs Overshott, 'if the Lauderdales don't find themselves in some kind of financial trouble one of these days. The Duke cannot say no to her, and she cannot say no to herself. You should *see* the green closet, Molly. You'd never believe it. The entire ceiling and halfway down the walls painted with copies of Caravaggio, and you know the kind of thing *he* was good at, don't you?'

'Naked cupids, nymphs and satyrs,' Mrs Overshott rattled off, twinkling. 'Did you feel threatened, dear?'

Chuckling, Phoebe held out her arms to embrace the companion she had left behind, the dear middle-aged handsome lady who smelled faintly of aniseed and mint, who had risked the plague to nurse Phoebe's parents, yet had survived. Her complexion was pitted with the scars of smallpox, but her brown eyes had never lost their beam of understanding, her awareness of Phoebe's humours, however well concealed. 'Threatened?' said Phoebe, hugging her. 'No, not by the satyrs.'

'Ah,' said her companion. 'Come and tell me all about it over a dish of tea. Was the Lauderdales' tea gilded, too?'

'Yes,' said Phoebe, giggling. Together they passed from the panelled hallway into the tapestry-lined dining room that glowed with the soft mellow tones of apricot and dusty blue, burnt orange and ochre. 'But you must not think I disapprove, Molly. For the Lauderdales, it's a perfect setting, grand, loud, showy, spacious. The—'

'Who was there? The Duke, I take it?'

'Yes.'

'Ah,' said her companion again. 'Perhaps I should have been with you, then.'

Phoebe had never concealed any of her concerns from Mrs Overshott, for she had a way of listening that made the sharing of confidences not only easy but valuable too. So Phoebe sipped her tea and rudely dunked her biscuit while telling of the fiasco at Ham House, which she felt sure had placed her lower in Sir Leo's estimation than she was before. 'If I'd not been so furious with him, I would never have agreed to such a charade. I suppose it serves me right for planning a revenge. It backfired, didn't it?'

'Easy to be wise after the event. But his actions in your room suggest to me that he must hold you in affection, Phoebe, whatever his sudden coldness means.'

'I cannot believe that,' Phoebe whispered, turning the little tea-dish round to study its pattern. 'He was all fired up, like me, and probably still angry, and you know what men are like when they've won something, don't you?'

'Yes. It may be no more than an overflow of energy, Phoebe, but I cannot believe that a man like Sir Leo would have gone as far as he did unless he meant to place you under his ownership. He may have a reputation with women, but he would not dishonour a woman, a guest in his employer's house. He must have meant something by it.'

'But he couldn't wait to shake me off, Molly, after that.'

'And then he gave you a good dressing-down, which he need not have bothered to do unless he wanted you to know the reason. I think you've misread the signs. Why would he have sought a discussion in the first place? Why would he have accepted that particular method of settling your dispute? It was very unortho-dox, I agree, but it brought matters to a head, didn't it? I can see all kinds of signs that he cares more than you think.'

'I don't know,' Phoebe said, shaking her head. 'I doubt it.'

'See how you feel after a night in your own bed, love. You did well to recover so quickly. That must have been difficult.'

Phoebe reached for the hand that moved across the polished table, taking it to her cheek to hold it there. 'I had to,' she said. 'They were all watching. What I want to know is how Elizabeth discovered about my fencing lessons when I thought to keep it to myself.'

'Perhaps you should ask Signor Luigi in the morn-ing.'

'No, there'll be no more lessons, Molly. I think it's a waste of time. I shall have dancing lessons instead. Or perhaps the lute. I still have Tim's, you know.'

But despite the negative tone of her conversation with Mrs Overshott, who seemed to have little difficulty in seeing through the problem, the small signs Phoebe had perversely overlooked now took on an importance worth another viewing. His kiss, for one thing. His intimate caresses, for another, which, while they had led nowhere, were not the kind of thing a man of his calibre would bestow on an honoured guest in his master's house without a very good reason. Molly was right about that. So why had he gone so far before telling her she was free? Well, he had provided her with the answer to that in no uncertain terms. *I'm two steps ahead of ye, and my second name is not Martyr,* he had told her before going on to deny that his potent kisses had anything to do with mere curiosity.

The mists began to clear. He was aware of her ploy. He was not to be duped in the way she'd intended. He would dictate his own terms and she would follow, not the other way round. She had misjudged him, for he must have known what effect his brief lovemaking would have upon her, how she was, even then, ready to give herself to him, how she would be both humiliated and left wanting more. He would call her to heel once she'd had time to simmer down, for he was not a man to be manipulated by a woman. How could she ever had believed otherwise?

Did that mean that he wanted her, after all?

This was what she must find out while there was still time, for who could tell when the Duke would demand his presence on the next journey north? She could hardly return to Ham House so soon after the disastrous visit, but a chance meeting somewhere might just provide her with an indication that all was not lost or, conversely, that she had better forget him altogether. Still smarting, still unsure, of one thing she was more certain: if she did not seek him out, he would certainly not seek her.

The aristocrats with the prestigious title of Keepers of Richmond Park were no other than the Lauderdales themselves, so it was not exactly by chance that Phoebe and Mrs Overshott decided at breakfast next morning that a ride in the park would be good for their health. The possibility that certain others might also be of the same mind was not spoken out loud, but the two women knew each other's thoughts well enough to make it unnecessary. So, dressed in fashionable velvet habits and wide plumed hats, they cut across the loop of the River Thames to the enclosed parkland that the King's father had considerably enlarged, taking in a sizeable bite of Mortlake, for which some disgruntled owners had still not been compensated.

Two grooms accompanied them to open gates, and soon the ladies were joined by friends and hailed from carriages which, on any other day, would have contented Phoebe. But while she scanned the green tree-studded acres to find what might be a party from Ham House, her attention wandered and her admirers could hardly fail to note that something had happened to dampen her usual equanimity. So when the whisper went round that she'd been staying at Ham while the great Duke himself was in residence, the reason for her preoccupation became plain. The scandal concerning the Duke's handsome secretary was only three years old, and a man had died for love of Mistress Laker.

When at last her impatience was rewarded with a distant sighting of Sir Leo Hawkynne on his unmistakable grey Andalusian surrounded by a group of friends, Phoebe's courage deserted her. 'I cannot,' she whispered to Mrs Overshott. 'He's with his friends. What will it look like? I shall not know what to say. Let's go home. I feel sick.'

'That's not like you, love.'

'I know. I'm *not* me.'

Never having met the Duke's secretary, Mrs Overshott would have liked to persevere, but knew better than to insist when Phoebe was already heading for home.

On the next day, ostensibly to satisfy Mrs Overshott's burning curiosity to see the recent additions to Ham House, Phoebe donned another of her modish riding habits, this one of deep gold and black, to call on her friend the Duchess who would presumably welcome the chance to conduct another admirer through her rooms.

The Duchess was, naturally, happy to see them both, but did not for one moment believe that this alone was the reason for Phoebe's return so soon after that contentious visit when nobody's plans had been effective. She saw how the light disappeared from Phoebe's expressive eyes when she was told that the Duke and his secretary were out riding with Elizabeth and Katherine that day. 'And their brother too,' the Duchess added. 'Thomas arrived yesterday, quite unexpectedly. What a pity you've missed him. I know he'll want to see you again. How long has it been?'

'Oh, dear,' Phoebe said, recalling the distant figures she'd seen in the park the day before, 'we seem to spend our lives just missing each other. Whenever I arrive at Court, Thomas has just left on some mission or other.' Smiling ruefully at Mrs Overshott, she followed the Duchess into the dining room above the hall where the high white-plastered ceiling and blue curtains came as a relief from so much gold leaf.

Thomas Tollemache was one of the Duchess's sons by her first husband. The eldest son, Viscount Huntingtower, had extensive estates to manage in distant counties but, being nearer to Phoebe in age, Thomas had known her better than his two sisters.

His chosen career in the army had kept him away from home for months at a time, and for him to be at home at the same time as his stepfather was most unusual.

'Court life is a very hit-and-miss existence, my dear, as you know well,' said the Duchess, leading them through a succession of doors with a vista of rooms that spanned the length of the north front. 'Even Sir Leo has seen the need to have a place of his own these days. He's taken them to see it.' She smiled indulgently, waiting for Mrs Overshott's murmurs of praise. 'I think he's been inspired by my renovations. He's spent a fortune on having it brought up to date.'

This was news to Phoebe. 'His own house? Where, my lady?'

'Just across the park from you, in Richmond. Now, from the drawing room we go into the long gallery, which,' she said, turning to Phoebe, 'has too little light for my taste. Portraits…ancestors…mostly mine. And the late King Charles up there. And through there is the Duke's library on one side, and the state apartments on *this* side.'

Inwardly, Phoebe groaned. 'Will he be living there soon?' she asked.

'I believe that's his intention, my dear, but it will all depend on his work with the Duke, I suppose. John tends to work his staff very hard.'

'I didn't realise he could afford to—' Phoebe

stopped, aware that she was thinking out loud. 'I thought…well…'

The Duchess looked at her and waited, observing the conflict between polite interest, blatant curiosity and the matter that still weighed heavily on Phoebe's heart. 'You thought he was a fortune-hunter like many men of his age? But didn't he tell you—no, he wouldn't, would he?—that his father died a year ago? He's inherited, you see. He's a wealthy man now, Phoebe dear, and I dare say,' she added, smiling at Mrs Overshott, 'that he might have mentioned it if you'd not been too busy snapping at each other's heels.' The reciprocal glance verified what Mrs Overshott herself had thought, that Phoebe's most pressing need was not for more vistas of rooms but for some motherly advice from her two most trusted friends. The Duchess led them onwards a little more briskly through bedchamber and closet, staircase and passage until on the ground floor she opened the door to a pretty new room looking south and east. 'Now this,' she told them proudly, 'is what I shall call my White Closet, Molly dear, when my white silk hangings are up. I had Verrio do the ceiling for me. Divine Wisdom presiding over the Liberal Arts. What do you think?'

More rollicking cupids in very solid clouds, with huge females, was what Molly Overshott thought. 'Wonderful,' she whispered. 'Truly remarkable.'

'It is, isn't it? Come and sit a while. I do my letter-writing in here, and yes,' she added, noting the interest, 'that's my own dear mama on the over-mantel. They say there's a likeness, but I cannot see it.'

There was indeed a likeness, though the mother had a gentler forehead and none of the pouches beneath the eyes that years of childbearing and high living had conferred on her daughter. The bronze bust of the mother gave them no indication about the origin of the Duchess's red-gold hair, either.

'My lady,' said Phoebe, settling into one of the lacquered cane chairs, 'I owe you an apology for what happened. It was quite inexcusable. Not how a guest ought to behave.'

'No need to apologise, Phoebe, dear. Really, no need at all.' The Duchess leaned forwards to lay a kind, podgy hand on her guest's. 'It was too much to expect that your differences could be resolved in two days. Quite unrealistic.'

'But our quarrel was made public, and that was not what any of us wanted, least of all me. I don't know why I took part in that ridiculous contest, except that my anger got the better of me. It was certainly not the best way for me to take my revenge, was it?'

'With a man of Sir Leo's calibre, probably not, in hindsight, but I thought the outcome would be an agreement, not a deeper rift than ever. That was the disappointment, for me. If it was revenge you sought, then it really was a waste of time. You must have realised that Sir Leo would win.'

'I never thought it would solve our problems, my lady, but I wanted to salve my pride, vent my anger and teach him a lesson.'

'Ah, this pride we women hold so dear.' The Duchess sighed, rolling her eyes towards Mrs Overshott. 'But when it's a Scot you're dealing with, Phoebe, you may as well put your pride in your pocket. Scots have enough and to spare for the whole of the British Isles. I should know. My family are Scottish, too.'

Phoebe was unresponsive for so long that Mrs Overshott felt obliged to say what her friend clearly found difficult to say for herself. 'I think, my lady, that Phoebe has never come across a man quite like Sir Leo, who apparently cares less for her than she does for him. She has always been able to choose quite freely, and none of her friends has ever been so critical of her. It's difficult to be sure how Sir Leo feels towards her when he's so provoking.'

'Then you can take it from me, dear,' said the Duchess, 'that if Sir Leo was not *very* interested in Phoebe, he'd most certainly not have expended so much energy in something as one-sided as a fencing match with a woman. What he was hoping for, as were the rest of us, was for Phoebe to accept defeat gracefully.'

'Which I could not do, my lady,' Phoebe said, more forcefully than she intended, 'when the only indication of his feelings for me were of disapproval. His manner has been very far from lover-like. Quite the opposite, in fact. I dared not risk it.' Her voice dropped to a whisper, as though the admission was too shaming to be heard. 'I was afraid.'

'Of Sir Leo? You thought he intended to chasten you?'

'I thought to chasten him, one way or the other.'

'Then the rapiers *were* the wrong weapons, weren't they? I ought not to have…er…'

Immersed in her own thoughts, the hesitation meant little to Phoebe, but Mrs Overshott glanced enquiringly at their hostess with a sudden dawning of comprehension. This was quickly followed by some energetic but furtive searching of her bright eyes which, to the other two, appeared to be studying the folded hands on her lap. In no time at all, Mrs Overshott's observations had exposed an anomaly in the perfectly appointed private closet where not even a fringe was askew: a slender box of polished wood with silver mounts lay across the curved stretcher below the Duchess's writing cabinet, a box long enough to be a case of rapiers.

CHAPTER FOUR

FROM THE DUCHESS'S delaying tactics, tea, a visit to the stillroom and dairy, it was clear that she hoped her family would return before her guests' departure. But it was on the first mile out of Ham that they met the Duke of Lauderdale and his entourage on their way home from Richmond where they had been treated to an inspection of Sir Leo's latest acquisition.

Master Thomas Tollemache's grin stretched from ear to ear with a genuine pleasure that accentuated the likeness to his sisters. 'Mistress Laker! At last we meet. I thought I'd have to come over and dig you out of your bolt-hole.' He laughed.

Phoebe smiled and inclined her head to the Duke. 'Your Grace,' she said, 'Master Thomas, well met indeed. And Mistress Betty, Katherine, Sir Leo. You remember Mrs Overshott, of course.'

Over shoulders, greetings were exchanged from high saddles while horses wheeled impatiently, and though Phoebe knew better than to continue her dispute with Sir Leo before the Tollemaches, she still found it difficult to smile at him as she did at his companions. Once, she caught his eye, which she thought might be showing admiration, but the memory of his mouth upon hers was still too recent, and her attention changed quickly to his hands before sliding guiltily away. With the admiration, she thought she might have detected a glint of amusement, as if he'd known the reason for her visit to Ham, when anyone with her kind of animosity would have kept well away for a time. So, while a part of her cared too much, another part urged her to bestow a wider smile in the direction of Thomas, who had always found a soft spot for her.

The Duchess's son had filled out with the years, red-gold hair tied back with coloured ribbons, eyes of merry blue, a grin approving and teasing, losing no time in telling her, with all the insensitivity of a twenty-five-year-old soldier, what scandalous goings-on he had discovered about her recent visit to Ham. 'So you thought to teach our cocky friend a lesson with the rapiers, mistress,' he called, loudly. 'Well done. 'Tis time someone took him down a peg. I would do it myself, if I dared.' He looked round at the faces, enjoying the laughter which he thought was at his expense. 'Never mind, you can practise on me, now I have a few days to spare. Shall I call on you in the morning? Will you don your lad's clothes for me, too?'

'Aye,' called the Duke. 'Take the girls with you while Sir Leo and I get on with some work. Can you stand a day with this whelp, Mistress Laker?'

Phoebe's hands clenched on the reins as she politely prepared to perjure herself. 'Indeed, my lord. Mrs Overshot and I will look forward to it.'

Waving and calling, they parted company, with Phoebe outwardly cheerful and inwardly despairing, casting a last glance at Sir Leo's back as if willing him to turn and reassure her that he understood. But he was already talking to his master, to all intents a passing stranger to her.

'Damn…damn!' she muttered, out of earshot. 'The very last thing I want at the moment is a day of empty chatter with those three. Can you stand it, Molly dear?'

'It's only one day, love. We can manage one day between us.'

Phoebe's instincts, however, told her that one of the reasons for Thomas's eagerness was to do with the rivalry he had fostered since Sir Leo had accompanied their stepfather to Ham House. Four years older than Thomas, better looking, more athletic and more dan-

gerous to women than he would ever be—the chances
to cut Sir Leo out of the chase did not come often
enough for Thomas's liking. It was also apparent to
Phoebe that, having heard about the contest from his
sisters, he would assume, as the sisters had, that her
outburst signified a total rejection rather than the complex emotional turmoil about which they knew nothing. Whatever tenuous understanding she had with Sir
Leo would be completely overlooked by this brash
young man in his endeavour to take her part against
him.

She was not much mistaken, for the next few days
were tediously uncomfortable and not at all how she
had wanted to use her time. Each invitation from
Thomas and his sisters offered the possibility that Sir
Leo might also be with them, but he was not, and
Phoebe was close to despair when she and Mrs Overshott
were invited to an archery contest at Ham House
where, they hoped, Sir Leo would be on one of the
teams. At last their patience was rewarded, even
though young Thomas was less than happy to be op-
posed by the rival who excelled at archery as much
as every other sport.

   Just before mid-day, they were joined at the butts by
the Duchess, rather breathless and flushed as if she had
been engaged in a more energetic sport than archery,
which had the effect of verifying what Mrs Overshott

had suspected for a few days. Sir Leo had little to say and, as long as he was there, Phoebe seemed rather subdued and content for the Duchess's family to give full rein to their natural competitiveness. But Thomas's sustained attempts to draw her into his rather petty arguments over scores, his gauche possessiveness put on, she thought, for Sir Leo's benefit, and his patronising attempts to give her practical instruction she didn't need, began to irritate and embarrass her, though to his sisters Thomas could do no wrong.

The Duke and Duchess were too absorbed in each other to notice their son's mischief-making but, lifting a contemptuous eyebrow, Sir Leo pulled the arrows from the target without comment, which made Phoebe sure he was rather disgusted at the spoiling of the light-hearted fun.

Signalling to Mrs Overshott, she went with her to sit on one of the stone benches just inside the Wilderness, beyond the shooting butts. 'We should make our excuses to leave,' she whispered.

'Too late,' Mrs Overshott replied, nodding towards the house. 'They're starting to set the tables for a meal. Look. On the plats.'

Over on the green shapely lawns, known as the plats, white cloths were being thrown over trestles while servants had begun to file back and forth with trays of food, buckets of ice, cider and wine in bottles stamped with the Duke's crest, massive pies and hams, loaves and fruit tarts, jugs of cream, sauces, salads and shellfish enough for a dozen families. The meal would have been the same whether the Lauderdales had guests or not, but Phoebe knew there would be no leaving now until well into the afternoon.

Both guests were surprised to find that, rather than remain at a distance as he had been doing, Sir Leo placed himself beside Phoebe before Thomas could do the same. He merely frowned, saying nothing while his stepfather was there, but the tension tightened as the sulky young man ate his meal as if he'd been cheated of the tastiest morsel, certain that it was not accidental. For her part, Phoebe felt the safety Sir Leo was offering and was relieved that he had identified her discomfort at Thomas's unwanted attentions. Unlike Thomas, he made no show of one-up-manship, courteously helping her and Mrs Overshott to the food, as he ought, while conversing easily with everyone at the table, even gently teasing the two sisters, making them blush with pleasure. It was a performance, Phoebe thought, meant to demontrate to the Duchess's son how to put guests at their ease.

To an onlooker, the scene must have been idyllic, sunshine on white cloths, sparkling silver and glass, colourful food and clothes, animated conversation, the discordant chink of cutlery and birdsong. Less easy to detect was the blossoming of extra senses when shoulders and arms touched in passing, the fleeting brush of fingers sent straight to the heart and held in the skin's memory, the warmth of a rare glance that sent coded, unreadable messages. Phoebe hardly tasted anything, believing Sir Leo was experiencing the same feelings she was. It would not matter so much now, she said to herself, if they were unable to speak privately, for she knew there was little she could have said that Sir Leo could not perceive for himself. Indeed, they spoke seldom to each other, Sir Leo saying more to Mrs Overshott on the other side of Phoebe than to her, which enabled her to study his face at close quarters in the most innocent of diversions.

The Wilderness, where the shooting butts were, was laid out in radiating compartments of hornbeam hedges and maple trees, not wild at all but avenued with grassy walks and adorned in the central space with classical figures on pedestals and orange trees in boxes. Mrs Overshott wanted to explore this area where the Duchess had told her there were four small summerhouses. Phoebe politely accompanied her. Mrs Overshott walked on ahead. 'Over here, I think,' she called.

The family were still sitting near the house from where their argumentative tones could be heard as Phoebe tried, without bending, to read the inscription on one of the pedestals. 'Venus de Medici. Now who was she? Molly?' In the shade of the trees, she felt a warmth behind her and, before she could turn, an arm encircled her waist, pulling her back against a hard body which she knew instantly was not Thomas's, for this man knew how to hold a woman helpless, how to turn her forehead towards his lips. She felt his words on her skin. 'Just a reminder, wee lass, not to get too involved with that young lord over there. He's not for you.' His hand caressed and cupped her face and kept it upturned to his, showing her what he meant so that she had no opportunity to pretend ignorance. His kiss was thorough, controlling and...yes... jealous too, telling her something of the anger he'd done so well to conceal. But his reminder was unfair and not well timed, after his previous courtesies. It was unexpected and not altogether welcome; not at all what she wanted from him on such a day when feelings had started to run high, with misunderstandings building like thunderclouds. She pulled angrily at his hand, prising it away from her neck. 'You have no right to do that,' she spat, 'and I need no reminders. You forfeited any rights when you told me I was free, sir. You cannot do this, Sir Leo.'

From behind the flat-topped hedge, they could not be seen from the house and Mrs Overshott was out of sight. Phoebe would like to have asked him, if he'd not provokingly told her what she already knew, to take her away from these well-meaning but meddlesome friends, to tell him how her heart was softening, to beg him for a little more time, patience, tenderness, perhaps. But the day was going disastrously wrong, and all she wanted was to go home.

'Still fighting me, then?' he whispered, restraining her with a hand across her bodice. 'So why were you in such a hurry to come back to Ham when it holds such bad memories for you? Are they as bad as all that? Eh?'

Squirming and twisting, she freed herself at last, smarting at being found out before she'd had a chance to explain her reasons. 'To show you how little I care, Sir Leo. And your warning is not needed either, thank you. When I wish to be courted, I shall not be looking for a young pup like that, nor shall I want a man to knock me over the head with his club and drag me into the nearest cave.' With an irritable shake of her shoulders, she wiped the back of her hand across her mouth and turned to face him, ruffled, hurt and infuriated by his assumptions, when she had thought he was beginning to understand. 'Now leave me to make up my own mind, if you please, about how best to live my life while you concentrate *your* efforts into keeping well out of my way. You were keen enough to do that only a few days ago, sir, so try to be consistent, will you? What's done is done, and that's how it will stay.'

'If you knew how to keep your feelings on track, Mistress Laker, how is it that half an hour ago you were relieved to be in my company? I was not imagining that, was I?'

'Not so difficult to explain,' she bit back, catching sight of Mrs Overshott through the trees. 'You were simply the better of two not-very-appealing options, that's all.' She did not watch his face to find out the effects of her lie, but Mrs Overshott was facing him as she approached and could see the flash of white teeth quite clearly.

Phoebe's natural reaction to Sir Leo's untimely warning was to enter into Thomas's plans for the afternoon, if only to show that she needed no one's assistance. But any pleasure she might have derived from this caprice remained beyond her reach, for by now she was thoroughly tired of his attempts to keep her engaged in self-indulgent small talk, to score points off his sisters and to bore her with tales of his soldierly exploits. Mrs Overshott, on the other hand, walked apart with Sir Leo and appeared to be sharing a sober conversation with him that took far too long, to Phoebe's mind. The afternoon was sweltering and her whalebone stays had begun to bite into the tender flesh under her arms, her shoes stuck hotly to her feet, the midges pestered, and her straw sun-hat clamped her brow like a crown of thorns. 'I think, Master Thomas,' she said, 'it's time we were taking our leave of you. I wonder if someone would be kind enough to summon my coach.'

Regarding her with reproach, the two Tollemache sisters protested. 'But if *you* go,' said Katherine, as if

Phoebe had a duty to consider the consequences, 'Sir Leo will go too. I think he only stays for your sake, you know. He was on his way to Richmond this morning to his new house, but he changed his mind. I don't believe you've seen it yet, have you, Mistress Laker?'

'Not yet. I believe it's rather splendid.'

'Oh, yes, Mama has given him lots of advice,' said Elizabeth. Then, in what appeared to be a renewed attempt to pull the reluctant protagonists together again, she called out to Sir Leo, who was at that moment returning from the Cherry Garden with Mrs Overshott. 'Sir Leo, Mistress Laker would like to see your new house, I believe. Shall you allow it?'

As if that same thought had already occurred to him, Sir Leo stopped. 'Of course,' he called. 'Any time. We'll arrange something.'

Rising from her cane chair, and trying not to wince at the sharp stab of the stays, Phoebe smiled at the sisters. 'Good. Then that's settled,' she said. 'Now, we really must not impose upon your hospitality a moment longer. Molly, dear, we must go and take our leave of the Duke and Duchess. Shall we go in?'

With a last wave from the window of the coach, Phoebe sat back against the blue velvet cushions and closed her eyes with relief, snatching off her straw hat and kicking off the clammy shoes. She squirmed with the release. 'It's really too hot for any more good manners, Molly. I cannot wait to take this apricot thing off. The bones have made a hole in me, and there's something inside the bodice prickling my back.' Her fingertips explored under one arm. 'It will have to be altered,' she said, stuffing her lace handkerchief into the space.

'Oh, dear,' said Mrs Overshott. 'Which gown will you change into?'

Phoebe thought it was a rather odd question to ask, but easy enough to answer. 'Oh, the old faded blue cambric without stays. What did you and Sir Leo talk about?'

'Mostly about his house. I was hoping we might take a detour through Richmond so that we can drive past and take a look, but if you're too—'

'No, we can do that,' Phoebe said quickly. 'It's not much out of our way. Did he tell you where it is?'

'One of those on the river's edge, on the Petersham road.'

From Petersham and Ham, the road branched; the lower branch was the older track that followed the river bank, the upper one, made more recently, went on over the hill and down again into the village of Richmond via a drier route. Sam Coachman had by this time already turned on to the lower road but, because his mistress had closed her eyes, her chaperon being careful to say nothing that might open them again, they were approaching the first cottages in

Richmond before Phoebe felt the coach slow down and bounce to a stop. Its occupants were jerked upright before a pair of black wrought-iron gates that enclosed a cobbled courtyard with a large redbrick house beyond, though the details were unclear.

'Where are we?' Phoebe said. 'Is this the house? How did Sam know…?' Puzzled and rather disorientated, she leaned out of the open window but, in doing so, found herself face-to-face with the man who, without her knowledge, had ridden behind them all the way from Ham. Sir Leo Hawkynne. His abrupt opening of the coach door, with all her weight leaning on it, might have precipitated a very undignified fall on to the ground had Sir Leo not caught her, scooped her out of the coach into his arms, and swung her round towards the magically opening gates, followed by his obedient horse.

'No!' she cried. 'What are you…Molly…my shoes… put me *down,* sir!'

Her wriggles and protests, beating fists and kicking feet had not the slightest effect on her progress, nor did Mrs Overshott follow her through the gates with either shoes or assistance. The gates clanged shut, the coach lumbered away and Phoebe was carried, squealing with rage, through the wide front porch into the cool entrance hall where the scent of pinewood shavings and paint still lingered in the air.

'Welcome to Ferry House,' said Sir Leo, lowering his guest's feet to the tiled floor. 'Not quite what I had in mind for your first visit, but I'm all in favour of bringing plans forward, if need be.'

'This is *monstrous!*' Phoebe growled. 'What do you think you're doing, sir?'

Placing himself between her and the door, Sir Leo made a barrier too great for her to pass, though her first thoughts were naturally to escape. Which he knew. 'It was what you said at Ham that gave me the idea,' he said.

'I said nothing about abduction, Sir Leo. Of that I'm quite sure.'

'No, but about dragging you off to my cave, wee lass. Now *that* was inspired. You wanted to take a look round, so now you can. See? Is it not a fine place?'

'It may be the finest place in all Richmond, sir, but I'm not staying to find out. I want to go home. I want my coach. And I want my companion. Why has Mrs Overshott left me here? Is she being abducted too?'

'No, she's gone to get you some clothes. You'll be staying here a while.'

'I shall be doing no such thing,' she cried, looking round wildly for a way out, 'even if I have to walk to Mortlake in my stockinged feet.'

The manservant who had been nearby to open gates and doors had disappeared like a ghost and, although the hall was light and in no way oppressive with new pine panelling and sparkling chandelier, Phoebe was in no mood to accept her confinement without making a great deal of fuss about it. Never before had anyone physically manhandled her into a place she didn't want to go, and the awful fear of being kept away from her dear familiar possessions, her own four walls, servants and especially Molly, was quite unacceptable. There was fury in her eyes as she whirled round to face him. 'Sir Leo,' she said, 'this may be a game to you, but to me it is not, I can assure you. You cannot keep me here. Now, open that door and let me out. *Immediately.*'

But before she could see what he was about, Sir Leo had caught her waving arms and pinioned them behind her back out of harm's way, enclosing her like a warm envelope with her face buried in the white linen ruffles of his shirt. Her howls of anger became croaks followed by a torrent of unladylike oaths and epithets she'd learnt at Court, screeched into his neckband, venomously and with gusto, spiced with every grudge she had held against him over the years as well as many others wholly undeserved. A lesser man would have wilted under her tongue-lashing.

A few moments of this, and she realised from the vibrations in his chest that he was talking to her. 'Yes, sweet lass…hush now…you're quite right, I *am* all of those things and more. But in one thing you exaggerate. I have never carried a woman off by force until now.'

'You never…had…a house…until now…did you? You great ugly *lout!*'

'Well, no, but that's not the reason. The truth is, I've never wanted to. I've waited far too long to get you to myself, Mistress Phoebe Laker, and if this is the only way, then so be it. I'll have no more damned interference from the Ham House family to pull us apart or push us together. There's been far too much of that silly nonsense in the last couple of weeks.'

'You've been talking to Mrs Overshott. You *have,* haven't you? You decided this together, today, conspiring about *my* future. Betrayed by the woman I trusted with my life. Oh, how *could* she do this? Let me go, damn you!'

'No, I won't. Hush, lass. Easy now. Just listen to me, will you? Mrs Overshott agrees with me that we need to find out about each other without help. Alone. You know next to nothing about me, and you're certainly not going to discover anything with the kind of help you've been getting, are you? So now it's time to do things my way.'

'I don't *want* to know anything about you, and I don't want to do anything your way. Not *this* way. How d'you think it's going to look for an unmarried gentlewoman to stay alone with a man, without even her companion or her maid? You were the one, remember, to be so scathing about my unconventional ways in the past, so how exactly is your plan going to help my marriage prospects? Is it your aim to cause another scandal? To ruin me completely? Ah, yes, now it begins to make some sense. I suppose you can hardly wait to gallop off back to Court to tell them all about how Mistress Laker—'

'Enough!' His method of stopping the tirade was highly effective and, even with whalebone stays jabbing into her and her wrists aching in his grasp, Phoebe's train of thought was so sidelined that, when he gave her a chance to breathe, those irritants faded against the tender rapture of his kiss.

But he was right; she knew so little about him, and men were capable of such duplicity in their dealings with women, whether at Court or outside it. He had already backed away from his first acrimonious victory, leaving her bewildered and angry. True, he had seen through her own vengeful ploy, but that was no excuse. Men were not supposed to disarm women so easily when there were so few weapons to fight with. If a woman could not use her conduct as a weapon, what else was there?

'Now *will* you listen to me, termagant? Your Mrs Overshott will be here in an hour with a trunk full of your belongings, and your maid, too. They will have rooms near yours, and you will be staying here with me for however long it takes to make you mine. No more protests, if you please.'

Her lips held the warm imprint of his mouth upon hers, and her mind strayed into other dangerous territory. 'What do you mean, to make me yours? You said I was free,' she whispered.

'I know what I said.' Carefully, he released her wrists and held her arms as she swayed unsteadily. 'Come through here into the parlour. You need to sit.'

The difficult day, the unrelenting heat, her emotions and furious responses suddenly began to take their toll of her, and she was glad to be supported for the few steps into an adjoining room lined with colourful tapestries and carved wainscoting. Her shoeless feet made no sound on the polished oak floor. A large leaded window had a cushioned seat across its width, and one of the casements had been opened wide to let in the scents from the garden beyond. She made her way towards the light to sit next to the open window, breathing in the aroma of cut grass and wallflowers. This, she thought, could not be the garden still in a mess, for the low box hedges were neatly clipped, and white roses spilled over the high brick wall to meet a bank of foxgloves and blue monkshood.

When she turned again to the room, a tray of pretty blue-and-white Chinese tea dishes had been placed upon the table, steaming with clear pale liquid, a plate of tiny biscuits beside them. It was fragrant and soothing and, as she took her first sips, the surface rippled in time with her trembling. Without doubt, it was the most bizarre situation she had ever been in, and one she had no idea how to handle. The fencing had been a contest for which she had put in place contingency plans against her failure, but this was different, for although she had wanted to know more about Sir Leo's true intentions, she had never expected to be informed so soon and in so bold a fashion. Or had she misunderstood him?

Shakily, she replaced her dish on the tray. 'What did you mean,' she repeated, 'to make me yours? Have you brought me here to dishonour me? Is this supposed to be the easy way nowadays? To abduct a woman *before* gaining her consent?'

'The easy way. Oh, dear, shall I ever be allowed to forget that, I wonder?' he murmured. Taking a biscuit, he put it whole into his mouth, picked up a low upholstered stool and, placing it below her, took her feet and put them on it. 'You are the most remarkable woman,' he said, munching. 'Even when you're dog-tired to the point of exhaustion, your tongue is as sharp as a dirk. D'ye hone it every morning, mistress?'

She glared at him, refusing to answer his jibe.

'Well, now,' he said, sitting at the opposite end of the window-seat, 'it's like this. I recall saying that I would not wed any woman who was as set against the match as you, but your Mrs Overshott, wise woman that she is, kindly pointed out to me that, so far, I've given you very little opportunity to feel any different. Have I? No. So, since no polite invitation from me is likely to get you here before I have to go off again on my duties, Mrs Overshott agreed that I don't have a day to lose. Besides, the Duchess's son is not going to leave you in peace, and her two daughters are not going to leave *me* in peace, either. So it's best if we both make ourselves scarce, isn't it?'

'Oh, I *see,*' Phoebe said, as if the light had suddenly dawned. 'So it's all about fitting me somewhere into your busy timetable to see if you can change my mind in…how many days…or is it *hours* before you must go? It's no wonder you're in such a tearing hurry, Sir Leo.'

'I've already given you the answer to that, lass, if only you'd listen instead of galloping off on your high horse. However long it takes, is what I said. And, no, you need not get all in a pother about it. I do not intend to ravish you while you're a guest in my house. In fact, I shall not lay a finger on you until you say you want me to.'

'Mmm. So I could be here for quite some time, then.'

'You *will* be here for some time, Mistress Laker, one way or another. You're going to marry me and this will be your home. There are still some finishing touches to be made, but I hoped you'd help me with those.'

Her expression was highly sceptical, to say the least, eyes half-closed, head tilted just too far back, her glance sliding off his face with barely controlled derision. 'Hah!' she breathed, tonelessly. 'Thank you for the tea,

Sir Leo. Perhaps I should come to see your house another day when you're feeling better.' She stood up and
gave her skirts a gentle shake. 'These rapid changes of
mind can be so confusing, can't they? What will it be
next, I wonder? Tch! I can hardly keep up.'

'Phoebe.'

She sighed, but made no move to go. His gentle use
of her name came like a caress, deep and velvety-soft,
tinged with sadness and regret for the misunderstandings that held them in this tangle. To carry her off in
this manner was a strange way to smooth out the problems of the past three years. Nor was it the way to woo
a woman. Or so she'd thought only that afternoon.
Strangely, however, she had heard something in his
tone, felt the urgent desire in his kisses, even the anger
too, but different from the victory-kiss after the contest. And when he had sat beside her, unquestionably
to be her protector, she had never felt safer or more
cherished. Even now, despite the noisy protestations,
the thought of being constantly in the care of such a
man felt like sailing into harbour after a particularly
lengthy storm.

'Phoebe,' he said again, 'come to me.' Holding out
a hand, palm upwards, he waited for her eyes to signal her intentions, moving up from boots to breeches
to buckle to chest, where they lingered, then up to his
mouth and finally to his eyes, looking above all things
for honesty.

They were brown and openly desirous but, more than that, Phoebe saw what she believed was something like love. Sighing, she closed her eyes and, in that brief moment, he was before her, holding her by the shoulders and tilting his head to look deeply into her face. 'Phoebe, I mean you no harm. You've never been afraid of the unconventional, have you? Neither have I. But what I have in mind is not for gossip-fodder, in case that's what you thought, lass. It's to make up for lost time after a foolish, callous, jealous remark that I made wounded your pride. I've regretted it ever since, not only for the life that was lost but for the damage it's done to you, too. Now I have to make things right between us. I *have* to, lass, for there's never been a moment when I haven't wanted you for my wife. Like you, I thought that contest at Ham might help to settle things, but you…'

'But I hated you too much for it ever to settle anything,' she whispered.

'Yes. And now? Will you give me another chance? Will you let me show you what a good choice I am, if I tread very carefully, wee lass?'

Her lips struggled not to laugh at his turn of phrase, but there was something in what he said that took her by surprise. 'Never been a moment?' she said.

'Never. I swear it. I want you. Forget the worshipping the ground remark. I was angry and fired up. I'll settle for affection, if that's all I'm worth.'

'No,' she said, touching the wave of hair that swept his brow.

'No?'

'No. I think I can probably do more than affection, Sir Leo, if I try.'

CHAPTER FIVE

IN A VILLAGE the size of Richmond that had just begun
to expand after the demolition of the beautiful royal
palace, it was never going to be possible to keep secret the irregularities of the few nobility who lived
there. They and their activities were, after all, one of
the main topics of gossip, along with marriage, birth,
illness and death and, of course, the weather.

Sir Leo Hawkynne's purchase of one of the larger
houses built beside the River Thames overlooked the
one and only ferry and was therefore known to everyone. As they stood on the ferry-boat, they had time to
scrutinise the scaffolding and builders' huts, and to
comment on the daily progress of the alterations and
extensions, and when at last the building was revealed

with its garden sloping down to the river, its summer-house and steps and all the details that came with wealth, there were plenty of envious mutterings about his bricks being reclaimed from the old palace itself. It was quite untrue, as it happened, but when tongues stopped wagging about that, they began to wag about the women he'd taken to live with him.

After a few days, however, the gossip abated, for Mistress Laker and her kindly companion were not at all like men's usual mistresses, who'd taken to flaunting themselves at every opportunity. Some said she and Sir Leo had married, but that also was untrue, Mistress Laker having decided at the outset that she would take full advantage of her host's hospitality to find out exactly what kind of a man he was who could abduct a woman on her own doorstep and get away with it. In broad daylight.

No longer doubting his sincerity in wanting to marry her, the sense of peace that came with this new-found knowledge was enough to calm all her doubts and fears. Now, there seemed to be no hurry to make something happen but to let it happen, naturally without the distressing rancour of the previous weeks. She began to laugh, to accept his teasing without retaliation, to allow him to impress her as he obviously wanted to do.

With Ferry House she was impressed from the start, with its views across the river and countryside, its white moulded ceilings reflecting the light, large airy rooms furnished with a distinct lack of tassle and fringe, decoration without fussiness and not a naked or gilded cherub to be seen anywhere. Polished oak and pine, antique rugs and stout Scottish-made cupboards might have been rather outdated, but the way the older heirlooms blended with newer pieces, pale curtains and cushions, was nothing short of inspired. Phoebe's own beautiful room that overlooked the river and the road to Twickenham was conveniently placed next to one for Mrs Overshott, and a smaller dressing-room closet for Constance.

But after the first two days, Mrs Overshott declared that she would return to Mortlake to keep an eye on things during Phoebe's absence. She promised to visit them regularly, to bring whatever was needed, to join them for dinner occasionally and to accompany Phoebe whenever propriety demanded. Otherwise she believed they would do well enough without her.

Until then, they had stayed within the confines of the house and gardens, having much to occupy them, especially outside. It was the kitchen garden, Phoebe discovered, that was still in a mess, the builders having trampled it down to construct a new kitchen, still-room, dairy and laundry on that side of the house, stables and coach house on the other. Plans for a new garden were drawn, materials listed, plants ordered, and Phoebe's nights were restful with the sleep of physical exhaustion. While Mrs Overshott had been with them, conversation had been kept to general and domestic matters, which Sir Leo thought rather too safe. There were things about his guest he wanted to know, yet it was with an extraordinary feeling of guilt mixed with relief that they waved Mrs Overshott off to Mortlake and wandered down to the river garden like children left without parental control.

'So,' Phoebe said, 'one prisoner released and the other retained. Am I still your prisoner, Sir Leo?'

'Indeed you are, mistress, although I hope you don't feel like one. Do you?'

'Deliciously so, I thank you, sir.'

He chuckled, opening the door of the little gazebo that perched like a pepper-pot on the very edge of the lawn where a wooden retaining wall shored up the bank. Round the hexagonal walls, cushions were set on benches below the leaded windows, and a small table in the centre had been laid with a silver coffee-pot and dainty mugs that seemed to complement the rustic setting and Phoebe's faded blue cambric gown. 'Then since you are mistress of the house, perhaps you would pour out the coffee. I seem to recall that the last time we were in a similar riverside location, you were not quite so relaxed.'

Frowning, she handed him one of the mugs. 'Don't,' she said. 'I'd rather not think about that.'

'Why, lass? Because of the two halfwits, or because I was there?'

Things had moved on since then, not so long ago in days, but certainly in relationships. She had been on edge, ready to leave Ham House, ready to fly off the handle, and tense with the premonitions of a show-down after Sir Leo's first approach. In the viewing-platform at Ham, he had gallantly come to her rescue and his touch had remained with her for hours. She knew it could not be the first time he'd pinned a woman's sleeve, but she would never ask him if it was true that women begged for his favours, as she'd been told. If they did, she could well understand it.

'Neither,' she replied. 'It was because I didn't want you, of all people, to see that kind of disrespect. You were sure to think I had once allowed it, but I had not. You believed I was promiscuous, and I was not. I simply had friends, men and women, with whom I had easy outspoken relationships, as we do at Court, with music and dancing and…yes…some flirting, too. There was nothing wrong. Noisy, perhaps, but not wrong, and there was no immorality, either. They all knew, even those two halfwits, that I needed a houseful of people to mask the emptiness I felt.' All this she said to the passing wherries on the river. The people on the ferry might just have been able to see her lips moving.

'Emptiness, sweet lass? The loss of your family, you mean?'

'I was only twelve when the plague came to London, and Mrs Overshott would not allow Tim or me near our parents once they became infected. How she survived it I have no idea, but she nursed them until…until the end. As you said, plenty of others suffered in the same way, but not to be allowed to say goodbye is…and to have no place…' Her voice trailed away, tightened by the memory of loss.

'Hush, lass. Say no more.' He came to sit beside her and took her in his arms, cradling her head upon his shoulder. ''Tis a terrible thing indeed. You were a close family?'

'They were wonderful parents,' she said, holding his hand over her cheek. 'I didn't realise it until I lost them. Then Tim in the following year. Our new home at Mortlake was to have been a safe haven, but when Tim went, it was like a reminder to me that I was supposed to make something of my life, and I had no idea what to do. Friends came to comfort me, and Mrs Overshott was always there for me to turn to, and as I grew older the house became a meeting place, rather like a glorified coffee house, for women as well as men.'

'And then I opened my big mouth, just to help things along.'

Phoebe sat up, demurely, brushing back her mop of curls and hitching a finger into the neckline that had slipped further than it ought. 'You were not the only one to comment on my range of friends, Sir Leo, but you can claim to be the first to hurt me. Don't ask me why.'

'I don't need to ask you why,' he said, softly. 'I had seen you and I knew you'd seen me at Court, yet I could never get near you and you did your best to make sure I didn't, fencing yourself in with your parasites.'

'They were good friends. They were loyal.'

'Yes, as long as you fed and watered them for nothing.'

'I needed them.'

'You needed a man, lass. And you were scared of me.'

'You had a reputation too, you know. I expect you still do.'

'Yes, for speaking plainly and truthfully. For treading on toes, like my master. Few Scots are born courtiers. You may blame the King's grandfather for flooding England with them, but we're here to stay. You'll be marrying one.'

'I don't think I ever totally agreed to that, did I?'

'No matter. I shall get an agreement from you before long, mistress.' His face had moved closer as they quibbled, making her push back against the leaded panes until she could evade him no longer. His mouth brushed over hers, sending ripples of pleasure down to her knees, nudging and lapping at her lips until they parted under his as she closed her eyes.

'You said,' she whispered, 'that you'd not lay a finger on me.'

'I'm not doing that, wee lass. Am I?' he murmured.

That time, it was to go no further, though a part of her wished it had. But she had begun to talk to him about herself and her lost family, which in itself was an unusual event. And because Phoebe had mentioned to Mrs Overshott that she might learn to play the lute, and because her brother's instrument was still at home, it had been brought to Richmond along with her gowns and writing desk. So that evening, in the private garden, Sir Leo gave her a first rudimentary lesson on it, although it took him over an hour to tune its sixteen strings.

She was already proficient on the harpsicord and spinet, but the lute was not an easy instrument to play; after a time, he took it from her and began to accompany himself in a haunting song by Dowland. When he looked up, he saw that she was stifling sobs with her hand over her face.

Putting the lute aside, he drew her again into his embrace, rocking her gently. 'What is it?' he whispered. 'Your brother?'

Mutely, she nodded, making a strangely forlorn sound in her throat.

'I should have known. Every young lad sings that at some time.'

'"Come again. Sweet love doth now invite,"' she

whispered. Had he chosen the song on purpose to offer her the chance he was waiting for?

He was close. Close enough to repeat those intimate caresses taken with her consent but without permission. And now, when the barriers had begun to fall, he waited for the signal she didn't know how to give. Practised in the art of flirtation, she had never gone beyond that, and now in her inexperience she yearned to find out more from the only man she had ever wanted to show her. Her brother's lute, her brother's song, the man whose arms were around her, and the memories that had begun to hurt less, becoming sweet and beautiful in one peaceful summer evening soothed her anger. What reason was there to hold back now except how to find the way forwards? Lifting his hand, she closed his fingers into a fist and brought it to her mouth, kissing his knuckles with the lightest touch of her lips. 'Was my fencing as bad as my lute-playing, Sir Leo?' she said, coyly.

The question took him by surprise. 'Och, lass! D'ye want the truth?'

'No,' she said, smiling. 'Not if it's as bad as that.'

'I could have been put off easy enough by the lad's clothes, you know. That was unfair. Affects a man's concentration.'

'Serves you right. It was the only advantage I had.'

'Well,' he deliberated, 'your three years' practice didn't exactly give you the stamina of a grown man, did it, sweet lass? You're still as soft as butter. And you don't think like a fencer either, do you?' The last words were spoken into her hair as his hand escaped from hers to pull carefully at the laces of her bodice, loosening it as if the mysteries of a woman's dress were well understood.

It was the blue cambric gown without stays, and she felt the luxurious easing of her breasts as they were freed from constraint beneath her chemise, though never before with this kind of excitement. It was, she thought, as if he were urging her to permit this freedom by doing nothing to stop him, but by the time his hand had slipped through the unlaced bodice on to the soft warm linen, the very idea of stopping him was already far away, taking her reservations with it.

Burying her face into his shoulder, she trembled as his hand found her breast and held it as though, after all, he needed no permission. She heard his deep voice speaking into her hair, almost harsh with pent-up desire. 'This is what I wanted to do, lass,' he said, gently moving his palm across the nipple. 'This…and this…taking a hand to ye, not a sword. It was the look of ye that made me sae mad. I wanted to tire ye with loving, not with sword-play. I could see your lovely body, and I wanted ye, there and then.'

'But you cut my button off.'

'Aye, lass. It was all I could do not to cut your shirt off. I *could* have.'

'Brute.'

'I could be a brute, too. It would be easy, with you. I could have thrown you down on that bed up there and taken what you were offering me.'

'I was *not* offering—'

'No, and you were not saying nay either, were you?'

'Don't, Leo.'

'Don't what? This…or this?' Tender and beguiling, his words accompanied the deftness of his fingers as he drew the chemise away to join the wide-open bodice, revealing her nakedness to the fading light and the new stars. 'Ah, Phoebe! You came within an inch of losing everything except your anger, that time. But I didn't want you like that, I wanted you like this. Soft in my arms. Trembling for me, not half-dead with fighting, and not afraid of me, as you were.'

With half-closed eyes, she turned her head to watch his hand move over her skin, capturing first one breast and then the other, teasing the buds with his lips, sending hot waves of desire through her body. It was true, she had feared him, the Duke's man, his scathing tongue, his authority, his experience of women older and more worldly than her. In love with him even then, she had kept him on the edge of her dreams, only reluctantly allowing him in, wanting yet hating, hurt by his dismissal of her as being hardly worth the chase. She had wept, having no means of redress except to show him how wrong he was.

'Have you kept me waiting long enough now?' he said, raising his head to look at her. 'Shall I show you what you've been missing?'

'I wanted to be sure, Leo. I had to be sure. I have too much to lose.'

'A woman always has more to lose, and I played my hand badly, clumsy devil that I am. You were right to reject me. But I never stopped wanting you, and if I'd been free to go where I would, I'd have come to tell you so and risk being turned away at your door. But now I've got you here, sweet Phoebe, and I cannot let you go again. Let me show you how much I love you, dear heart. You'll not regret it, I swear.'

The hand continued to explore her, insatiable in its fondling, setting her alight, robbing her of thoughts, twisting her body in his arms to follow his caresses, greedily seeking more. 'You were right on one thing, Leo,' she said. 'I would have been an easy conquest for you. I would have laid myself at your feet if you'd snapped your fingers for me. You were the only man I'd ever have given myself to. Even when I was planning revenge, you managed to turn me inside out with one sweep of your hand. And I have a hundred questions to ask that women are supposed to ask at such times, yet I cannot recall even one. Take me to bed. Show me what I have to do. Teach me all you know, Leo.' Hiding her burning face against his chest, she breathed in the scent of him, dissolving the last of her fears. Her head lifted to seek him again, while the touch of his lips and hands held her senses in a limbo of delight. "'Come away. Sweet love doth now invite,"' she said, quoting the song.

His white teeth caught the last of the dying light. 'Doth it, indeed?' he said. Hooking an arm beneath her knees, he lifted her into his arms. 'Then who am I to resist such an invitation from the woman I've loved for sae long?'

As her room slid gently into darkness and the night spread its warmth over them, her took her carefully through every phase of loving, revealing the mysteries of her body that she had known nothing of, that could only be unlocked by a lover's hand, never by her own. She had not needed to protest her inexperience, for he could tell it was all new to her, the places to be kissed, her wonder at her own responses, her delight in his magnificent body, the growing fierceness of her ardour long before he expected it.

What he could not tell was the way her memory taunted her with the added thrill of being loved, at last, by the very man who had once held her in contempt, even though she now understood the artifice. Winning Sir Leo Hawkynne and having held him off, fought him and bound him to her, and then fallen in love more deeply than before was the stuff of dreams and not to be taken lightly. After his efforts, he deserved her respect, her devotion and her trust, for he was a man of substance, not a lad with his first love.

The moment, when it came, was for Phoebe the peak of all her desires as well as being a gift as great as any she could bestow, one she'd withheld despite many persuasions. It was for her the most natural thing to be close to him along every surface, to have him fit perfectly inside her, smoothly throbbing, making her moan and cry out at the power in him that could possess her so utterly. That was something she'd not been told to expect. That, and his wonderful muscle-bound body, toned and virile, holding her under him with his hair touching her face, his kisses luring her mind, his deep tones whispering of her beauty in words too intimate for daylight, words she received with sighs and smiles and all her senses stormed.

'I want this to be good for you, sweet lass,' he breathed into her hair. 'I want you to remember the first time you gave yourself to me, without shame or resentment, but for love of me. Is there love for me yet, Phoebe Laker? Or shall I have to do more to earn it?'

'There has always been…ah…love for you, Leo. I was hurt only because I cared deeply what you thought of me. Forgive me. I hated *and* loved you. Ah…Leo! Something…is hap…happening…'

There was something else that no one had told her of, except with meaninglessly extravagant words too vague to make sense. Her own attempts to speak be- -

came cries and inarticulate sounds as his loving swept her on ever faster into a tide of sensation, her hands clinging, raking his back, her mewing gasps suspended on the crest as he arched above her, groaning softly into the tangle of dark ringlets that spread across the pillow. His weight upon her was gentle, like a human blanket that wrapped with tender fingers, rewarding her with breathless kisses and praise for her courage.

'Don't go,' she whispered when her breathing began to settle. 'Stay there, beloved.'

Leaning upon one elbow, he looked into her eyes, dark and gleaming like deep midnight pools, damp-lashed. 'Did I hurt ye, sweet lass? Are those tears?'

'No, Leo. I'm not hurt. Do other women weep at such times? I don't know. Something happened, and I don't think I shall ever be the same again. Perhaps this is what it means to become whole.'

'I've waited sae long for this, sweetheart,' he said, pushing away her tear-drop with the soft heel of his hand. 'You're mine now. Wholly mine. Ye'll be marrying me now, Mistress Laker?'

'Yes, I'll be marrying you now, Leo Hawkynne, I thank you.'

Moving out of her, he drew her into his embrace, smoothing her wild hair off her forehead, kissing her damp skin. 'What a woman,' he murmured. '*What* a tigress for our bairns.'

* * *

The next day, Sir Leo suggested a trip to London. 'I have my barge ready,' he said. 'We could be there by mid-day, if we start early tomorrow.'

'You wish to go to Court?'

'No, to the Royal Exchange where your family's shop was. I know it's been rebuilt since then, but…'

'But it's changed hands now, and I don't know who the new owner is.'

'No matter. I thought a pilgrimage might help to lay a few ghosts.'

'It might. Who knows?'

The heat had become oppressive overnight and the sky was heavy, the breeze off the river stronger from the south-west, hitting the long graceful barge with rough waves each time the oarsmen pulled into a bend of the river. Each man had served a seven-year apprentice-ship and was entitled to wear the uniform of the Thames Watermen with two badges on the sleeve of the pleated coat, one for the Waterman's Hall and the other for the Duke of Lauderdale, their employer. Rowing strongly with the tide, they came into the Chelsea reach well before noon, the shelter of the buildings making a welcome respite from the con-tinuous blasts of the wind.

Leaving the barge just short of the bridge, Sir Leo summoned a hackney carriage to take them to Cornhill, giving Phoebe a chance to see some parts of the town that had recently been rebuilt, and to compare her memories of ten years ago with the clean new buildings of brick and stone that were growing in their place. The original stone-built shopping place of the Royal Exchange had suffered less than most and had been restored very much along the same lines as before, four sides of stalls and two-storey arcaded shops set around a vast open square.

The crowds of browsers, shoppers and merchants made it difficult to move forwards with any speed, once they had descended from the hackney, and all Phoebe could do was to point out where the goldsmith's shop had once been, on the ground floor where some of the other jewellers were. Telling him that she didn't suppose it would go by the name of Laker now, he was undeterred, leading her by the hand through the throng towards a young aproned apprentice yelling a familiar name. 'Laker's! Finest gold and silver for your table, earrings for your lady. This way, sirs!'

A cold shiver ran along Phoebe's arms, and she pulled her cashmere shawl further over her shoulders, shocked by the use of her father's name, though there was no law to prevent it. They stopped outside the display of silverware that the young man guarded against thieving hands, and on the pretext of looking, Phoebe gave in to a moment of unease. Despite the renovations, this was the place where her father had traded, the place where her brother had died. Here. On this very spot.

Sir Leo appeared to sense her apprehension, giving her time to regain her composure before entering the dim interior, where well-dressed customers sat at tables with assistants hovering, just as they had in her father's day. It was dim and quiet after the roar outside, a long wooden counter marking a barrier behind which were shelves of gleaming gold, plates of every shape and size, ewers and chalices, rings, pearls and pendants hanging below, chains of office, badges and bracelets, hat-pins and filigree pomanders. An elderly bespectacled gentleman sat behind the counter, weighing coins on a fine brass balance.

'Master Laker?' said Sir Leo, knowing that he was not.

The gentleman's expression changed instantly from preoccupation to pleasure as he saw the cut of his customer's fine mulberry velvet suit and that of his lady companion. The balance was dropped and pushed aside. 'Why, no, my lord. Laker is the previous owner's name. I kept it because it's well known. After the fire, you see, I bought the plot, as we were allowed to do when the owner could not be traced. Very sad. Started my own business from scratch. Your lady…?' He glanced at Phoebe with a smile. 'Looking for something special?'

'The lady is Mistress Phoebe Laker,' said Sir Leo,

'daughter of Master Adolphus Laker, the banker and goldsmith whose name you have borrowed. I am Sir Leo Hawkynne, private secretary to his Grace the Duke of Lauderdale. And your name, sir?'

The man rose slowly from his stool, his mouth making a perfect *O,* his brown watery eyes showing the whites all round as the information registered. Then, gathering his wits with a discernible effort, he lifted the hinged counter and came round to their side, bringing the stool with him and placing it reverently beside Phoebe. 'Please to be seated, Mistress Laker...oh... this is...this is something I've waited for....how long? Well, since I visited the building site to see how they were getting on with...you know...the new premises. And you, my lord, may I offer you a glass of my best...?'

'No, I thank you, Master...?'

'Addiman, my lord. Samuel Addiman at your service.' Frowning in disbelief, he shook his head several times. 'Tch! This is...*unbelievable,* sir.'

'What is, Master Addiman? What is it you've been waiting for?' Sir Leo leaned against the counter beside Phoebe, clearly as puzzled as she was.

'Well, it's like this,' he replied, directing his explanation at Phoebe after a furtive glance down the shop. 'I've been hoping that someone connected with the Laker family would one day appear, because although the ground floor and cellars were buried when the upper floor fell in…' He paused, seeing how Sir Leo's hand came to rest upon Phoebe's shoulder. 'Er…yes. The thing is that hardware shops like ours didn't suffer quite as badly as those selling fabric and fur, for instance. Or the haberdashers either. So when they started to clear away all the rubble, there seemed to be pockets where the fire had done very little damage, you see.'

'You mean paperwork? Bills? Order books?'

'Oh, no, Mistress Laker. No paperwork survived, unfortunately. But there were some empty strongboxes that the owner found too heavy to remove, and there was something else that must have been dropped.' At this point, he scurried round behind the counter again and disappeared while Phoebe looked up to meet Sir Leo's eyes, as clouded as her own.

Puffing a little with the weight, Master Addiman heaved an oak chest on to the counter, chose a key from the bunch at his waist and unlocked the lid using a series of complicated turns that took him some time to execute. From one corner, he brought out a small linen-wrapped parcel tied round with string, and a label which he read out to them. 'Found on premises, October 1666. Unfinished item.' Replacing his spectacles at the end of his nose, he passed the parcel across to Phoebe. 'The workers passed it on to me,' he said, 'which was remarkably honest of them. Naturally I gave them a reward. If you'd like to open it, mistress, you may be able to shed some light on the mystery.'

Phoebe had begun to shake, not only in anticipation of what she might find, but also for the unease she had felt outside, a premonition that something significant was about to happen again, after all the happenings of the past weeks. Fold after fold, the linen fell away until, nestling at the bottom and still shining, was a lump of solid gold in the shape of a heart. It was no larger than a wren's egg. At the top, waiting for a chain, was a delicate ring.

Gasping with amazement, she held it up and caught the blue-white flash of a diamond embedded in one side with star-points radiating from it. On the other side was engraved the name 'Phoebe,' and underneath it in the point of the heart was a full moon of white enamel enclosed by seed pearls.

'It must have been meant for you, mistress,' said Master Addiman. 'I believe the Greeks called one of their moon goddesses Phoebe. Do you know who might have had it made?'

She could hardly speak. Instead, she held it up for Sir Leo to see. 'Mistress Laker's brother ran the shop after their father's death,' he said. 'He was only eighteen, but he managed to keep the business going and to build a house at Mortlake too. He was a remarkable young man.'

'This must have been what he came back for,'

Phoebe whispered, 'on that night. He had to come back for something he said was for me, and he'd nearly finished it. He was learning the art of gold-smithing from the shop manager.'

Master Addiman was absorbed in the workmanship, hardly listening. 'There are two pearls missing,' he said, 'and it wants for a chain too. You shall have one from me as a gift. And if you can wait a while, I'll find two more pearls and put them in. From a brother to his sister. Well, well…what a day this is, to be sure.'

'I would rather it stayed as it is, unfinished, if you please. But I feel I should pay you for it. It's a very valuable piece, Master Addiman.'

'Won't hear of it, mistress. I would never have sold it, you see, and the chances of a lady named Phoebe Laker coming to claim it must be one in a million. No, what you've told me fits like a hand in a glove. Here we are now, here's the chain I have in mind. Ah, per-fect. See?' The chain he threaded through the ring was a generous one with finely twisted links, and he passed it back to her from the end of his finger. 'Take it. It's found its rightful owner. Mystery solved.'

Her hands trembled as she accepted it and wrapped it again in the linen. Then, on impulse, she leaned for-wards to place a light kiss upon each wrinkled cheek. 'Thank you, Master Addiman,' she whispered. 'You have done more than solve a mystery, sir.'

* * *

On any other visit to London, they might have shopped in Cheapside or gone to see the menagerie at the Tower, but already the sky had taken on a greeny-grey cast, and rumbles of thunder could be heard over the raucous street cries and the hubbub of noise chanelled down every street. The purpose of the visit seemed to have been accomplished, even though they had not quite determined it beforehand, and now they both agreed that a quick return home was important. Yet it was not the threat of a downpour that kept them immersed in their own thoughts as they felt the pull and lurch of the boat through the water.

The journey upriver was more difficult than the previous one on the tide, for it had not turned yet, and the oarsmen had to battle against both wind and current while Phoebe and Sir Leo huddled together for shelter under the open-sided roof of the barge. Rain began to spatter them well before they reached Richmond, but the men were spurred on by the promise of extra pay and, although drenched and tired, they reached Ferry House long after other river traffic had abandoned their journeys.

The storm was now at its height, unleashing its fury on the two who ran for cover with clinging clothes and hair like rats' tails, breathless with cold and beaten by the unrelenting force that swept across the river. Immediately they were the centre of attention, stripped of sodden clothes and wrapped in blankets, hair rubbed and warm bricks placed underfoot, food set before them, hot punch at their elbows. By this time their faces had begun to thaw and Phoebe's teeth had stopped chattering enough for her to dismiss the fidgeting servants, leaving them in peace by the fireside.

Basking in the comfort of loose dressing gowns and the crackling fire, the high whine of the wind and the rattle of rain on the windows, the events of the day swirled around Phoebe's mind like scenes from a dream from which she had yet to recover. Only a hand's reach away, the little parcel lay on the table and she'd had time to be sure, between London and Richmond, that its future was to be not only a reminder of her brother's love but as something else too, just as symbolic.

Sir Leo lounged across a cushioned day-bed of walnut and rattan with one arm across the back as if waiting to enclose her, should she wish it, his eyes watching for her to tell him her thoughts. His gown was tied round the middle, but gaped open to reveal a deep V of bare chest where brown hair darkened the upper part, and he had already seen how her eyes strayed there, looked away, and returned. He sat in silence, knowing how she was choosing words and finding them all inadequate, wondering if actions might be better.

Finally, unable to demur any longer, she took the

linen bundle and, rising with some difficulty through a swaddle of loose robes and rugs, she shuffled over to him and sat down with a bump, tripping over herself like an infant learning to walk. He pulled her against him, dislodging the wraps that had begun to slip, making it difficult for her to move without revealing more than she had intended. 'I have something for you,' she said.

As if on cue, her words were drowned by a crack of thunder that reverberated across the sky with a white flash, lighting the room in shadowless detail. Not expecting her announcement to be upstaged so promptly, she let out an involuntary yelp of fright, throwing herself across him, clinging to his woollen robe, her damp curls tucked beneath his chin. She had intended her well thought-out declaration to be a delicate and touching affair. Now things were not going entirely to plan.

His arms tightened around her and she could feel his laughter. 'What, sweet lass?' he rumbled as the thunder crashed again.

The competition was too great; the lightning took centre stage. Reaching up to his head, she saw the glint of laughter in his eyes and the smiling lips preparing to try again with his question. 'Please forget it,' she muttered through the din. 'Just kiss me, Leo.'

Her request might not have been heard above the cacophony of sounds, but her arms invited and there seemed to be no delay before his mouth was upon hers, hard and hungry, as if he'd held himself to breaking point throughout the day.

Their loving this time, wild and spontaneous, would not wait for them to reach the greater comfort of Phoebe's bed. This time, she could not wait upon every preliminary, as she had before, for it was as if the storm itself drove her into a frenzy where her cries were muffled by the noise outside. He would have waited to take her in more comfort, but this day had been unique in every sense, and her astonishing surge of desire was like a spark to his tinder, igniting them both like a forest blaze after drought. Their coupling took on a dream-like aspect lit alternately by the fire's glow and by lightning, one moment plunged into deep shadow with blinding flashes to penetrate their eyelids, the next moment relying on touch alone to guide them, which deterred them not at all.

Phoebe opened to him like a flower to the heat of the sun, and as the cracking thunder and lashing rain mingled with her moans of bliss, they were sealed in the roaring blaze of their desires, oblivious to everything but their passion. It took them both by surprise, leaving them speechless and with hardly enough breath left to laugh at their greed, or at the unusual use of the day-bed and, later, the hearth-rug.

As they quietly recovered, untidily coiled inside Sir Leo's gown while the storm passed overhead, their lethargy took over from where their energy had left off, with their hands idly smoothing in mutual comfort. Phoebe, suddenly remembering something it had been holding, began to search through the folds of the blanket on the day-bed.

'What is it, sweetheart?' Sir Leo mumbled.

'I was about to give you something.'

'I thought you just did.'

'Not *that*. There's something else. Somewhere.'

His fingers brushed over her forehead, holding her hair away. Then he covered her with the blanket and stood up, as graceful as a cat. 'It's here,' he said. 'We've been lying on it. I fear Master Addiman might be scandalised by such irreverence.' Placing it on her lap, he pulled up to the day-bed and pushed a cushion behind her, sitting himself at her feet. Phoebe unwrapped the treasure and placed it on her palm, holding it out to him. 'It's for you,' she said. 'I want you to have it, with my love. It's meant to tell you that you hold my heart next to yours, but now you already know that so…oh…I don't know what…only that I worship the—'

'Hush, sweetheart. Don't say it.' His arms enclosed her and held her to his chest, his hands sweeping down her back. 'I know,' he said, nuzzling her neck. 'I know what it tells me, and if you really want me to have it, then I will, but it was meant for you as a message from your brother.'

Easing herself away, she placed the chain over his

head and arranged the heart upon the silky brown hair, smiling at the contrast. 'There. That will keep it polished, won't it? Wear it for me, Leo, if you please. Tim would be pleased by it, too.'

'My sun and my moon,' he said, looking down at it.

They held each other, heart to heart, as a log fell and sent a shower of sparks up the chimney. The rain gusted wearily against the black windows, and from behind a bank of angry clouds a full moon began sailing through the tattered remnants of the storm like a disc of white enamel edged with watery pearls.

CHAPTER SIX

THE STORM HAD passed, but the discoveries of that night answered a host of age-old questions and inadequate half-truths that, courtesy of flirtatious friends, had whetted Phoebe's appetite but never satisfied it. Sir Leo told her all she wanted to know without inhibition or false modesty, of which he had neither. His body was perfect and he was comfortable with it, happy for his beloved to profit from its boundless energy while being careful with her newness.

They slept, made love, and slept again, waking to the realisation that their long-standing feud had gently faded away into the night. They took a long time to rise.

'You know what the Duke's first words will be, don't you, sweetheart?'

'Will he be angry?'

'No, he'll say, "Aboot time too, m'lad. What kept ye sae long?"'

'And the Duchess will insist it was all her doing.'

'Well, she did have a hand in it, I suppose. She's also found a husband for young Betty.' The startling news was casually delivered.

Phoebe's head turned sharply, her tongue ready with the comment, in a moment of unashamed jealousy, that perhaps she would now stay out of *her* future husband's hair, and what a pity the Duchess could not have done the same for young Katherine.

'Och, she will, lass,' he grinned.

'How do you know that?'

'Because they've been casting about for some time.'

'Then why could you not have told me?'

The grin broadened. 'Because it was more fun not to. Did they ruffle your feathers then, wee lass?'

'Not at all, sir.' She sniffed. 'They're only untutored girls.'

'And you,' he said, rolling himself above her, 'are very *tutored* now, are you?'

They took an even longer time to dress, and Constance began to wonder if it was always going to be like this. She went to speak to Sir Leo's valet who, reminded of something, gave her a shirt of his master's with instructions for what to do with it.

* * *

Their first call, after noon, was to take their news to Mrs Overshott at Mortlake. Shedding a tear, she hugged them both and said she was sure it had been meant, all along. Another tear was shed when they showed her Tim's gift, lacking two pearls, and the story of how it came to light was, she told them, not as strange as all that since strange things happened often where love was involved.

Fortunately, and to their profound relief, Master Thomas Tollemache had returned to his regiment two days previously, which allowed them to make known their news without his nonsensical remarks to spoil it. The Duke's first comment, however, was exactly as his secretary had predicted.

Likewise, the Duchess's reaction, with more justification.

It was their daughter Elizabeth's response to the news that took them by surprise, for her face crumpled and, before her mother could ask her what on earth ailed her, she had fled from the room as if her world had suddenly taken on an ugly reality too distressing to behold. 'May I go to her, my lady?' Phoebe said.

The Duchess shook her head. 'It's only the talk of marriage,' she said. 'She's to meet Argyll's eldest son next week and already she's getting herself into a fash…er…fuss about it.'

'She's still very young, my lady,' said Mrs Overshott.

'It's a good match. That's all a woman can ask for,' the Duchess said.

Later that evening, at Mortlake, Mrs Overshott expressed the opinion that any young woman might ask for anything instead of a dose of the Duchess's matchmaking. 'Too many cooks,' she said. 'That was mostly your problem, too.'

'I'd like to know,' Phoebe said, 'which particular cook told her about Signor Luigi Verdi giving me fencing lessons.'

'It hardly matters now, does it, love? Though you might have wondered where the case of rapiers came from and who provided the lad's clothes,' said Mrs Overshott, picking up a white garment from the top of the mending pile. She held it up for inspection, lifted an eyebrow, folded it again and passed it to Phoebe. 'This is one for you, I believe.'

Phoebe took it without comment. 'Where *did* they come from?'

'Probably from the Duchess's own closet.'

Phoebe stared at the garment for some time and then, instead of replying, shook it out, found the long slit on the sleeve, and proceeded to search for a strip of fine lawn from which to make a patch. There were some questions, she thought, that were best left open-ended.

About an hour later, a guest was announced.

'Sir Leo? I thought we had agreed…'

He bowed, and replaced his plumed hat. 'Mrs Overshott, ma'am. Mistress Laker. We *did* agree to leave today free, I know, but I've found that I cannot do it, after all.'

'Do what, sir?' Phoebe's heart began to pound.

'Spend a day without you, sweet lass. I've come to your door, you see, begging you to see me, to favour me with a smile. Anything.' His face, though not exactly smiling, held a twinkle behind the eyes that was not entirely innocent, and his mouth would not keep still.

'Ah,' said Phoebe, recognising the game with some relief. 'Are you by any chance the gentleman who said he'd never be coming to my door?'

'I regret to say that I am that man, Mistress Laker.'

She couldn't keep it up. Lifting her arms to him, and regardless of Mrs Overshott's presence, she took his face between her hands and kissed him. 'Then you are most welcome, Sir Leo. Come and sit with us while I finish mending your shirt. I cannot think what you've been doing to tear it so.'

'It happened in a careless moment when my attention was being distracted,' he said, soberly.

Stitching away in her corner, Mrs Overshott did not see the blush that stole along Phoebe's neck. But Sir Leo saw it, his smile full of mischief.

PART TWO 1803

CHAPTER ONE

AFTER THE BRIGHT midsummer sunshine of the garden, the cool hallway of Ferry House was almost black until Phoebe's eyes adjusted to the dimness. Scooping up the letter that lay on the silver tray of the hall table, she was unable to read its details until, passing into the sun-washed parlour, she saw that it had been franked, sealed with red wax, and addressed not only to her on one side but also on the reverse with that of the sender. The only person to send her franked and sealed correspondence was her mother in London, but this handwriting was surely a man's, bold, large and stylish.

She turned it over. "Ransome," it read. "Greenwater, Mortlake, Surrey."

Viscount Ransome. Phoebe's hand pressed hard against her ribs where a deep resonance had suddenly become uncomfortably loud. Sitting on the padded arm of the nearest chair, she quickly broke the seal, spread out the folds and read the briefest of messages.

Dear Madame Donville,
I beg to inform you of my intention to call on you at Ferry House on the morning of the sixteenth day of July, 1803, to discuss a matter of some importance. I trust that this short notice will not inconvenience you.

I remain, Your Humble Servant, Ransome.

Phoebe frowned. *Yes, my lord. Yes, it* will *inconvenience me greatly. I'd as lief have my brother Ross and his moaning wife call on me at no notice at all, than you. And* that's *saying something.*

Tomorrow. He was to call on her tomorrow on a matter of some importance. Which could surely mean only one thing: the unfinished business of three years ago when she had forfeited her mama's protection in London to place herself well beyond the reach of men like him, her well-meaning mama having insisted, as she always did, that this time she had found her a suitor who would do very nicely. For various excellent reasons, Phoebe had strongly disagreed, as *she* always did, and had then snatched at the chance of starting a new life here in the peace of Richmond. In less than a week, she had fled.

If she had known at the time that Lord Ransome would purchase a house not far from her brother and his wife in Mortlake, she might not have been so keen to move in this direction, Mortlake being only across the bend of the River Thames. But although she had not been by any means penniless, Ferry House had cost her nothing to buy since it belonged to her eldest brother Leon, who had found no use for it and had never visited.

Studying the handwriting, she could see how close it came to revealing what she already knew about the man, self-confident and aggressively direct, even when requesting to be received. In fact, this was not a request at all, was it? Whether she was inconvenienced or not, he would be visiting her. Yet it was not his habitual arrogance that had once put her off wanting to know him better, but his reputation for fast living in the *beau monde,* the excesses, the waste, the lack of responsibility. It was a style that had once been hers too, before her widowhood, so she knew exactly what it entailed, what kind of people, what kind of ethics. After that, she had rejected it for a life out of the public eye, more wholesome and private for her grief, and better by far for the young daughter she must bring up alone, Claudette. She had not regretted it for a moment, not even the irksome proximity of her older brother

Ross and his sickly but remarkably fecund wife Josephine, who visited too frequently and without warning.

There was an older sister, too. Mimi, Lady Nateby, and husband George lived in extended family conditions in nearby Twickenham, their brood increasing every two years, their infrequent visits to Ferry House reflecting their unconcern with Phoebe and her young daughter of eight-and-a-half. It barely signified—she and Mimi had never been particularly close.

Brother Leon, the eldest of them all, had been the one to offer practical help when Phoebe had most urgently needed to escape their mama's ceaseless matchmaking. Like her, Leon had wanted none of it and, so far, had managed to hold on to his bachelor lifestyle that allowed him to waste his inheritance as if time might run out on him. Once Phoebe had left the family home on Harley Street, her mother and her much younger new husband had moved to St James's Square, leaving Leon to do pretty much as he pleased, without interference, with what wealth remained to him after his addictive gaming at London's best clubs. With the family now split apart and Phoebe tucked safely away in his house at Richmond for as long as she wanted it, Leon appeared gradually to have forgotten his siblings' existence. All of them. Only his mother, Lady Templeman, knew exactly what he got up to.

For the first two years, he had intermittently sent funds to Phoebe when his winnings were high, but this generosity had dwindled to nothing over the last year, and she had now ceased to expect any more help. Her large well-stocked kitchen garden was, however, a source of income, providing fruit and vegetables for the house, the villagers, and for many of the local inns and coaching houses. Consequently, she was managing to live quite comfortably and to support several dependants and a staff of seven, one of whom was Claudette's governess. So the very last thing she needed, she told herself, folding the letter up and stuffing it into the pocket of her apron, was a visit from the exquisite Lord Ransome, who apparently laboured under the misapprehension that a twenty-six-year-old widow with a young daughter must now be desperate to know what he had to offer. Even one who had run away three years earlier in order not to hear it.

Guiding his team of showy chestnuts across the park towards Richmond, Lord Ransome gradually slowed them to a walk as the house came into view. Through the trees he could see that it was more extensive than he'd thought, though the brief information he had received only a few days ago in London was sadly insufficient in every respect. It had been a pleasant surprise to him to learn that this was the house to which Leon Hawkin's sister had fled three years ago, but the knowledge had also caused him to revise his plans, which would now depend, he supposed, on the lady herself. He was under no delusions. She would take more than a little persuading, for she was no innocent chit of a girl.

Smiling, he recalled the haughty, heavy-lidded dismissive blink of her amazingly dark eyes, refusing even to please him with an answer to his invitation, as if he'd invited her to an orgy instead of a drive in Hyde Park. Any other woman would have blushed, stammered and accepted, but not Madame Phoebe Donville, lusciously dark, aloof and self-contained, daring a man to lay a finger on her for whatever reason.

Undoubtedly, her personal tragedy had made a big difference to her, placing her at a distance from the frivolous superficiality of the *haut ton* as if she had just discovered how close life was to death, and how grief afflicted the high-born as well as the lowly. He had seen her before her whirlwind marriage to Claude Donville when she had been willing enough to flirt, to dance all night, to accept every invitation and to reject suitors with a nonchalant laugh. He had not been one of them then. Nor could he have called himself a suitor after her widowhood either, when her pushy mother had pursued every likely candidate on her daughter's behalf. No, he had never got that far. But neither had anyone else.

Unlike Madame Donville's pushy mama, he himself had been able to tell when a young wife with an infant was disinclined to put herself back on the marriage mart so soon, while she still grieved over the terrible events concerning her husband. And although he would have pursued her had not Donville got to her first when she was a lass of sixteen, as a young widow she had eventually put herself beyond anyone's reach, quite literally.

The half-smile remained, remembering how his disconsolate friends placed bets on her remarrying, or not, within the year, and how they lusted after her while pretending that she was too hot to handle, too cold, too prickly to bed, too contemptuous of their empty flattery to offer them the slightest hope. Well, it would be interesting to see how La Dame Donville would react to his news, and whether that celebrated composure would show any sign of melting after three years in rural Richmond.

At last he came upon the large redbrick house behind the iron gates. Stone urns brimmed with bright summer blooms like fountains of colour dripping on to a cobbled courtyard. Through a gate at one side he could see steps leading down to green trellises blanketed with white and pink roses, borders spiked with delphiniums and foxgloves. Without a doubt, he thought, some hard work had gone into the making of a garden like this.

The house was another revelation, seventeenth century with newer additions, a central porch with a gable, and two wings forming a letter *E* with the main façade. High walls with double doors and a gateway extended backwards to form a rear courtyard, every part of it neat and clean, its angles softened by trees and topiary. She would not willingly leave such a place, thought his lordship as he drove through the gates into the courtyard.

His groom ran to the horses' heads, but already a young coachman man had come rushing from the stable-block, eyeing the chestnuts in silent admiration, if one could ignore the whistle through his teeth. 'M'lord,' he said, touching his hat, 'the mistress is expecting you, but I'll take you in through the front, if you please.'

'Stay with the horses,' Ransome told him. 'I can find my way.'

The short walk gave him a chance to see the view from the opposite direction: the rise of Richmond Hill at the front of the house and the river close by on the other side, peaceful, secluded and spacious. It was close to paradise here. Pheasants strutted across his path as he reached the front porch, removed his hat and entered, giving the bell-handle a gentle tug in passing. The hallway was dark after the bright sunlight, and she seemed to appear from nowhere before his eyes could adjust.

He was used to assessing any female at one glance or, at the most, two. This time, while noting the tall slender figure, his eyes were riveted by the perfect oval of her face and the long neck sloping flawlessly into her wide shoulders, her bountiful hair piled high in black silken curls with no widow's cap to cover it, the huge almond eyes behind half-moon lids and the lofty brows that tapered to fine points on her temples. The full mouth did not smile in greeting, nor had he expected it to, though her voice held no hint of the annoyance she must be feeling. Nevertheless, his bow was punctilious.

'Lord Ransome,' she said, executing a shallow curtsy with a graceful incline of her head. 'I have no butler or footman, as you see, and my housekeeper is otherwise engaged. Will you come into the parlour?'

Their eyes met for a second review, probing for the exact level of remembrance, criticism or approval. As greetings go, he thought, that was probably as good as he'd any right to expect. 'Madame Donville,' he said, 'thank you for receiving me at such short notice.'

'I'm convinced there must be an adequate reason for it,' she said, leading the way into the parlour. The sun was still on the other side of the house, but the previous day's warmth still lingered in the pale green panelling and on the polished floor scattered with mellow Persian rugs. Light from the sash windows bounced off an arrangement of ox-eye daisies and sweet peas, mirrored in the table top. 'Is there some news from London that brings you here?' she said. 'My mother? My brother? I have not heard from Lady Templeman for almost ten days.' Immediately, she could have bitten her tongue, for she had not intended to part with even the smallest snip of information, either about herself or her family. It was as much as she could manage to invite him into her private parlour although, on reflection, she had little choice in the matter. He was not the kind of man to whom she ought to give *any* personal information, for there was no knowing what he would do with it.

She watched him as carefully as a cat watches a bird too large for her to catch unawares. He was powerfully built, but he moved as gracefully as a greyhound, every gesture practised and polished, his hands strong and clean. Yet there was no disguising the bulge of calf and thigh beneath gleaming Hessians and tight buckskins. His dark blue coat fitted smoothly over broad shoulders that would not have disgraced a prizefighter, and not even the folds of his plain white neckcloth could hide the muscled neck and strong square jaw emphasised by trimmed sideburns.

She sat, indicating that he should do the same and, as he flicked aside the long tails of his coat, she saw the top of his head where thick waves of dark brown hair had been raked back from his forehead to reveal a widow's peak, which, she thought, was a style few men could manage as well as he. Oh, yes, he was as handsome as she remembered him, and well worthy of his nickname, Buck Ransome, which had not been awarded exclusively for his appearance, either.

She had debated, during the sleepless hours of last night, whether she ought to ask Cousin Hetty to be present at this interview, but had then decided against it. After all, she was a mature widow in her own home in the company of a mature acquaintance, and he was unlikely to do or say anything to shock her. If it was indeed a proposal he'd come with, she would rather dear Hetty, her companion of many years, didn't hear it. Arranging the folds of white jaconet muslin over her knees, she folded her hands on her lap and waited, quite unaware of the picture she presented to her visitor. The sun had lightly bronzed her skin, but fashionable peaches and cream were for her a thing of the past, and now she told herself that his detailed scrutiny of her meant nothing. He would do the same to any passable female, of that she was certain.

'You may be sure, *madame*,' he said in reply to her questions, 'that I have good reason for disturbing your peace. I would not have come without one, after our last unprofitable meeting in London.'

'May I offer you some refreshment after your journey?' she replied, not lifting a finger to convince him of her sincerity. It was not the way a perfect hostess ought to behave, she knew, but she suffered no pangs of guilt. As for his reference to their last meeting, she had banished it from her mind along with many other uncomfortable encounters forced upon her by Lady Templeman, in her zeal.

'Thank you, no,' he said. 'Not if it means you preparing it yourself.'

'I *do* have servants,' she retorted, letting go of more information.

'I gathered as much. The place is immaculate. Perhaps you'll show me round before I leave?'

'Unlikely, my lord. I have a house to run. Now, would you mind *very* much telling me what I've done to deserve so much of *your* precious time? If you have no news from my London relatives, then I cannot imagine what else could interest me.'

'Three years have had little effect on your sharp tongue, *madame*. My interesting news, as it happens, *does* concern your eldest brother.'

For the first time, her eyes widened enough to show him the blue-whites. 'Leon? Oh…is he…is he all right? When did you see him? Where?'

'The Surrey climate suits you well,' he said.

She knew she deserved that. 'Tell me about Leon,' she demanded.

'He's all right. No harm. We met at Brooks's a few nights ago.'

'Then you've come…ah…I see. He was at the gaming tables, of course. And you've come to tell me he's lost more money. How much? Who to? Does my mother know?'

'He was at the tables, as you say, *madame*. And Lady Templeman probably knows by now, as will a good many other people, that he lost again. How much? He lost the entire Ferry House estate and all its contents.'

There was nothing for him to see. No histrionics. Phoebe's composure was uncanny, but he could feel the shock his words had caused, settling deep in her heart and refusing to move, and he was sorry for it.

'To you,' she whispered, hoarsely. 'He lost it…to *you*. Why else would you have come with such news?'

He nodded, once. 'To me. I have his note here…' His hand moved towards his breast pocket, but was halted by her cry of despair.

'No! No, I don't want to see it!' The words were rasped out with the last of her breath before a sob held it and let it out again, slowly. 'Don't show me,' she whispered. 'I suppose he was…inebriated…was he?'

'His writing reflects that, *madame*. But in case you're thinking to claim invalidity on that score, may I remind you that—'

'You don't *need* to remind me, my lord,' Phoebe cried. 'Drunk or sober, a debt of honour must be paid. I've been his sister long enough to know that much. Did you get him drunk on purpose?'

A steely coldness crept into his eyes. 'I shall pretend

you did not say that,' he told her, sternly. 'Nobody needs to induce your brother to make bets while he's in his cups, *madame,* nor is anyone responsible for stopping him. He's free to do whatever he wishes with his own person and property.'

Phoebe leapt to her feet, shaking with fury, her eyes flashing in a manner Buck Ransome had often longed to see, but not for this reason. 'Not while *I'm living in it*!' she cried. 'He *forgot,* didn't he? He forgot I'm here keeping his property in good repair, lavishing money on it, keeping people in work.' Flinging an arm into the air to signify the extent of the improvements, she gasped as a small table-easel and its watercolour-painting flew across the room, hitting the floor with a crack. 'All for nothing! For *you!*'

'A rather premature analogy,' he murmured as the door opened.

A concerned face appeared in the gap as if she had not been too far away. 'Can I get you anything, dear?' she said, her grey eyes wandering over the scene in alarm.

Phoebe was having trouble with her breathing, so Lord Ransome answered for her. 'A tray of tea, if you please. And quickly, woman.'

'Oh…er…yes,' said the lady. 'Is that…?'

'It's all right, Hetty dear,' said Phoebe, soothingly. 'Lord Ransome's manners have their own kind of charm. A tea-tray would be very welcome.'

He rose from his chair as the door closed and began to pick up the pieces. 'Lord Ransome's manners, however, are usually less destructive than some ladies of his acquaintance,' he said, softly, placing the component parts upon the table.

'I beg to differ,' Phoebe retorted. 'They're a good deal *more* destructive when you accept other people's homes in payment of a bet. I would call that *disgraceful,* my lord. I suppose it didn't occur to you to renegotiate?'

'No. I had no idea you were living in it at the time and, even if I had known, I may not have attempted to renegotiate, as you put it. A bet is a bet. Take it or leave it. And the more I see of this place the better I like it. With or without you.'

'Unfortunately, my lord, that is exactly how I feel about it too, so you can renegotiate with *me,* because I'm not moving. I've put too much time, money and effort into Ferry House to hand it over to you, of all people, simply because you chose to take advantage of my brother's weakness one evening. There are people living here who depend on me.'

'Yes, I know you have a daughter.'

'It's not only my daughter I'm thinking about. There are others.'

'Oh, I didn't realise. How many?'

'Please don't be facetious, sir. You may have won my home, but that doesn't allow you to make ridiculous assumptions about my situation. Indeed, my personal affairs have nothing to do with you, nor will they ever. All we need to settle as quickly as possible is that I am allowed to live here as unhindered as I have been since I came. It's taken me all this time to put the place back to rights, and there is still more to be done, as and when I can afford it.'

They had come to stand where they could read each other's face more clearly and, even before she had finished speaking, Phoebe knew that it was not going to be as straightforward as she would have liked. If he'd had it in mind to allow her to stay, unhindered, he would hardly have rushed from London with news that could have waited months, presumably. She prompted him. 'You wished to see the place, naturally.'

'Naturally, *madame*,' he agreed, smoothly. 'But let us get a few facts straight, shall we? It will prevent misunderstandings in the long run. I am now the rightful owner of Ferry House, lock, stock and barrel, however you may wish it to be otherwise. And since your brother clearly states in his promissory note that he forfeits the *whole* estate and all its contents, including the tenants and livestock, that includes you too. You are a tenant, are you not, *madame*?'

The almond-shaped eyes widened again, flashing with rage. Any lesser man would have stepped back, but Ransome was unwavering. 'That is utterly *ab-*

surd,' she replied. 'It cannot be. Leon would not…
could not have meant that.'

'I can assure you he did. He may not have remembered that you were here at the time he made the bet,
and I was hardly in a position to remind him of it. But
this is a matter of honour, Madame Donville, and debts
must be paid in full.'

'Honour my *foot*!' she said, moving away. 'I had
nothing to do with *my* brother's debt. I refuse to be
drawn into it, and I won't be owned by anyone. Ever.

'And if I were, my lord,' she continued, blithely
contradicting herself while rounding on him again,
'I'd not be owned by the likes of *you*. Heaven forbid,
but I can do better than *that*, if ever I need to.'

She had come perilously close, closer than she intended and much too close for her own safety. She
ought to have known better, but there was a furious and
reckless fire ablaze in her that morning, waiting since
yesterday to be fuelled by his presence, his arrogance,
his deep voice and the inflexible choices that were no
choices at all. She had hardly slept, sure that she knew
the reason for his visit, fearful and excited by the danger he presented. She had intended to give him the kind
of snub he deserved for his presumption and now, to
her cost, the well-prepared put-down was as useless as
her protests. She was no match for him, after all that.

She flung up a hand to ward him off, but it was
caught even before she could think, taken to the small

of her back and pushed, bending her to his body like a green willow. Overpowered by the width of his chest, her other arm was useless in holding him away and not even a yelp escaped her before his mouth took hers in a kiss that told her in no uncertain terms how he could make her change her mind.

Along the whole length of her body she felt it, through her thighs and knees locked against his, through her aching shoulders, even through her hair that he held in one hand, keeping her immobile. Distantly, she heard herself plead for breath, for release, hating herself for weakening, for not fighting harder. But when the kiss softened in response, she found herself lingering to taste him and to fill her nostrils with more of his scent, opening her mouth under his to breathe him in more deeply. *Savage. Brute. Mannerless ruffian,* she told herself. *What did you expect from him? Charm? Sweet words? What a fool!*

Struggling wildly, she opened her eyes to the daylight and twisted away from the heady danger of his lips. Her own lips tingled, shamefully. 'Barbarian!' she gasped. 'Get out of my house!'

But he took her chin in his hand, forcing her to look at him. 'I shall leave you to think about it, *madame*, as well as how not to cross swords with me with your sharp tongue. Because I can stop you. Tomorrow, we shall discuss the details.'

'Don't come back!' she said, wrenching herself out of his arms at last. 'You will not be allowed in.'

'Tch! You are remarkably forgetful, Madame Donville. *You* are the one who can be kept out, remember. Not me.'

'Then there is nothing to discuss, my lord. I shall be staying here whatever your feelings are, and insulting me in such a manner will not change anything. After that feeble demonstration of lordship, you can surely have no more need to boost your confidence. And if it was intended to humble me, it didn't.'

'Good, I'm relieved to hear it. So we may discuss your late husband's patriotic activities without restraint, I take it. Excellent. I bid you good day, *madame*. Don't come to the door. I shall easily find my own way.' He bowed, picked up his hat and gloves from the hall table as he went, and she saw him stride past the window like an owner, adjusting his grey beaver upon his dark hair as if the kiss was of no consequence to him. In two strides he was in the phaeton, taking his whip and reins while the groom swung himself up on to the rumble-seat as the horses pranced and plunged and, with a rattle of hooves, dashed off through the gates.

But the words that lingered in her head alongside his punishing kiss were the ones she had dreaded hearing since the tragic death of Claude Donville. *We may discuss your late husband's patriotic activities without restraint.*

The rattle of the inner door announced the arrival of the tea-tray borne by Hetty, whose astonishment appeared in every crease of her well-worn face. 'Oh, gone?' she said, looking across at the window. 'Already?'

Keeping her face averted while struggling to tidy her loosened hair, Phoebe could only mutter through the hair-pin in her mouth, 'Not a moment too soon, Hetty. Pour a cup out for me, will you, dear?' With the back of her hand, she pressed comfort upon her tingling lips, and she could not take the cup and saucer Hetty offered for the shaking of her hands.

'Oh, my *dear*,' Hetty whispered. 'What has that dreadful man said to upset you so? I ought to have been with you, oughtn't I? What has he done?'

Phoebe's voice trembled. 'I don't know, Hetty. I don't know what he's done.'

But Hetty's grey eyes were still sharp, and she knew Phoebe's lips hadn't been as swollen at breakfast.

CHAPTER TWO

Passing the glasshouse and the patch of tall artichokes, the dainty figure clothed in various shades of blue, some of them mud-spattered, peered round the corner of the potting shed where the sun glared against the pink-toned brickwork. 'Mama, there you are. I thought you might be. Hetty said you preferred to be alone, but you don't mind me, do you?'

Clearly, Claudette was an exception to most generalities, being Phoebe's only beloved child and likely to remain so and, for that reason, very special. She had not been spoiled beyond what one might expect, but her years of being the centre of her mother's world had taught her that, if she questioned the rules with enough care, she could usually manage to have them bent in her favour. Cousin Hetty had given her the facts as she saw them, knowing that the bond between Phoebe and her daughter was of a quite different order from that of Phoebe and Lady Templeman, who would have meant what she said about being left alone.

'No, *chérie*. I don't mind you at all. Come and sit by me.' Patting the warm cushion, she moved the soft muslin skirt closer to her thigh while Claudette took her hand between her own, gazing at the tearful face with open curiosity.

'You've been weeping,' she said in her newfound motherly voice. 'Are you unhappy, Mama? Your Viscount didn't stay long, did he? Did you hope he would?'

Phoebe's tears had dried, but she had not thought to smile quite so soon. Squeezing the nearest hand, she selected one of the easier questions. 'No, *chérie*. Lord Ransome stayed the usual time for a gentleman's first call, perhaps a little longer. Now, tell me what you and Miss Maskell found down at the riverside. Did you see the coots and moorhens?'

Assured that her mama was not as distressed as she'd been led to believe, Claudette obliged her with a full account of the river's wildlife, some of which she and her governess had brought back to the house for closer examination. It was never difficult to engage Claudette's interest in anything, with so much to be discovered on the doorstep. She was a bright, energetic young lady with her father's innate charm; some might have said that she was precocious, having been allowed to contribute to her elders' conversations whenever there was a chance, contrary to most parents' approach. But at Ferry House there was no authoritarian father to be humoured with displays of feminine subservience, only three women and a child who took all meals together with the freedom to say what they pleased, within reason.

Claudette was now fluent in French, both written and spoken, for in spite of Claude Donville's tragic fate, Phoebe had always encouraged her daughter to write regularly to her French grandparents who had remained in England. At home, the four of them often lapsed into French for Claudette's sake, the use of *chérie* being a favourite endearment.

Looking down upon her glossy curls and catching the laughter in those black-lashed eyes, Phoebe saw glimpses of Claude Donville and his celebrated allure that had once ravished her heart. She had been a mere sixteen years old when she'd first fallen under his spell, too young to exercise any discrimination until much too late. Thinking of little except how quickly to cement the brilliant match for her youngest daughter, her mother failed spectacularly to discriminate on her behalf, talking down anyone who urged caution on account of Donville's nationality. As far as her mother was concerned, Monsieur Claude Donville was connected to one of France's oldest families, was utterly in love with her daughter, well mannered and, most of all, wealthy.

Phoebe was married before her seventeenth birthday. The fact that hostilities between France and England were in abeyance at the time was an indication that there was nothing for them to be concerned about. This, in spite of the fact that, only two weeks before the wedding, the French king had been cruelly executed by a howling mob on the rampage for anyone bearing an ancient name, a title or disproportionate riches. Claude Donville had two of these and had fled to England as a refugee some time before, as had many others.

The new Madame Donville, soon pregnant, had understood that her wonderfully courageous husband was obliged to make return visits to his estates in France in order not to be classed as an *émigré,* forfeiting everything to the dreaded Committee of Public Safety. Time after time he came back to her with the news that he had managed to sell property, increasing their prosperity, soothing her fears.

Then came the time when he failed to return, and she learned a week later that he had become yet another victim of the ghastly guillotine. The trumped-up charges, she was assured, were malicious and loaded with envy, but the Committee needed no more than that to act without a trial.

Broken-hearted, distraught, Phoebe had been persuaded to return their London home to members of the
Donville family and to move back to live with her
mother and older siblings, where Claudette was born
at the end of November 1794. Married for less than a
year, Phoebe was now the mother of a child who would
never know her father.

But no sooner had she begun to reconcile herself to
the terrible manner of her husband's death and the
grief of not having said a fitting farewell, or having his
body to bury with dignity, than another blow fell upon
her unreal world that threatened to turn her love and
admiration crazily upside-down. French refugees
abounded in London and elsewhere, friends of her
husband and family, some of whom had lost everything to the new regime. One of them felt unable to
keep secret what he knew about the manner of Claude
Donville's death and, for no other reason than a desire to put the record straight regarding the way he
himself had lost his entire family, told Phoebe what
he knew. Far from helping others to keep hold of their
estates in France, Donville had, in fact, secretly been
supplying the Committee of Public Safety with false
evidence to convict them on any trivial charge, such
as growing cattle fodder instead of corn, or express-
ing sympathy with critics of the new dictators. As a
reward, he had been allowed to pocket some of the
confiscated wealth, loading his own coffers with

blood-money. This was now Phoebe's, for he had left it all to her.

One of her weightiest problems then had been how to reconcile what she knew of her handsome, charming and brave husband, with what their French friends had decided, except one, to keep secret from her. Another problem was to decide whether his supposed gruesome death by guillotine was better or worse than being shot in cold blood by those who had found him out, which was precisely what had happened. Either way, what she herself had known of him in their short time together and what she had just discovered, were so incompatible that, for a long time, she could not believe it, nor could she believe it had happened to her. This was the kind of nightmare that others suffered, outside her experience. The only thing of which she *could* be certain, during those distressing months, was that she carried his child to be her comfort and solace. The other certainty was that as few people as possible must know that her husband had betrayed his own countrymen for money. Especially it must be kept from her mother who had engineered the match and who would probably not recover from the shock.

The consequence of this bereavement was that once her sister Mimi and brother Ross had found suitable marriage partners, nothing would satisfy their mother as much as a new husband for herself and *then* to begin, all over again, to search for Phoebe's second husband. If she had known the real reasons for her widowed daughter's aversion to her plans, she would probably have left her alone to bring up her daughter in peace, but she did not, and her machinations were relentless and embarrassingly conspicuous.

By that time, Phoebe's mother, now married to Lord Templeman, was stepmother to two young men who saw their new stepsister as fair game for their flirting and for exercising all the attention-seeking ploys young bucks use when competing with each other. According to their immature reckoning, four years was quite enough time for her to have got over it, and what with their persistent and annoying attentions, her mother's unremitting attempts to force the pace, her new stepfather's irritation with a four-year-old infant, Claudette's needs, and Phoebe's own fear of being exposed as the widow of a traitor, the need to get away from London became her top priority.

Added to all this was the inevitable guilt of needing to retain the wealth Donville had gained by dishonest means, money that would give her independence when the time came. In one way, it became an aid to remaining chaste to the memory of the man she had loved. But the guilt was a high price to pay for it, and it was this as much as anything that encased her in a distant world where no one was admitted except her daughter and, at times, Cousin Hetty. She had learned to her cost that men were not what they seemed, and too much was at stake for her to allow another man into her future. Her future was Claudette, and no other.

It was at this point that Lady Templeman, in desperation, introduced the Right Honourable the Viscount Ransome as a possible suitor. The biggest catch on the marriage mart, he was every ambitious mother's dream for her daughter: titled, wealthy and good looking. The desperation was in the fact that some found Lord Ransome's straightforward manner rather offputting and, although his whims and fancies were slavishly emulated by every beau from seventeen to seventy, the younger women were frightened by his tendency to be blunt, at times. The older ones, who found his dangerous good looks and directness exciting, were already married. Lady Templeman, however, had been convinced that, with more co-operation, not to say encouragement, from Phoebe, Lord Ransome would have made more progress with her than anyone else, for he had appeared to be making an effort to gain her interest. Which was quite remarkable when, to everyone's knowledge, he rarely lifted a finger to make himself agreeable. It was always the other way round.

But Phoebe had discovered from her elder brother as much about Lord Ransome's lifestyle as she wished to know, and had decided early on that he would not be the one to succeed where others had failed. She had observed him before and after her marriage to Claude,

and although such men always aroused a flutter of excitement and quite a lot of fantasy to keep one warm
in bed, Phoebe did not believe him to be good husband
material unless his partner was prepared to close her
eyes to his future infidelities. And Phoebe's faith in
men had been severely shaken, after her widowhood.

She knew no more than that, except for one important thing. Having travelled across Europe on the
Grand Tour, Lord Ransome had acquired a large circle of aristocratic French friends, one of whom was the
embittered young Count whose family had been victims of Donville's treachery, the one whose resentment had caused her so much anguish. Whether Lord
Ransome had been told of this or not, it was a risk
Phoebe dared not take. What he might or might not do
with such information—if he was in possession of it—
she did not know. Why he would want to know her better, in the circumstances, she did not know either.
Perhaps, she thought, he did not care as much as he
ought, which would be puzzling indeed. All she knew
was that the association was a dangerous one, that her
mama was making a thorough nuisance of herself over
the matter, and that she, Phoebe, was desperate to escape.

Then Leon, dear Leon, had made his offer. Ferry
House might be a bit run down, he told her, but here
is my biggest coach, four nags, a coachman and two
footmen. Pack your bags and go. Handing her the key,

an old cast-iron thing wrapped in newspaper, he told her what to do about her funds and how to find a builder, and within a week, to the sound of much wailing and protest, she was on her way to Richmond to find this magical bird-songed place where water lapped at the edge of the garden. And at last, Phoebe and Claudette, Hetty, her companion, and Tabby, the governess, were in paradise. It was here where her bad dreams were replaced by good ones.

'Are you listening, Mama?'

'Yes, *chérie*. I'm listening. Go on. The village children joined you.'

The villagers of Richmond had been quietly delighted to take young Claudette under their wing and to have tenants at Ferry House after years of neglect, while the men gave her all the free advice she could need to renovate the outbuildings and gardens, her brother Ross and his wife offering only ill-concealed envy.

'Just the hem of my dress got wet, Mama. I had bare feet.'

'Then you should change it before we sit down to luncheon unless, of course, we take it outside on the terrace. Shall we picnic today?'

'Oh, Mama, *may* we? Shall I go and tell Mrs Ted?' In a bound, Claudette ran off up the path through the herb garden, jumping over the dozing cat, to the kitchens. Mr and Mrs Ted Clough were the cook and her handyman husband who lived above the kitchen range and worked tirelessly to make Ferry House beautiful for their mistress. To Claudette, they were more like doting grandparents than the one in London who had not yet found the time to visit, in spite of promises.

She watched her go with a familiar pang of regret that the child had rarely been carried in a man's arms, never walked hand in hand to church with her father, or ridden out with him. These were sacrifices Phoebe had been prepared for when she had decided not to remarry, but she had not fully appreciated the impact it would have upon a daughter on the brink of womanhood. It was a situation fraught with dangers. She, Claudette, had already begun to ask questions about her father, and the piquant idea of being sent off to the riverside with Miss Maskell while her mama received a Viscount intrigued her as only a girl of that age could be.

Once more, Phoebe's exploring fingers roamed across her lips to discover if they were really as swollen as they felt, chastising herself for not having had Hetty with her, as she ought. The events of the morning crowded in again, pestering her to find a way out of a problem that threatened the happiness of so many others, apart from herself. And what about poor dear Leon? After being the one to bail her out of an impossibly difficult situation, he was the one to plunge her into the next one from which there appeared to be no comfortable escape. At the same time, he also needed help to protect him from opportunists like Lord Ransome who, apparently, could not wait to take advantage of his weakness.

Cursing the man under her breath with words no lady ought to have known, she caressed her aching wrist, pulled her shawl over it and stood up, looking across the large walled garden lush with vegetables. 'Well, my lord,' she muttered, angrily, 'you'll not wrench this off me so easily, whatever your clever schemes. I've not done all this simply to hand it over to you on a plate. And as for owning me, too, put it out of your mind. *Nobody owns me.*'

'Beg pardon, ma'am?' said the gardener's lad, passing her with a basketful of peas.

Eating al fresco was one of Claudette's chief delights, whatever the season, and Phoebe had had a stout rustic table and benches made for the terrace on the river side of the house where they could eat while looking out towards the nearby bridge. In the distance, cornfields were ripening and the high sunny wall at one side gave them shelter, as it did to the kitchen garden on its opposite face.

Miss Maskell had been almost one of the family since Claudette was four years old, as petite as a wren, brown and merry-eyed and of indeterminate age since no one younger than a centenarian could possibly know as much as she did about everything. In fact, she was only one year older than Phoebe, and she knew everything thanks to her education by her professor father, a penniless academic. If she tended to throw into every conversation the knowledge she'd soaked up like a sponge, the other three indulged her because she was kind and quite adorable, and far above the usual type of governess. Tabby Maskell and Cousin Hetty had grown fond of each other, for here there was no jealousy or snobbery. Tabby was never cold-shouldered away into the schoolroom at mealtimes or on social occasions, and Hetty took on many of the responsibilities while never impinging on those of Phoebe's personal maid, Miss Cowling. Nevertheless, with her white hair and rather old-fashioned dress, she had more than once been mistaken for the housekeeper.

On this occasion, knowing what she did of Lady Templeman's early efforts to bring Phoebe and Lord Ransome together, she could make an educated guess at the reason for the distress, and although she was no stranger to the Viscount's personal brand of etiquette, she had not expected him to renew his interest with the kind of immediacy he had apparently shown that morning. She hoped sincerely that he would not return to upset dear Phoebe again, just when she was finding some peace at last.

* * *

Phoebe knew that Hetty's ignorance of the true situation could not be allowed to continue, particularly as it involved her and Tabby Maskell as much as Phoebe herself. Lord Ransome had promised to visit her again tomorrow, no doubt with a time limit for their removal. The dreadful truth would have to be told, and the sooner the better, so after Claudette was in bed, she gathered in her parlour to tell them the news.

Predictably, both Hetty and Tabby were more sympathetic and supportive than distressed, and with touching loyalty declared that, like Ruth to Naomi, wherever Phoebe went they would go also. If she recognised the problems with that sentiment, she was far too overcome with thanks to call attention to them. They stayed up far into the night talking about the reasons, the alternatives, the organisation, about Claudette's future as well as their own, yet the one fact that seemed to come round for discussion rather too regularly was that Lord Ransome had found the means to avenge himself for the indifference Phoebe had once shown when, if she'd had a mind to it, she might have encouraged him. It was useless to speculate, Phoebe told them, when the end result would be the same.

She was less prepared, however, for his astonishingly early arrival next morning, long before the usual hour for a gentleman's call, so that it was Claudette and

Miss Maskell who met him as they came into the courtyard from the side garden with a basket of roses. Claudette, who had never met a real Viscount before, half-expected him to be wearing a red velvet ermine-edged robe with a coronet on his head rather than the double-breasted tailcoat with a high stand-fall collar and a grey striped waistcoat showing below. They watched with interest as he swung out of the saddle and stood before them, sweeping off his tall hat and performing a faultless bow.

He noticed Claudette staring at his gleaming boots. 'Hessians,' he said, smiling. 'From Hesse, you know. May I introduce myself? I'm Ransome. And you must be Mademoiselle Donville. Am I correct?'

Prompted by the reminder in the small of her back, Claudette curtsied. 'You are correct… er…my lord. May I present my governess, Miss Maskell?'

'Your servant, ma'am.' Ransome nodded, giving Tabby ample opportunity to see why Phoebe had not been quite herself since yesterday. She made her curtsy, and could see no reason to object when he offered to introduce them to his horse. It was, Tabby thought, a perfect way for him to make Claudette's acquaintance, for she had no fear of the great black creature. What would she say though, she wondered, when the Viscount claimed her home for himself? Would she withdraw the friendship so quickly given? Ought they to have shown the same disapproval as Madame Donville?

The answer to that was seen in Phoebe's stony expression as she came out of the front porch, bristling with the disapproval Tabby had identified, yet reluctant to break the instant rapport between her daughter and the Viscount, who were so engaged that it was a few moments before they noticed her.

But in that small capsule of time, Phoebe's heart played her false before it remembered the reason for his visit. Here was a man, it told her, an athletic and virile creature with the most disagreeably insolent manner, unbearably good looking and probably well aware of it, walking into her house as if he owned it, which he did, and striking up an immediate friendship with her daughter when it was common knowledge that few men even recognised the existence of young girls until they were old enough to be either seduced or married off. Phoebe's heart also reminded her once again, in that short pause before she spoke, how it felt to be held in those arms, pressed against that hard chest and ruthlessly kissed.

Pushing the errant thoughts aside, she stepped forwards into the sunlight, refusing to be drawn into a discussion about single and double bridles, maintaining the unsmiling face she had prepared since she'd heard the clop of hooves on the cobbles. She had been upstairs at the time and had not had time to finish tying up her hair, so she had no idea how lovely she looked.

Tabby Maskell was quick to remove her charge, leaving her mistress and unwelcome guest to face each other with some indefinable spark between them, keeping them both silent for far too long. Looking over her shoulder, Tabby saw that neither of them had moved or spoken before she and Claudette reached the door.

Drawing off his leather gloves, he sauntered towards her. 'You were never one for friendly greetings were you, *madame*?' he said.

'My friends would not agree with you, my lord. Will you come inside, or do you prefer to give me more bad news out here where there's nothing much for me to break?'

His eyes twinkled in the sun, but his reply was to hold out his hat in the direction of the porch and wait for her to lead the way. 'Oh, mistress of the sharp tongue,' he murmured. 'Your ancestors—'

'If you were at all concerned with my ancestors,' Phoebe snapped, 'you would have guessed that Ferry House has been in the Hawkin family since the late sixteen hundreds. My ancestors would never have believed it would pass out of their hands with so little effort.'

'So, if we are to leave the ancestors out of it, may we speak of your delightful daughter? She does have the look of *this* lady,' he said, stopping to look at the portrait on the wall above the hall table. He placed his hat, gloves and whip on the polished surface, peering at the woman wearing seventeenth-century dress, clearly related to Phoebe. 'But then, so do you.'

'Lord Ransome, am I to understand you came so early in the morning solely to talk about family likenesses?' Phoebe asked as she led the way into the parlour. 'Or is this small talk meant to soften me up ready for the *coup de grâce*?'

'You should ask me to sit down, you know. I'm glad you've changed your mind about allowing me inside. So much more comfortable.' Holding up his long coat tails, he lowered himself into a wing chair upholstered with china-blue velvet, sat back and stretched out his long legs, showing not a wrinkle in the skintight breeches.

Phoebe placed herself, very upright, on the slender couch. 'Please be seated, my lord. As you pointed out so gallantly on your last visit, I am hardly in a position to prevent your entry, am I? Even so, I do not intend to pack up my possessions and camp out on the village green so that you can move straight in. You have at least two houses to live in. Probably more.'

'Yes, several more.'

'Tenanted, are they?'

He smiled at that. 'The farms on my estates are all tenanted, certainly, but Ferry House is simply a house, isn't it? With a sitting tenant.'

'Rather more than that, my lord.'

'Oh? Do enlighten me, *madame*.'

'The place was almost derelict when I first came here. My brother had no use for it, and no one had rented it since my father died. Leon didn't want to spend any money on renovating it, and that's why he lent it to me. Fortunately, I was able to repair it and to employ people who needed some security. Three of these I brought with me, but most of the others are all either too old or too… well…vulnerable, to find work elsewhere. I took them on without references and I've had no trouble so far. The gardens were in a terrible state, but now we grow all our own vegetables and fruit, and we supply two or three inns in Richmond, too. We use all our own dairy produce, and sell it at the local market, and the money it earns is used on wages and running costs. It would be such a pity to lose all that.'

'And the money you inherited from your late husband?'

'Yes, I wondered how long it would be before you brought up the subject again. Most of that money, my lord, went on new roofing, floors and plastering, windows and doors, fittings for the kitchen and stables. Everything. I also rebuilt the attics for my staff, for it seemed to me that since I could not refund my late husband's gains to the rightful owners, it should be used to help others less fortunate than me. So now you know. It's out in the open, and all I ask is that my family never gets to hear the truth. I have learnt to live with it now, but it would do *them* irreparable damage. My brother Ross, who lives near you at Mortlake, is a solicitor, you see, and he would not take kindly to any hint of a scandal in the family. Nor would my brother-in-law, Lord Nateby. Not to mention my mother and *her* husband.'

'Templeman? No, he manages to find an opinion on every subject under the sun whether he knows about it or not. He'd certainly have plenty to say.'

'So you know exactly what happened, do you?'

'Oh, yes, Madame Donville. I do. The young Count who told you is an embittered young man who doesn't see himself as fortunate to be alive. But I believe he regrets what he has done, now his friends have told him how wrong he was. I don't think you need be too concerned that he will repeat it outside of the circles the French move in.'

'I'm rather more concerned, my lord, that *others* will.'

He could hardly have failed to understand her precise meaning, but he said no more on the subject, passing on to a relation about whom she had said very little. 'And your eldest brother Leon? Has he seen Ferry House since your renovations?'

Phoebe went to stand by the window that looked out on to the formal garden at one side, at the white roses that fell like a waterfall over the pink bricks, the little topiary bushes cut into corkscrews. Her voice was only just loud enough for him to hear. 'No,' she said. 'He hasn't. He ought not to be in London at all. It's

not the life for him. He's an artist. Ideally, he should
be living here in Richmond, where he could paint to
his heart's content.' Idly, she picked up the watercolour painting, the victim of her outburst yesterday.
Its frame lay in pieces along with the small easel on
which it stood. 'This is one of his watercolours. I believe he has real talent, but my mother never encouraged it and he won't try to sell anything. He needs
looking after. He needs a wife. And a patron. I ought
to go to him. He was the one to help me when I needed
it most.'

'And do your family support what you're doing
here?'

Phoebe looked at him over her shoulder. 'No, my
lord. Nor will they do so now, when I need help again.
I'm more sure of that than of anything.'

'May I see the painting?' He was up on his feet to
take the paper from her, holding it to the light. While
he studied it, Phoebe studied him, wondering what
kind of women had felt the touch of his skin next to
theirs, had touched the long dark sideburns and the
cleft in his chin, the thick waves of hair with a dent
where his tall hat had been. 'Surely this is Marble Hill
House?' he said. 'It's remarkably good.'

'You recognise it? It's the view from—'

'From Ham House, just across the river. Yes, I
know it well.'

'My sister and her husband live just here, through

the trees.' Phoebe's finger touched the woodland at one side of the house. 'I'm surprised you know the place, my lord. I thought…' Her shoulders shrugged as she turned away.

'You thought I spent my time either in gaming, at the races, or in turning widows out of their houses. Or perhaps in taking the last penny off any man too far under the table to know what he's doing.'

'Reputations like yours usually begin somewhere, don't they?'

'As did yours, *madame*. You may believe it to be an invention, nevertheless.'

'Unless some mischievous person re-invents it.'

'For what purpose?'

She shrugged again, taking the painting from him. 'Retribution, I suppose. It's what people do, isn't it, when they've been rebuffed?'

'Ah, so you remember that, do you? Your mama's *strenuous* efforts to get—'

'Please, stop! I really do not want to go over that old ground. It can serve no useful purpose, can it? My mother has quite given up trying to interfere in my life, I'm happy to say. So much so that she has not been here either, to see where my daughter and I live.'

'You may not wish to cover old ground again, Madame Donville, but you have just implied that I am holding some kind of grudge for the failure of Lady Templeman's ambitions. It's an interesting theory but, you know, I have never yet had to rely on anyone's matchmaking. When I set my sights on a woman, I usually manage things without any help at all. And opposition is more of a challenge.'

'And indifference, my lord? Total uninterest? That usually works.'

'Oh, I believe I can tell the difference between the real thing and that which is feigned,' he said, softly.

Lowering the painting, which she'd been pretending to examine, she saw that his eyes had narrowed. Piercing like darts, they seemed to penetrate her thoughts most disconcertingly, revealing her doubts about him and his intentions, and about her other more physical appraisal of him that, try as she might, she could not succeed in concealing. A woman of strong emotions, she had never been good at hiding her loves and hates and now, when these had begun to take on aspects of each other, the confusion in her eyes must be there to be read by a man as experienced as Buck Ransome.

Why she allowed him, then, to do what he did was a total mystery to her, for if someone had told her that she would permit his fingers to slide over her throat, slowly, tenderly, like the kiss of a moth's wings from her chin to the low neckline of her muslin day-dress, she would have told them they were imagining it. Indeed, it had all the elements of a dream, for she stood there like a sleepwalker, held by his eyes and by the warm fragile caress that travelled down and back up again. She was aware of nothing but that and the powerful nearness of him. Yesterday, he had roughly subdued her scorching tongue and now he had taken another liberty, as soft as swansdown, yet just as unsettling. No respectable woman would have allowed it.

'No, my lord,' she whispered. 'No, you cannot do that. If you are trying to remind me of what might have been, I do not need it. There could never have been anything. Even if I'd not still been grieving, you would never have been the kind of man I would…well…' She gulped, aware that she was trembling and breathless.

'Would what, *madame?* Marry? But situations change, don't they?'

'Unfortunately, they do. But on that topic there would never have been a change of mind, my lord. This is why you must never, ever, touch me again. *Never.* My widowed state may indicate to some men that I am available, but that is not so. I shall never be available to a man of your persuasions. I shall be no man's mistress, so if that's what you had in mind as the price of my tenancy here, then you are mistaken. My suggestion that you should re-negotiate did not include that kind of thing.'

'Do you know, Madame Donville, that thought had never entered my mind, either? My attempt at a re-negotiation would have nothing to do with mistresses. I'm sorry if that's what you thought. What I had thought is that, in return for your tenancy of Ferry House, you might offer me something more permanent. But if, as you say, your mind is quite made up about the kind of man you would even *consider* marrying, then it looks as if our discussion may have to end here.'

The discussion did, however, have to wait for a few moments until the maid had deposited upon the side-table a tray loaded with a chocolate pot and small blue-and-white mugs. To Phoebe's thanks, she smiled and curtsied before limping to the door.

'Has she had an accident?' said Lord Ransome.

'In a way, yes. She was a street-walker when I found her, badly beaten up. The authorities would have imprisoned her, but I persuaded them to let me have her. She's lived here for two years now.'

'Ah. One of the vulnerable dependants.'

'I have two such maids-of-all-work. One was in the workhouse up on the hill. But what did you say a moment ago? I think I did not hear you correctly.'

'If you continue to shake the chocolate pot like that, *madame,* you'll get more on the tray than in the mugs. Here, allow me to pour it out. You sit down.'

She had expected to feel annoyance, even anger at this meeting, having no intention of letting her home go without a fight. But she had not expected to feel this kind of confusion or anything like the helplessness she was now experiencing in the company of this unusual man. In London, she had never allowed him to come as close as this. Now, here in her home, he filled the room with his great frame, making her feel more womanly and desirable than she'd felt for years. No other man of her acquaintance would have dared to speak and act as he did. But then, what madness in her had allowed it? 'I ought to send for Mrs Spindelow,' she said. 'If you had not arrived so early…'

'Drink your chocolate. We can manage well enough without a chaperon.'

'Hetty has been a good friend to me. We have no secrets.'

'She knows about Monsieur Donville, does she?'

'No,' Phoebe whispered. 'No one knows of that except you.'

'Except me. So, we need to talk about your future, *madame,* and how to get round the obstacle of my ownership. And we don't need an audience to do that.'

'Your ownership of me? Lord Ransome, I may look like a typically helpless female, but I—'

'No, I wouldn't say that.'

'Please allow me to finish.'

'I was hoping you would. It sounds interesting.' Taking his chocolate, he swallowed it in one gulp and replaced the mug with a smile. 'Yes? Helpless…?'

With a noisy sigh, she looked up at the ceiling, silently invoking patience. 'Lord Ransome, I think you really are the most irritating, overbearing and rude man I've ever met. Did you know that?'

'I might have guessed as much, from your expression,' he said, still smiling. 'So you could never accept me as a husband, then? Pity. We both have so much to offer.'

CHAPTER THREE

THERE WAS THAT look again, he thought, as if she had made her mind up about the nature of his offer, even before she'd heard it. He knew she would take some convincing but, since their first meeting yesterday, he had discovered that side of her which only her late husband had known, that part she kept hidden beneath an icy front since the disastrously short marriage had ended. What a fool the mother had been to allow it. He had known Donville, the heart-breaker and oath-breaker. What a pity it had been Phoebe Hawkin he'd set his sights on, a girl of sixteen who knew no better than to fall for his Continental charm, thinking that that alone was enough to feed on.

Yet he had felt how she burned inside for the touch

of a man with courage enough to storm the barriers, how she had melted under his kiss, how his caresses had shaken her. She was interested. Excited. Curious. Defensive. And angry. Very angry.

Contradictions came easily to her. 'No, we don't!' she replied sharply. 'I have nothing to offer you, Lord Ransome, except to be a caring tenant for your property. And you have nothing to offer me that I want, *except* this house. My home.'

'All these *exceptions, madame,*' he said, rebuking her. 'They're the basis of our negotiations, surely? If you could bring yourself to listen to what *I'm* saying instead of listening to your prejudices, you'd have more reason for hope. I *am* offering you the continued tenancy of the house. I am also offering you something else, but unfortunately you appear to be completely set against it, even before you've given it a moment's thought.'

'I don't think I want to,' she whispered, looking sideways at his boots. 'I've spent years trying not to think about it. It happened to me once, and I was taken in for all the wrong reasons, and the pain of it is still with me. I cannot afford to let anyone into my life like that again, my lord. Tell me I'm wrong. Tell me that was *not* what you were talking about.' Warily, she glanced across at him, and he knew that their thoughts were running parallel at last.

'You are *not* wrong,' he replied. 'Marriage is what

I'm talking about. But you are not sixteen any more, and you are not being taken in by anyone. The offer is quite straightforward. I need a wife, and you need to keep your home.'

He might have expected a noisy refusal, an outburst of passion with all the whys and wherefores, but instead she sat very still, twisting the wedding ring on her finger, her eyes searching the room, resting on the well-chosen items, the silver chocolate pot and china mugs. She had taste and breeding, sensitivity and compassion, honesty and courage, qualities he admired in a woman. But Madame Donville had more than that after being so deceived, and now she was as vulnerable as those poor creatures she had taken under her wing.

'Is this what you meant about owning *me* as well as the house?' she said. 'If so, my lord, I must tell you that every finer feeling in me rebels against the concept. I never owned Ferry House, but I *have* owned myself for the past nine years, and I've grown used to it. I do not need a master. Is there no alternative to this? Could you not simply allow me to carry on as I have been doing? Would not owning the house be enough for you? You surely cannot be lacking female companionship.'

'I am lacking a *wife,*' he said, 'and you are not only living in my property, but you have the qualities I'm looking for. I believe that, between us, we could deal tolerably well together. You have proved that you can manage a household, and more. You do the accounts yourself, do you?'

Phoebe frowned at the impertinence. 'Of course I do.'

'Remarkable.'

'And are you going to ask me if I sing, play the pianoforte and harp, paint and embroider, make cherry wine and raspberry vinegar? Would you like to inspect the linen cupboards and quiz the coachman? I do have horses too, you know.'

'Do you ask your guests if they would like a second cup of chocolate?'

'No. Not when my guests pour it out for themselves.'

'*Touché.*' He smiled, uncrossed his legs and sat up. 'Will you take another, *madame*? It calms the nerves, I believe.'

'There's nothing wrong with my nerves that a little co-operation from you would not mend. Could you not consider my requests?'

'I have done.' Deliberately, he poured the chocolate into both mugs and placed one beside her. 'You see, I am quite house-trained. And I have understood your reservations too. I am not riding rough-shod over them but, on the other hand, I know they can be overcome, if only you will make a few concessions.'

'Concessions?' The liquid in Phoebe's mug slopped

as the word exploded. 'You think that marrying against my better judgement is a *concession,* my lord? Giving up my freedom to someone I don't even *like*? Having a man live in the house I've built up with care? A stepfather to my daughter with a reputation like *yours*? You call those concessions, do you?'

'Having a good sound roof over your head,' he threw back at her, 'is not to be sniffed at, these days, when so many sleep rough on the streets. Having loyal staff and a well-run household with horses in the stables, with or without a coachman, is more than some widows can expect, Madame Donville. If I were you, I would think carefully about your options when generous ones are so hard to come by.'

'You'd turn us all out, then? Is that one of the options?'

'We're still discussing the positive ones. I'll tell you when we've reached the negatives. Just start using your common sense, woman, and leave your sqeamishness out of it.'

'Thank you. I will. I shall go and speak to Leon about my squeamishness.'

'When I last saw him he was in no condition to talk to anyone. What he needs is to be brought here to Richmond. Better still, I have a friend who lives not far from here who would lend him a little place where he could recover, be near his family and perhaps start to paint again. You said he needed a patron. I have someone in mind.'

'You would do that, for Leon?'

'As part of our agreement, I would do whatever I could to help him. Anyone who can paint like that should not be wasting his time at the gaming tables.'

'That's not what you thought when—'

'No, he's kept very quiet about his talents, hasn't he? But this might turn out to be the best thing that's ever happened to him. It's up to you.'

Phoebe looked into her mug at the still-untouched chocolate, then replaced it on the tray as she stood, clearly unhappy with the choices she was being expected to make on behalf of so many people. 'He needs help. I owe it to him. But you have placed me in an impossible position, my lord.'

'On the contrary, *madame,* you are in a very *possible* position. I may not be the most perfect choice of stepfathers for your daughter, but I have a suspicion that such a paragon would be impossible to find before it ceases to matter. She seemed to find me easy to talk to, and I found her quite delightful. Do you not think it's time she had a father? She's never had one, has she?' She could do with a few brothers and sisters too, he thought, watching Phoebe's agitated movements reflect her thoughts. He knew what she was about to say well before she spoke, half-turning to him, turning away, turning back.

'Give me some…some time, please? Or are you in a hurry to take possession of the house?'

Not of the house, he thought. 'No, I have my new place at Mortlake. The builders will be there for another week or so, but I can manage.' He went to stand behind her as she looked out of the window to where Claudette, Miss Maskell and Hetty sat together on the stone bench by the wall, their feet hidden by low box hedges. Phoebe's hair gave off a perfume that he tried, and failed, to recognise. Delicate, floral, haloed with a ring of light. Sheening like a starling's plumage. 'I have an idea,' he said to the back of her head. 'Tomorrow, I shall call for you after luncheon and take you to this friend of mine. He's an artist and collector, and you can talk to him and his wife about your brother and see if you think they could help him.'

'Who are they?' she said, not moving.

He could feel her tremble at his nearness, though there was no contact. 'They live down the road at Ham. You'll like them. Everybody does. Then, if you think you've made enough concessions, you can give me your answer.'

There was no obvious sarcasm in his voice, but Phoebe was quick to pick up on the irony. 'Yes,' she said. 'Thank you. That would be helpful. But this surely cannot be the best way for you to find a wife, Lord Ransome? You know very little about me, apart from the one thing I don't want anyone to know. And I know very little about you, none of which I like the sound of, although my mother did. But then, look who *she* approved of as a suitable husband for me.'

'So the best thing would be for you to stop listening to what others say about me and start finding out for yourself, wouldn't it? I shall be here just after noon tomorrow, *madame*. I bid you good day.' Bending his head, he placed his lips just above the neckline of her muslin gown and kissed the nubs of her spine, one by one. She stood without moving as the warmth of each kiss moved upwards into her hairline.

Then he remembered the scent. It was myrtle.

The three figures out in the garden appeared to hold her attention as bees buzzed lazily and the cat came to find the sunniest patch on the floor, while Phoebe's thoughts, if they could be called that, stirred her body and melted it. The back of her neck held the warm tenderness he'd planted there, sending tendrils of excitement probing downwards deep into her womb and beyond, tightening, relaxing, stopping her breath, parting her lips, stifling her cry of longing. *Damn him... damn him.*

Both hands slid down to comfort and press, telling her quivering empty parts to be still, to keep on waiting as they had been doing, to be patient. But his hard warmth still lingered upon her back and, although he had not held her, he must have known what his closeness was doing to her, adding a new dimension to his bald statement that he needed a wife. Cleverly, insidiously, he was telling her that she needed a husband. Not just any husband, but a man in his prime, experienced, ruthless and audacious, the only one able to invalidate and banish her jaded memories of Claude Donville's ineffectual lovemaking. Far from satisfying her cravings, childbirth had only intensified them, creating a relentless conflict between physical desire and the need to spare herself more heartache. So far, no one had come close to upsetting the balance. Until now.

So unfair, she told herself, turning away from the window. So unfair. Losing her home to one of London's most notorious rakes. Marriage to him as the price of it. And Leon, to be rehabilitated and cared for, also at a price. A father for her daughter, most unsuitable but better than none. Questionable. Security for those unfortunates who worked for her. How could she possibly let them down? Who would take them on? Who would run this place, and where would she and Claudette go? Impossible to answer. Meanwhile, she would accompany this overbearing man to see these friends at Ham, whoever they were and, however great her reservations, she would have to keep Leon and Claudette at the top of her list of priorities.

There was also the dark shame of her late husband's treason to consider, which Lord Ransome would presumably not have mentioned if he'd not intended to use it as a lever against her. No, he had not said he would, but nor had he said he wouldn't.

* * *

If she had also wondered how long it would be before there was some reaction from the rest of her family to Leon's latest delinquency, she had not long to wait. It was just after lunchtime when they arrived. It always was.

On any other day than this, Phoebe would have put a cheerful face on it but, as her brother Ross and his wife Josephine had visited only last week after seeing friends in Richmond, another visit so soon could only mean one thing—that they'd heard the news from Mama in London, who knew everything that went on in the capital as soon as it happened. Much as Phoebe would have appreciated some sound advice on the problem, Ross Hawkin's advice as a solicitor tended to be so doom-laden and riddled with clauses that she would rather he stayed away altogether. Requesting Hetty to warn cook of the unexpected luncheon guests, she sent Claudette upstairs, telling Tabby Maskell to make her look more presentable, or they'd never hear the last of it.

The carriage doors opened, spilling out Mr and Mrs Ross Hawkin and three-year-old Arthur, already howling and clinging like a limpet to the nearest leg. 'Do come inside,' Phoebe called over the din. 'Have you lunched yet?' She knew they would not have. Cook would be ill. Or they'd been held up in town and thought they'd call on the way home. Or that they couldn't stay, but if Phoebe's cook had prepared something they might as well stay and help her eat it, her garden being so much larger than theirs, better stocked...et cetera...et cetera. It was a favourite theme, the size of Ferry House compared to theirs.

Not waiting to guage the state of Phoebe's mind, Josephine flung her crimson satin arms around her sister-in-law in an exaggerated embrace of sympathy that was physically difficult to reciprocate, Josephine being well into the family way by seven months or so. It gave Phoebe the chance to cut it short, though her hands were caught and held, obliging her to take the full force of the shocked words and pained expression. 'Oh *dear,* Phoebe. What a business this is, to be sure. You must have heard from Lady Templeman, as we did. Such a nasty *horrid* shock. We must go, I said to Mr Hawkin, to be with your *dear* sister in her hour of need, for even though it's nurse's day off, we could not be staying away when we need to discuss what's to be done. Is that not so, Mr Hawkin?'

Supressing her cynicism with difficulty, Phoebe released her hands, sure that any discussion with Ross and Josephine would be unlikely to produce a solution to the problem, neither of them having offered her anything of a material nature in the entire three years of her living near them. As a perfectly healthy and fertile individual, Josephine had found that a pretence of delicate ill health was useful for not getting involved in anything that required even the smallest effort. It had always puzzled Phoebe that her brother accepted it when he was as keen as a terrier to denounce anyone else for not pulling their weight. Needless to say, his elder brother Leon was a front runner for his condemnation.

'Dreadful business,' he growled, pecking Phoebe on each cheek. 'Can't imagine what a state Leon's got himself into to do such a thing. Dreadful!' He picked up his son, suffering the limpet's strangling arms around his collar and cravat.

By the time they reached the pleasant gold-and-white dining room, Hetty and one of the maids had transformed the recently-cleared table with place-settings of polished silver and glass, as if the uninvited guests had been expected all along. Dishes of cold meats, new bread, warm cheese tartlets, bowls of pale lettuce and watercress, sugared apple slices and a tray of almond creams meant for dinner were brought in while Claudette and her governess took small Arthur away into the garden after an argument about whether his hunger was genuine or not. Instead of giving him a piece of watercress to solve the vexed question immediately, his doting mother offered him a cheese tartlet. The result was the same, and predictably messier.

Not unexpectedly, the free food took precedence over business, and as Phoebe watched it disappear almost as fast as it had arrived, she was obliged to wait for Ross's knife and fork to take a well-earned rest. 'A bad business,' he said again, dabbing at his mouth. 'Mama's letter arrived this morning. Leon was at Brooks's, apparently. Templeman's lads were there at the time. That's how she knew what happened.' Casually, he looked around the table for a further addition to his plate, then helped himself to another glassful of elderflower wine. 'Very nice. Almost as good as last year's,' he remarked.

'Then why on *earth* didn't they stop him?' said Phoebe, crossly. 'Don't they have tongues in their heads any more?'

'Well, for one thing, you can't prevent a man from putting up his own property as a bet if that's the currency he's got. If the other players accept it, there's no reason to interfere.'

'But the Templeman brothers are half-related to us, Ross.'

'They know nothing about Leon's estates, however.'

There was more than a suggestion of the lawyer in his manner, speaking while fidgeting with something else or sitting back with steepled fingertips. At twenty-nine, Ross belonged to Mortlake's most successful practice and rarely missed a chance to let it be known. Slightly thinning on top and already thickening around the waistline, his rotund features were more boyish than handsome. The row of gold fobs dangling below his pale yellow waistcoat was a show of ostentation

more valuable to him than the quality of his superfine
or the cut of his pantaloons.

'Has Mama not offered to come to his aid?'

'The simple answer to that, my dear, is Templeman.
Whatever Mama might wish to do for our family de-
pends entirely on our stepfather, and he has those two
stupid dolts of his own to help out. He's not likely to
bail Leon out, whatever he does.'

'Not even when he's losing his inheritance?'

'No. That's Leon's own affair, not his.'

While Ross buttered another slice of bread, his wife
saw her chance. 'What we need to know, Phoebe dear,
is what *you're* going to do. Obviously, if that *dreadful* man Ransome is going to take the place over, as
we feel sure he will, where does that leave you and
Claudette? He's already bought that place near us—
what's it called?—Greenwater, and our neighbours
are concerned that it's being extended to house his latest mistress. Well, you need not look so shocked, Mr
Hawkin, for I'm sure I don't wish to use the word if I
could find another more suitable. I had it from Mrs
Blackman next door whose husband spoke to the
builder's mate who told him it was to be the mistress's
house, and that's as plain as it gets, to my mind.
Viscount Ransome stayed there over the last two
nights, so I was informed by nurse who walked past
this morning. She saw his curricle outside, so perhaps
he'll eventually get round to calling on you personally,

Phoebe. Would you like Mr Hawkin or myself to be here when he does?'

A chill of heart-rending intensity crawled along Phoebe's arms as the news she had dreaded hearing was delivered with such unbearable lightness, just like any of the other gossipy tid-bits Josephine cluttered her mind with. He had a mistress all ready to take up residence at Mortlake when only a few hours earlier he had proposed himself as her next husband, placing kisses upon her neck, playing upon her powerlessness. Anger and nausea pulled at her innards. Already the pain had begun, even before she was committed. What would it be like when she'd gone too far to turn back? Could she do it? Could she bear the pain of having her self-esteem torn to shreds once more?

Until that moment, Phoebe had deliberately kept the news of the Viscount's visit to herself, nursing it like a jewel too precious to show. Now, however, as if to score a point against Josephine for her mealy mouthed disclosure about the mistress, she politely thanked her for the seemingly altruistic offer. 'No, thank you. Viscount Ransome has already called on me.'

Ross's knife clattered upon his plate. 'Been? Here? When, may I ask?'

'I have no objection to you asking, brother. He called yesterday.'

'Unexpectedly?'

'He sent a note. And, no, I did not receive a letter

from Mama, as you did. Apparently she thought you ought to know before me.'

'So if you'd let me know, Phoebe, I could have been here with you. Couldn't I?' said Ross, placing both hands on the table.

'And what good would that have done?'

'Well, for pity's sake! For family support. What else? Besides which, it is highly improper for an un-attached man to spend time alone with—'

'Oh, spare me, brother! I'm a widow of twenty-six. I have Hetty here and a houseful of women. We could have torn him to shreds between us if I'd called for help, but I didn't and, as you see, I'm still in one piece. I can manage quite well on my own, you know. I have done for three years now.'

'That's most unfair, Phoebe. We're only a couple of miles across the Park, and you've always been able to call on us if you needed to.'

'And we've always said,' Josephine joined in, catching the drift, 'how Ferry House is too big for you, Phoebe. It would have been much better for—'

'For *you* to have had it. Yes, dear, but Leon gave me the use of it in an act of kindness I shall not forget at a time when I needed help. He was the only one to *do* something. I only wish he could see it now.'

'I only wish he could too, sister,' snapped Ross, whipping his napkin off his knee and hitting the table with it. 'It's all very well giving it to you with one hand

and taking it away with the other. How much help will Leon be when you have to pack your belongings and leave, I wonder? Have you been given a time limit? What did Ransome have to say for himself?'

'I shall not be leaving,' said Phoebe, quietly. She looked at Hetty, who had not said a word so far.

There was a silence until Josephine, showing her hand too soon, said, 'It might be better if you did, dear. Ransome would not be a man to tangle with.'

'Ah, you're about to offer me some of that help whenever I need it,' Phoebe replied. 'So do you have a viable alternative? Are you saying we'd be welcome to live with you? No, I'm teasing you, dear. Don't look so dismayed. I know your house is so *dreadfully* small and, even if it wasn't, it would not work, would it? I have fallen women living in as maids, you see, and that's not quite your style, is it?'

'We shall get nowhere,' Ross said, 'with that kind of discussion. This has more to do with how to keep a roof over your head than with style, Phoebe. There's Claudette to think of, too. I doubt if Leon gave that small detail one moment of his attention when he gambled with your future, did he?'

'Don't abuse Leon to me, Ross, if you please. He's the one who allowed me some peace after what happened, and now he's in his own kind of trouble. I dread to think how he's living. Perhaps I ought to go and find out. I don't suppose you would go, would you?'

Ross ignored her request. 'Your first priority is to settle your own problem,' he said, pushing his chair back. 'If we could offer you accommodation at our home we would, but with the arrival of number two in September we shall have no space left for your ménage. Nor do I suppose Mimi is any better off at Twickenham, with Nateby's mother and sisters there, and the children too. I think you need a lawyer on this, you know, but I have to say it doesn't look too good. If he wants the place for himself, then it's between you and him how long you've got. You can hardly expect anything more when you made it plain you wanted nothing to do with him.'

'Oh, Ross, I was still grieving, wasn't I? No one with the least sensitivity would expect me to be sociable in those circumstances.'

'And Ransome is not best known for his sensitivity either, is he?'

She recalled the tender caresses of finger and lips, saying nothing.

'Dreadful man!' Josephine muttered. 'Mistresses! Disgraceful! But you'd make a very good governess, Phoebe dear. I've always thought so. You have good French, and you're good with children too. And Hetty dear…well, I really don't know what we could do with you, unless there was an old lady somewhere.' Arching her back against the load, she went to stand by the window, quite oblivious to her own appalling clumsiness.

'We don't have to *do* anything with Hetty, thank you, Josephine,' Phoebe replied tartly, laying a hand over her companion's. 'She is as much a part of my life as Claudette is, and where I go she goes too. I assume that if Lord Ransome spends most of his time at Mortlake with his mistress, he'll not be spending much time here so, if that is the case, he may allow me to stay. Nothing has been decided.'

'You didn't show him round, then?' said Ross, rising from the table.

'No, he came only to give me the news. He'll be returning tomorrow.'

Although Ross allowed his sister's blush to go unremarked, he could tell that the prospect of a further visit was not looked forward to with much hope, in spite of her defiance. 'Would you like me to be here with you?' he said.

'No, thank you. I cannot believe he'll throw us all out within the week.'

'Then allow me to give you some advice, my dear, before we go. Don't try to second-guess a man like Ransome. He may have unorthodox methods, but he's no fool, like our dear brother. He doesn't *ever* lose what he can't afford, and no woman has ever sued him for paternity, either. That much I know.'

Again, Phoebe felt the ice-cold prickle along her arms. 'Thank you for the advice,' she whispered. She would like to have told him that the second part of it was irrelevant, but Ross was a lawyer and he would never have offered any advice, free or otherwise, unless there was a reason for it.

Listening to the conversation that flowed across the table, Hetty had observed how the Hawkins couple had demolished the food, contributing little to Phoebe's comfort while greedily assessing the contents of her home. She had seen how Josephine surreptitiously peered at the hallmark on the back of the tablespoon, how she had held her glass up to the light to watch the sparkle of cut edges, fingering the lace border of the tablecloth, eyeing the gold brocade curtains from top to bottom.

Josephine Sadler had been glad to accept Sir Leo Hawkin's second son after Viscount Ransome had refused to show the slightest interest in her. But Ross Hawkin had always had to work for his living, and that had rankled with her when the elder of the two brothers seemed intent on wasting what he had inherited. She had rarely missed a chance to carp about the unsuitability of Ferry House for a young widow like Phoebe, and far from rejoicing in her good fortune after all her misery, envied all that she'd done to rebuild her life.

What was more, Hetty suspected that Josephine was perhaps alert to the possibility that Lord Ransome might resume his attentions to Phoebe after her initial apathy. Which is why, Hetty thought, the envious

Josephine had been quick to disclose Lord Ransome's plans for his newly acquired Mortlake property. To Phoebe, that would be a more serious reason for hostility than the masterfulness he'd shown her yesterday, for only Hetty understood how her dearest friend's heart had been more badly wounded by her husband's infidelity than by his death. It was also Hetty who noticed that, throughout the Hawkins' visit, not once had Phoebe uttered a word to discredit Lord Ransome or to blame him for wanting what was lawfully his, however distressing his method of acquiring it. Returning Phoebe's smile, she followed the others into the parlour.

Ross picked up the broken pieces of easel, replaced them and turned his attention to the watercolour of Marble Hill House. 'What happened here?' he said. 'Clumsy housemaid, was it?'

'Clumsy me,' said Phoebe. 'That's the painting Leon gave me.'

'Never noticed it before. It's good. Who's the artist?'

'Look in the bottom left-hand corner. Hold it to the light, Ross.'

'Ah…yes…what? This says, L. Hawkin. *Can't* be.'

'Yes, it is. Leon painted it five or six years ago.'

'Huh! Well, his hand won't be so steady now, will it?' he said, tossing the paper back on top of its wooden bits. 'Pity.'

'What's the pity for, exactly?' said Phoebe.

'Wasted talent. Well now, we must be off. Let me know if you want me to be with you when Ransome calls again. Tomorrow, did you say? Well, I shall have my hands full at the office tomorrow, but I can find some free time the day after, I suppose. Now, where's that child of ours, Josephine?'

'Oh, Hetty!' With a ragged sigh of relief and anguish, Phoebe gave herself up to the comfort of Hetty's lace-edged arms, breathing in the faint aroma of peppermint and snuggling her cheek into the soft white wispy hair. 'He's got a mistress at Mortlake,' she whispered. 'I might have known.'

'Does it make any difference, *chérie?*' Hetty said, smoothing a hand over Phoebe's back. 'Does it surprise you?'

Phoebe's chin nodded on the gentle shoulder. 'Come over to the window-seat. I have something to tell you. I have to make a decision, Hetty dear.'

That same evening, as the peachy sun flooded the river with colour, Madame Phoebe Donville and Miss Hetty Spindelow set off in the phaeton towards Mortlake with the intention of finding out for themselves what the mischievous Josephine was so sure of. They understood Greenwater to be one of those large white houses on the edge of the river, standing on Mortlake's main street. Lime trees made an avenue of dappled shade, and a large green plot at the side of one house was being eaten into by a new extension rising three storeys to the partly finished grey-slate roof. Not wishing to drive the phaeton right up to the house where they might be seen, Phoebe held the horses beneath the limes where, from their high seat, they could see over the wall.

Two of the builders were tidying away their tools, calling to someone down by the river to watch out. Then two small boys, one of them holding a fishing-net on a stick, responded to another deeper shout, running towards the house and straight into the outstretched arms of its owner. Caught, lifted and swirled round like a whirligig, they squealed with laughter and were set back upon their feet. Phoebe and Hetty, frozen with astonishment, were sure that this was Greenwater and that the man with a small boy in each hand was Lord Ransome, leading them back into the house. Their home.

'I don't want to see any more, Hetty,' Phoebe said, hoarsely.

'Time to go home, I think.'

Clumsily, Phoebe turned the phaeton round and headed back the way they had come, blinded by the orange sun and by a sudden rush of tears. 'I won't cry,' she croaked. 'I *won't*!'

'I think you should ask him about it, *chérie*. Tomorrow. If you accept his offer, you have a right to know.'

'Knowing any more isn't going to make a scrap of difference, is it? Perhaps Ross knew about this when he said Lord Ransome has never been sued for paternity. If he's quite content to recognise his own offspring, no one would need to sue him, would they? And judging by the size of that extension, he must have quite a large household.'

Was this what he'd meant when he'd told her to find out for herself?

CHAPTER FOUR

AFTER THAT REVELATION, it would have been surprising if Phoebe had slept soundly. On the one hand, the solution to her most urgent problem was there for her to accept or reject. On the other hand, the price of the solution was to be everything she had nurtured and kept inviolate, her freedom, her independence, her body and her property. How much did that matter when she would be allowed to remain here at Ferry House? And what of Leon, deeply in trouble? The reactions of Ross and Josephine had come as no real surprise, yet she would have liked it to be otherwise. They called on her hospitality whenever it suited them; theirs to her was severely limited. In this case, it was absent altogether.

The problems turned over and over, confusing in the darkness, waiting for the single blinding flash of illumination that didn't appear. Between the complications, sneaking in like guilt, came thoughts of the bold aristocratic male who'd turned her life upside-down, of those eyes that understood too much, piercing her guard, unsettling the peace of her days and nights. She thought of the aura of rugged power he brought into the room simply by standing there, wide-shouldered, slender hipped, the haughty tilt of his head, used to commanding. And being obeyed.

She recalled what she could of Claude, who seemed to shrink by comparison, slight of build, porcelain pale, delicate of hand, exquisitely mannered and superficial, clever enough to deceive her on all levels. She had been a girl. She would not tremble now if he came near her, as she had recently in Buck Ransome's presence. As a girl, she had appreciated the light weight of Claude, rather immature and full of himself. Now, when her sexuality had been awakened and left to starve, she had felt the rawness of her need, felt the seething white-hot ache leap once more into her thighs at the touch of Ransome's teasing hand, his lips on her skin, over her mouth, and she knew that his kind of loving would be the only kind her body craved. Turbulent. Unsparing. Consuming.

But he had a mistress and children and now, she supposed for the sake of his title, he needed a wife.

He would have a ready-made house to move into and she, the wife, would be his society hostess whenever he needed one, having already been trained to the role. How clever of him to see all the advantages in one quick glance, at no expense to himself. To her, that role would be a sacrfice as great as the others; the sharing of a husband with another woman, not far away, who had already given him sons.

Lord Ransome's phaeton, unlike Phoebe's, was a crane-neck, more weighty and solid on its bearings than a perch, but more prone to overturning on sharp bends. For a long-legged man, climbing up into the high two-seater presented no difficulty. For a lady wearing a gown of striped green lustring with a plain green sleeveless pelisse, the climb relied on two strong hands around the waist and a moment or two of trust when she felt herself to be completely reliant on his strength. The green-and-gold panels bearing the Viscount's crest were shallow, the seat velvet-covered, the Wilton carpet soft and clean, the poles and buckles silver-plated. After being used to her own sedate vehicle, Phoebe felt she might easily be tipped out of this one, bouncing on high springs. She knew, however, that Buck Ransome was one of London's best whips, his satin-skinned chestnuts some of the best that money could buy. He spread his feet across the foot-board, and there was nowhere for Phoebe to escape the warm intimacy of his thighs as he turned the phaeton through the gates towards Richmond.

'You said we were to go to Ham,' she said, 'which is in the other direction.'

'Yes, Madame Donville. But I have a mind to drive you round Richmond Green first, before we go up the Hill.'

'Why?'

'To show you off.' He glanced sideways at the gold-edged pelisse, the green gloves and boots, at the black curls that escaped the green-trimmed straw bonnet. Her beaded reticule and a small package lay on her lap, prompting him to compare, yet again, the young woman he had half-known in London to this fiery sharp-tongued beauty whose future he had just commandeered, to her fury. Still distrustful, still dismissive, her dark eyes did not slide away this time, but continued slowly down in a critical study of his blue coat and white breeches, lingering over the soft leather gloves and the reins running over them. He knew what she was thinking. Indeed, her blush told him that he was correct.

Steadily, over the rutted track, they pranced round the four sides of Richmond Green, past the elegant houses where Ransome knew she would be obliged to acknowledge the salutes and waves of those she knew. The gossip, he thought, might as well be accurate.

He drove the phaeton on up Richmond Hill, after

that, where a greater press of riders and coaches laboured to and from the Star and Garter, the upper Park Gates, and the stunning view from the top. He slowed the chestnuts to a walk as they wove through the crowd. 'I believe a number of French *émigrés* live round here,' he said. 'Do you know any of them, *madame*?'

'You can guess the answer to that, my lord. To keep my distance is the best for me, and for them,' she said. 'I have no idea how much they know, but I've never tried to find out, either.'

Expressionless, he looked straight ahead. 'After all this time, I think you may find that those who fled here from the Revolution are hardly seeking to settle old scores amongst their neighbours. They're simply relieved to be safe. And for another thing, Claude Donville was one of *them,* not us. They themselves dealt with the matter in their own way, and such treachery was not at all the isolated incident you seem to think it was. I could tell you of several such scandals, but that's what war does. It breeds the worst and best in men. You were a mere seventeen and about to become a mother when you were widowed. Time enough, they would say, for wounds to heal.'

'Their wounds, or mine?'

'Both. You refer to the money, I know, but here in Richmond they'll know what kind of a woman you are, what kind of child you have, what you've done

for the community, employing unfortunates, rebuilding the house, selling what you grow. They'll have
consumed some of your produce, no doubt.'

'So what are *your* plans for my gardens, my lord?'

'I've hardly thought about it but, since you ask, I see
no reason to change anything. Why would I? You're
surely not still concerned about this idea of revenge, are
you? You could accuse me of being opportunist, if you
like, but I have no time to be seeking revenge for anything. I wish you to be my wife because that seems to be
the best way to deal with this situation. For your sake and
mine. I don't need a mistress, I need a wife, *madame.*'

Phoebe seized her chance. Would he admit it, if she
pushed him just a little in the wrong direction? Art-
lessly, she tried it out. 'You don't need a mistress?
Oh…oh dear, I had wondered…but never mind.'

'Never mind what?'

'You've answered my question before I asked it.
I've been thinking, you see.'

'About my extremely generous offer?'

'About your offer, yes, and I wondered why you
would not prefer to have a mistress instead of a wife.
Is it perhaps because you already have one?'

'The short anwer to that,' he said, slowing the chestnuts and drawing them in to the side of the track, 'is
no, I don't. One woman at a time is enough, two would
be madness. A wife *and* a mistress is not my style.'

'Too expensive, you mean?' Phoebe said, watching

him closely from beneath the brim of her bonnet. His response had not been what she'd expected. Not at all.

He kept a hold on the reins, but now gave her his full attention. 'What *exactly* are you saying, *madame*? Come on. Out with it. Are you telling me you would *prefer* to be my mistress rather than my wife?'

'There are advantages,' she said, scanning the green Thames valley below.

'Not many. What happens at the end of an *affaire*? You're still a sitting tenant in my house and I'm back where I was before. No, thank you. What I need is a wife, a home out of town, and—'

'But you already have a home. In Mortlake.'

'That's a different kind of home.'

'Ah. I see.'

'I'd be very surprised if you did. What advantages do *you* see in being a mistress?'

'I could hardly expect you to understand.'

'Then try me.'

'For one thing, it would shock my family,' she said, hoping he would accept the reasoning. And the subterfuge.

'That's an advantage? Well then, *madame,* you can shock them even more by being my wife. Can't you?'

'That doesn't have quite the same shocking ring to it, and my mother would be quite pleased, I imagine. Could we not perhaps…compromise?'

His firm mouth twitched, then broke into a wide

smile that was almost a laugh. '*Compromise*? Did I hear you aright? Say it again?'

'I shall do no such thing. I was trying to be serious.'

'Well, then, I shall have to guess. What you mean, I suppose, is that you want more time, and you think that an *affaire* will keep me at a distance. Eh? Is that more like it?'

'No, that is not what I meant. Not at *all* what I meant,' she replied.

'Good. Then let's forget that idea, shall we? It's not bastards I want, but noble-born sons from a woman of quality. There are too many bastards in the world already.'

'But you've—' She looked down at her hands, biting back the words.

'I've what?'

'Nothing. Shall we go on? I think you've made your point, my lord.'

He waited to see if she had more to say, then lifted his hands ready to start. 'Yes, well…I think it's time I made my point rather more forcibly.'

'My brother and his wife visited yesterday, after you'd gone,' she said, rather too quickly.

'Oh? Offering to help?'

'No, nothing like that. Offering to be with me when you next visit, that's all.'

He set the phaeton in motion. 'Oh, is *that* all? Well, they won't be.'

'How do you know that?'

He made no answer except for the briefest of glances in her direction, and the burning that stole upwards from neck to cheeks stayed with her until the few houses came into sight that made up the village of Ham.

The track turned back upon itself, taking them beside the river towards redbrick walls, stable-blocks, and a view Phoebe recognised from her brother's painting. 'This is it,' she said, leaning forwards, pointing across the river to a white house perched on a green lawn on the other side. 'That must be Marble Hill.'

'And this, *madame,* is Ham House.'

Without breaking their spanking trot, the chestnuts turned in between blue-and-gilt painted gates towards a very large and imposing house of redbrick picked out with white along all its edges, three-storeyed, multi-windowed, set back in the centre with bays at each side. A very large, bearded and naked man made of stone lounged upon a rock in the forecourt, clearly a god from his crown of laurels and serious expression.

'But this is the Earl of Dysart's home,' Phoebe said, in awe. 'Is he really your friend?'

'I've known the Dysarts for years,' said Ransome, 'but he's only been an earl for four of them. His brother Lionel lived here before that, so the place was in a bit of a state until the sixth Earl and his lady took it over. He was a Member of Parliament until recently, then High Sheriff of Cheshire. A soldier before that. A man of the world.'

'So why on earth would he be interested in Leon, my lord?'

She didn't expect an answer while she was being helped down the portable steps by footmen. They came running at the first sign of visitors, liveried, white-stockinged, belonging to an earlier generation. One of them ushered the guests up the shallow stone steps and through the heavy oak door with coats of arms, plinths, pilasters and pediments. Entering at one end of a large hall, they were greeted by full-length portraits on every wall, the ancestors, and by two plaster figures balancing precariously on the mantelshelf, as oblivious to the comings and goings as the River God outside.

A man's voice, cultured and authoritative, floated down into the lofty hall from above. 'Buck…ah, there you are! I'm coming down. Wait there!'

Phoebe looked up to the grey-spindled railing round the first-floor gallery where a man's face disappeared from view, taking the command with it. The quick click of footsteps, the sharp trip of shoes upon the staircase must, she thought, belong to an agile man. Almost leaping from the grand staircase across to the chequered floor, a white-haired elderly man of military bearing came to meet them with such courteous enthusiasm that Phoebe was completely taken by surprise, having met few men of his age who possessed that kind of energy.

Both hands shot out to clasp Lord Ransome's, grasping his arm too, but it was to Phoebe his attention was directed almost immediately. 'Buck, my lad, good to see you again…but who…?' His white eyebrows lifted as he pulled himself erect, keeping his eyes on her face until she glanced uncomfortably at her escort.

'Madame Donville, Lord Dysant,' Ransome said. '*Madame,* allow me to present Lord Dysart.'

'But surely,' said the Earl, holding his chin as if it might fall off, 'surely this lady is Phoebe? Isn't she, Buck? Isn't she our Phoebe Hawkynne?'

'Madame Donville's maiden name was Hawkin, my lord. There is a likeness, isn't there? I was sure you'd see it.'

Phoebe had made her curtsy and was now aware of some mystery here, and that they would share it with her in their own time.

The Earl appeared to recollect himself. 'Forgive my *appalling* manners, Madame Donville. I am truly honoured to meet you. I don't usually delve into my guests' ancestry as soon as we meet, but in your case…well, perhaps if you would care to come with me, I can show you the reason for my astonishment.

Come!' Already he was heading again for the staircase, and Phoebe suspected that this was his way, immediate, losing not a moment of whatever time was left to him.

Ransome offered her his arm up the carved stairway, smiling secretively at his host's reaction, which he'd been reasonably sure of. They came to the gallery from where the Earl had looked down into the hall, where more ancestral portraits hung against a patterned turquoise wallpaper. The Earl stood back, looking up at a young couple in the costume of the late sixteen hundreds, the pale sheen of silk folds, frills of lace, satin ribbons and velvet. And the statutory King Charles spaniel. They were a darkly handsome pair, the man wearing a sword-sash across his coat, the lady holding a gold pendant with a moon on it, their free hands tenderly entwined. Two children nestled against them, a small serious-looking boy and a girl with a mop of black ringlets.

'Sir Leo Hawkynne,' said the Earl, 'was a Scot. He was secretary to the Duke of Lauderdale, who married the Countess of Dysart, one of my ancestors. And this is his lady, Phoebe. Now, do you see anything of interest here, Madame Donville? A family resemblance, perhaps?'

It was uncanny, she thought, to be looking back at herself in period dress, the same oval face framed by raven-black ringlets that both of them had tried to tie back with limited success. Dated 1684, the portrait represented almost one hundred and twenty years, several generations, yet the features were almost identical.

'I had no idea,' she whispered. 'I knew there had always been Leos and Phoebes in our family, but no one ever mentioned that the originals were husband and wife. I must admit that it gives me a very...*very*... strange feeling to be looking at my forebears, my lord. You must also get the same feeling when you see your ancestors looking back at you.'

He laughed. 'Oh, I can never get away with anything while the family are watching every move. But that portrait was painted for the Duchess who was apparently very fond of them both. Which is why you'll not have seen it before. I believe they had four children. Come to think of it, there was a Sir Leo Hawkin in my regiment, the 6th Foot. Could that have been...?'

'My father, my lord. He was killed when I was very young.'

'An excellent man, too. And you have brothers, do you, *madame?*'

'Leon is the eldest. I've brought something of his to show you, my lord.'

'So you all grew up fatherless? Now that *is* a tragedy. Show me, *madame.*' He led the way to the window side of the gallery where he seated Phoebe on

an enormous velvet-covered footstool while he and
Ransome perched beside her, receiving the unframed
watercolour from her as if he had already perceived
its value. Angling it towards the light, he studied it
without speaking, giving Phoebe the chance to watch
how his mobile features softened over the palette of
colours, the mingling of pigments, the delicate
draughtsmanship. His hair, fine and white, was short
enough to show the pink scalp beneath, the folds of
his face and the delicate lines following a merry path
rather than a downtrodden one. Ransome had told her
that his friend was a keen amateur artist, and a con-
noisseur, a term that applied to many men of too much
wealth and time. But of this man's genuineness she
had no doubts.

His was not a noisy kind of appreciation, however.
He nodded, looked across at Lord Ransome, and nodded again. 'A real painter,' he said. 'A great talent.
Why have we not heard of him, I wonder? Does he exhibit?'

The three heads pored over the painting in an intimate moment that somehow brought together so many
loose strands of Phoebe's life, holding them ready to
be tied. The Earl would have to be told of Leon's circumstances, and hers too, before they had any right
to expect an offer of help from him. Yet having
reached the point where someone, at last, had recognised Leon's one and only talent, the moment for

Phoebe was so charged with emotion after seeing and meeting the first Phoebe that she found it difficult to speak. One hand rested on the gathered bodice of her green-striped gown and pressed, trying to still the pounding there. Her lips parted to breathe in deeply, settling the words into line. She could scarcely stifle the sob.

The Earl saw her struggle. Tenderly, he laid a gnarled hand over her arm. 'Yes, I see, *madame.* Talent doesn't always walk in a straight orderly line, does it? All we can hope for is to have a share in it while it still burns. While your brother lives, then there is hope. Will you...can you...tell me about it?'

So she did, sparing nothing except the shabby facts of how Ferry House came to be owned by the man who sat beside her. About Leon's gambling and drinking, however, and about Lady Templeman's apparent inability to help her eldest son, she told him all, though whether that was more distressing than his wasted talents she did not venture an opinion.

None the less, it soon became clear to the Earl that the youngest sister of Leon Hawkin owed him a great debt of gratitude and that she had been brought to Ham House to seek help for him. For the generous, able, and well-connected Earl of Dysart, this posed no problem except whether—or not—the young man in question would accept his offers of patronage and a cottage on the estate, if he wanted it. That he would need some kind of rehabilitation went without saying, if he were to recommence his painting. The Earl would be only too happy to help him.

The practicalities were discussed at greater length as Phoebe and Lord Ransome walked slowly through the Fountain Garden on their way to the Orangery. A high brick wall afforded them some privacy from the house, where a fountain rattled joyfully, providing a bath for a queue of birds. 'I shall go to London tomorrow,' he said, 'to find him and bring him back.'

'I know you said your friend would want to help,' said Phoebe, untying the ribbons of her bonnet, 'but his offers are *unbelievably* generous. Commissions. A place to live, rent free. Could this be because he's found a descendant of the Hawkynne family, do you think?'

'I doubt it. It's because he's like that. He'll help anyone out, especially artists. He's a great philanthropist, too. He keeps open doors here at Ham, all the time. His servants idolise him.'

Phoebe pulled off her bonnet, swinging it by its ribbons. Her hair had caught on some of the rough bits and now, instead of being neatly bundled into a chignon, the curls bounced out like escaped watchsprings. Walking along the shady parts where the trees overhung the wall, she became aware of Lord Ransome's closeness, his scrutiny. She stopped and turned to face him. 'Why are you doing this for Leon?' she said, quietly. 'You were the one to benefit by his gambling and to find little sympathy for him.'

'Oh, for all the wrong reasons,' he said, without conviction.

'Not to make amends, then? Not guilt?'

Swiftly and without warning, he took both her shoulders in his hands, pulling her towards him with a suddenness she had no time to evade. Her arms had nowhere to go, bonnet in one hand, reticule in the other, her head pushed back and held under his, her skin already responding to the dangerous warmth of him, the hard pressure of his thighs enclosing her. With a hunger she had not anticipated, his mouth sought hers and tasted greedily, as if he could wait no longer to make his claim on her, this time without the excuse of anger for her harsh words.

His hands slid quickly across her waist and shoulders, fingers sinking deep into her hair, twisting her under his mouth, and the fire deep in her belly roared to meet his like a forest blaze, searing and scorching. Whether it was the emotion of her discovery, relief for Leon, or simply a release of denied longings, Phoebe had no way of knowing, but now it was as if, for the first time, the deep underground well of her desire burst upwards to flood her reasoning with an unstoppable energy, demanding whatever he had to give, without restraint.

She had taunted and rebuked herself, since his reappearance, about how reprehensible he was, how she could *never* want him, how imaginary her sneaking lust for him was. But now, like this, held hard against his chest, her body would take no more of her cowardly lies and rebelling against her anger and caution, bent into him and softened, pressing her aching breasts against him, giving him her mouth to search, explore and plunder. Eagerly. Wantonly.

She felt the steel of his arms shift across her, his hand splay across her buttocks, his mouth lift from hers just enough to speak. 'For you, woman,' he said, hoarse with emotion. 'For no one but you. Not for guilt, either. I have none. Only a need for you, that's all. Expect no apologies. When I find what I want, I take it. I've found you, and you'll be mine.'

Shards of fear mingled with her excitement. Hard words. Possession, not love. Ruthlessness, not tenderness. She had what he wanted, and he had what she wanted, but bargaining was out of the question when he had the upper hand, and already he was winning. Like any woman, her perfectly understandable objections melded with her body's hunger for loving, and because men's minds are not tuned to exactly the same pitch, he stood no chance of understanding her when she struggled furiously against him, balking at the reasons for his desire. It mattered. Beating his back with her fists, her submission turned into instant attack.

'Just like that!' she hissed, furiously. *'You'll be mine!* No, I *won't,* my lord. You didn't *find* me. I was not lost. And I won't be *taken.* I am not any man's for the taking. My needs are not so simple as a tavern girl's. Now let me go!'

He did let her go. Almost. Keeping hold of one wrist in a grip of steel, he made her listen to him while she, with head turned defiantly aside, was somehow relieved to know that he was not in the least bewildered by her about-turn after letting down her guard in a moment of weakness. 'Listen to me first. No…stand still…and *listen!* Your feathers are ruffled, but that's no reason to deny what you feel. All right, you expected…would have preferred…me to talk of love, but would you have believed me? No, I thought not. So what I said was the honest truth, no more, no less. I thought you could deal with that.' His voice softened. 'You're a woman, Phoebe, not a girl. There's no need to be angry with yourself for letting it all out, once in a while.'

'Don't patronise me. I didn't *let it out.* It *came* out. I had no choice. And if you think I do that once in a while, then let me put you straight on that, my lord. Nine years is not a *while,* it's an eternity. My husband made love to me three times in all. Yes, less than the fingers of one hand. He had a mistress in France, I discovered afterwards. He could hardly wait to get back to her, after he'd done what he needed to with me, an ignorant girl of sixteen.' The words came out in gasps, as if she'd been running, and by the time she had finished, his arms were once again around her, his hands smoothing over the green silk pelisse.

'Don't pity me,' she said into his shirt-front. 'I don't need anyone's pity, least of all yours. I have my daughter. And my life. I don't think I care any more, after this, whether my family discover the truth about him or not. Not one of them has lifted a finger to help us. They deserve to be shocked. Shocked to the core. It now seems that I have to turn to complete strangers for help, my lord. You, and the Earl. Ironic, isn't it? Complete strangers.'

'Well, from now on,' he said, gently brushing back the coils of hair, 'I'm not a stranger to you. I'm in your life, and I'm staying. But you need more time. I can see that now. If I'd known what you've just told me, I'd not have rushed you into a decision. So if you prefer to be my mistress for a while, then I shall accept that. Shock your family to your heart's content, it'll make no difference to my plans for you. Heaven knows, I've spent most of my life shocking people. I'm a dab hand at it. Come to me for advice on it, sweet nymph.'

Her shaky huffs of laughter made him smile and hold her closer, and for a few more moments she was content to stay there in his arms, listening to the tinkle of water and wings splashing, and somewhere the whinny of a horse. 'You're quite determined then,' she said, drawing away at last.

'Oh, yes, Madame Donville. Never more so.'

'Not shocked by my behaviour just now?'

'On the contrary, I'm delighted by it. I intend to provoke you again.'

'I don't suppose you'll find that at all difficult, my lord.'

'Excellent. I look forward to it.'

'That's not what I meant. I think we're getting into deep waters here. You were supposed to be showing me the Earl's newly planted Orangery.'

However, round the corner of the archway into the garden, a slender figure came to greet them with apologetic smiles, a rustle of brown-figured silk, and a Paisley shawl slithering off her narrow shoulders. Phoebe caught it just in time and handed it back, already smiling.

'Buck Ransome!' the lady piped in a reedy voice. 'And Madame Donville. I could not be there when you arrived, but trust a husband like mine not to offer you tea. Come inside, dears. It's waiting for you in the drawing room.' Chattering like a bird, she pecked the Viscount on each cheek, holding out a frail hand as if to make sure Phoebe did not run away.

'Lady Dysart, allow me to present Madame Donville to you. Phoebe, my dear, this beautiful lady is the Countess of Dysart.'

Nobody, but *nobody,* had ever called her 'Phoebe, my dear' in such an elegant and lover-like manner, and the sound touched her heart and plucked it like a harp string, vibrating its resonance through her body to comfort it. She made her curtsy in a daze, already loving the sweet elderly lady who had come out to find them instead of sending a servant, who took her by the hand like a mother with her daughter and stumbled over the grass until Ransome drew her hand through his arm like a son. Phoebe thought she had never met a more delightful couple than the Earl and Countess of Dysart.

Having made his wife aware of his newest discovery in Leon Hawkin, direct descendant of Sir Leo and Lady Phoebe, the Earl talked animatedly about his other young protégé, John Constable, who was doing work for him at the house in London, about his friend Sir Joshua Reynolds who'd had a house built up on Richmond Hill before his death ten years ago, about the Gainsboroughs he'd bought and the Van Dycks he'd inherited. About his own talent for painting he was less forthcoming, and it was Anna Maria, the Countess, who showed them his portfolio of water-colours in the library.

Since their arrival at Ham, much of their time had been spent in tending the estate and in making necessary repairs to the house, having found it overgrown and neglected. 'Did you notice our new River God on the forecourt?' the Earl asked them.

'Anna Maria, you *must* show Phoebe your Duchess's bathroom. Everybody should have a bathroom like that, I believe, yet I cannot persuade my wife to use it.' His enthusiasm was a joy to see, but it was when the conversation turned to the subject of families that voices chose a minor key, for the Dysarts had had no children and the nephew so loved by the Earl had been killed, aged eighteen. Naturally, Phoebe wondered whether that had something to do with their eagerness to sponsor young talent whenever they could find it.

Even as the two guests prepared to climb into the phaeton, information and instructions continued unabated. 'We're having a musical evening on Friday,' the Countess said, planting a farewell kiss on Phoebe's cheeks. 'You will come, won't you? Get Buck to bring you, my dear. Some string players from London. Some pieces by Mr Haydn and a bit of George Frederick Handel. A few singers. Starting at seven. A little supper.'

'Thank you, my lady. We shall be honoured.'

It was the first time for years she'd said such a thing, as if she was once again part of a pair. But as they bowled out of the gates and turned towards Ham, she knew in her heart that a giant step had been taken in a direction which, only a few days ago, she would have thought utterly impossible. Her anger in the garden just now had reflected the way she had set herself to think since Claude's death, that never again would she belong to any man, that no man would take her. Yet her impulses had clearly shown how outdated her protests were. Buck Ransome, that great arrogant, high-handed, handsome creature sitting close to her, taking up too much of the seat, had forced himself into her life and insisted on being part of it, and it was just such occasions as this that made her realise what she'd been starved of for so long. Companionship and conversation, gallantry, a man's protection, and yes...that, too. Madly, wildly, she had responded to him like dry tinder to a spark.

She had been shown another side to him too, one she would never have associated with the man whose exploits had often been the talk of the *beau monde,* gambling, womanising, all the usual excesses of youth. There at Ham House, he had talked knowledgeably about the newest alterations, materials and styles, about places he'd been and people he'd met, artists and scientists he knew, politics and literature, as easy with the older generation as he was with her. Courteously, he had commended her brother Leon to the Earl in a way she could not have done, personally vouching for his dedication to a commission which, the Earl suggested, would be to paint views of Ham House as the renovations took place. A pictorial record for his private collection. For posterity.

'How could you guarantee that?' she asked him as

the trees sped past them. 'Wasn't that rather a risk to take, knowing Leon's habits?'

'It's not too late to change him round,' he answered, keeping his eyes on the twists of the road. 'In London, he appears to have no support, only parasites. Here, with us, he'll have all the support he needs. He's not past redemption, *madame*.'

'Earlier, you called me Phoebe. I seem to have committed myself, don't I?'

'Don't take it too hard. It had to happen. And I'm not gloating. If it happened rather too quickly for your comfort, that's due to circumstances and my impatience.'

And his other mistress? How much will she know about me, I wonder? Yet he had said he had no mistress. Having seen what she had seen, how could she believe him? Why did he need another home at Mortlake?

'They called you Buck. Is that how they've always known you?'

'Buckminster Percival Ransome at your service, *madame*. Now you have it.'

'Buckminster?' Like dark orbs, full of laughter, her eyes turned to him.

'Yes,' he said, not returning her look of disbelief. 'I never thought the name Percy was one I could get used to. Not quite for me. Would you not agree?'

She hiccoughed as the phaeton bounced over a

bump in the road . 'Oh, I do indeed, my lord. And I could never be the mistress of a man called *Percy.*'

'I think I must have known that, somehow,' he said, permitting himself a smile.

The drive home, made in companionable silence, gave Phoebe time to reflect on what else Buck had known. About the portrait, for instance. That had been a shock, to find that she had worthy ancestors whose employer was fond enough of them to have their portrait painted. A Duchess, no less—an ancestor of the Earl of Dysart had known *her* ancestors, Sir Leo and Lady Hawkynne. And Buck Ransome had known all along of her ancient lineage, seizing the chance to show her the famous side of her family while playing down the infamous side. And then, to give the comparison a touch of humour, he had revealed to her the glorious name of Buckminster Percival. What an amazing man he was.

CHAPTER FIVE

THE LOW SUN filled every windowpane with an orange blaze, fading to yellow, then silver, as it sunk and dipped below the horizon, leaving Ferry House to its own grey-orange hues and a last squawking flutter of roosting starlings. In the garden, Phoebe walked alone with her thoughts, her grey-and-white cat moving alongside as if their direction was entirely coincidental.

Lord Ransome had not stayed long enough to discuss the new agreement with her, although he had allowed Claudette to lead him down to the river to be shown the baby frogs in the reeds, the cygnets and the ducklings. His manner with her was easy, more brotherly than fatherly, and it was clear that in each other's company, they had found something to fill a void. To Phoebe, that was more important than discussing the finer points of a relationship which had not quite begun.

Touching the fragrant tips of lavender as she passed, she wondered for the twentieth time how it had come to this so quickly, and why she had told a man of whom she could not approve the humiliating details of her brief marriage when she'd shared that information with no other person. Even now, after all these busy years, the seamy side of it wrinkled her nose with disgust for, as an innocent girl, she had been bitterly disappointed by her young husband's impatience with her ignorance. Teasing and boyish ridicule had quickly dampened the tender flame that had burned for him, and though she had assumed that, in time, this would mend under his instruction, his three attempts to stir her to great heights had been dismal failures. She had loved him, blaming herself, setting the scene with soft scented candles, satin sheets, all the trimmings of wifely seduction she'd been told were necessary. Perhaps she had expected too much. Perhaps they both had. Her later discoveries, when it was too late, had shed a dark and sinister light on the experience, and time had not softened its sharp edges.

It was therefore doubly astonishing that, after such a disappointment, the flame that had burned so low should suddenly and without warning be whipped to a conflagration by Ransome's first kiss taken, not given, yet fuelled by real passion instead of duty. For all her personal lectures to the contrary, this afternoon she had been sure he desired her. Satin sheets and scented candles would be an irrelevancy for them both. But was she not stepping into yet another three-sided set-up doomed to failure? How could she trust him when she'd seen the proof with her own eyes? Did she have a choice, when it was all about bargains?

Turning the corner of the high wall, she pushed open the door to the kitchen garden into the secluded place that picked up the last of the light on the glass of cold-frames and cloches. Beans climbed up tall cane steeples, and the feathery fennel swayed as she walked towards the glasshouse that leaned against the south-facing wall. The perfume of plants still damp from the gardener's watering can filled the evening air with mint and lavender, the green earthy scent of life. She stood still to breathe it in, noting the pattern of es-paliered apricot and peach trees on the nearest wall, the waxy fig tree with its green nubs of fruit. Tomor-row was one of the days on which they sent most pro-duce to the inns, when the men would be busily loading up the orders by dawn, having prepared them the night before.

The storage room was a specially built thatched shed for the preparation of the produce with sinks for washing, tables and bins for sorting, bunching and trimming, ready to be laid in baskets and boxes. Though she knew everything would be in order, Phoebe liked to see for herself who was buying it, and how much. Entering the dark warmth of the shed, she left the door open to let in just enough light to see the tables stacked with labelled containers, each one over-flowing with vegetables, herbs and early strawberries. The scent was almost overpowering as she passed along the rows, touching the cool leaves of rhubarb and beetroot, turning in alarm as the light suddenly dimmed.

His bulk filled the doorframe, making her heart lurch with recognition and excitement. 'You!' she whispered. 'You came back!'

She had no need to ask why or what for, when even before she'd finished speaking he was stripping off his coat and flinging it on to the nearest basket, pulling at his neckcloth, unbuttoning his waistcoat, advancing, wordless, reaching out to her with one hand, draping melons, cucumbers and cauliflowers with discarded clothing with the other.

To Phoebe, the act of love had been a bedroom ex-perience, carefully choreographed within certain spaces and with controlled guidelines, devoid of any spontaneity and seeding it in her memory with pain and sadness. A garden shed had never seemed to her like a possible alternative. But, if she had to admit it, Ransome's unconventional manners were infectious and more in keeping with her own way of living, these days. He knew how to shake her dormant emotions. She was already aflame. Raising her arms to receive him, she was gathered hard against his chest, her mouth being sought hungrily for the main course, the first of which had been at Ham House, cut short by a squabble. The craving for more had stayed with them both.

With a cry, she took his head between her hands like a great loving-cup, drawing it down to her with fingers deep in his thick hair, tasting the night air on his skin, the scent of his haste in her nostrils. The maleness of his powerful body was like a drug. Desire and need flared once again as his lips closed on hers, slanting hard across her, compelling her to forget, to go with him, to let him lead.

Breathlessly, willingly, she submitted to a world of sensation, of unreason, of a control that was not hers to direct, but his. Between the boxes and baskets their bodies bent and swayed in that first blaze of rapture, clinging, hardly pausing for breath. Pressed against the bench, she let his mouth move down her throat and felt the warm brush of his hair against her face, his skin on her lips.

More. She wanted more.

'Here,' she whispered. 'Look…under there, a pile of…'

Knowing instantly what she meant, he stooped,

hauling out a pile of folded blankets used for laying over the cold-frames in winter, spreading them along the wooden floor between baskets, watering-cans, pots and canes, taking her back into his arms as soon as it was done, gently pulling her down into a dark oblivion scented with earth and the tang of male vigour. Held captive by his weight, feeling the solid muscle of his chest and shoulders through his shirt, she moaned through his kiss and felt the excitement churn and flip inside her deepest parts as his hand moved over her, tenderly, like an evening breeze.

Under his exploring fingertips, the buttons of her bodice gave way easily against the strain of her aching breasts. She had borne a child and nursed her, and her figure had taken on the full roundness of a mother, her breasts still firm but no longer those of a girl. His touch set her skin alight, circling, weighing, stroking, telling him what his eyes couldn't see, making her cry out as he reached the firm peaks, readying them for his mouth. 'Beautiful earth-woman,' he whispered, teasing her skin with his tongue. 'Moon-goddess. Fruitful Phoebe. You said no man would take you. Isn't that what you said?'

'That's not what I meant, Buck. You know what I meant, don't you?'

Raising his head, he looked at her in the darkness so that she felt his breath upon her face, felt the smile, the silent laughter of triumph. 'Yes, I know what you meant, proud woman. You were afraid. Afraid that your fires were burning out of control. With me, the man you've tried to dislike for so many years. Eh? Don't think I couldn't see how you felt about me, my beauty.'

'I didn't. I didn't want you at all.'

'You didn't dare admit it. And now? Now I have you like this? Soft, and still argumentative? What is it you don't want from me, woman?'

'Nothing…you great…arrogant brute. Noth—'

There was no telling who moved first to quench the lie in mid-flow, but there was the smallest gurgle of laughter between them before their mouths forgot all words, seeking moistly, hungrily, promising, giving and demanding. She pushed his hands away from her breasts in an impatience to assuage the yearning, the emptiness that craved to be filled, then wildly, without thinking, she lifted her hips, writhing against the hardness that pressed upon her. Without more delay, he pulled at one side of her gown while she pulled at the other, easing it up around her waist, baring herself to his hand. With Claude Donville, this part had never gone well, his impatience having quite the opposite effect from the purpose, the pain of his entry completely overlooked in his selfish haste.

This time, however, the hand that caressed and fondled did so to the accompaniment of soft kisses over face, neck and breasts that scattered her mind until her

sighs became cries for him to take what she was offering, quickly. She had waited years for this moment.
She felt herself opening, aching, giving herself without fear of humiliation. Compliant at last. Quivering
with anticipation.

Holding himself above her, he flicked open the
buttons of his breeches and moved into the space
she'd made for him, seeking her moistness with a
gentle urgency that responded to her cries, pulsing
with a mutual need. He had known Donville, his
boasting, his amours, his disrespect of women, his
profligacy. What Phoebe had told him would account
for much of her resistance to another marriage. But
now he had witnessed for himself her innocent wonder at the ways of lovemaking, even an experience as
basic as this one, telling him what he'd only suspected, that she was every bit as unconventional and
spontaneous as himself. She was a creature of impulse, passionate and untamed, for all her house-
wifely skills.

So this time it was he who did the thinking, who
moved each exciting phase on according to her panting cries of ecstasy, her slow sighs that followed his
rhythm, her hands that searched under his shirt over
his moist skin. It was he who watched carefully for
each sign, who discovered a fiercer passion within
her than he'd supposed, who quickened the pace long
before he thought she'd be ready, reacting with aston-

ishing speed to his deep thrusts that rocked her on their earthy bed. She tried to stifle a growing wail of exhilaration, and he knew then that the explosion of tension that followed, and the cry, were an experience about which she had known nothing until now.

Euphoric, he released the unbearable assertive force he'd been holding on a tight rein for so long, groaning with an energy that shook them both, leaving them speechless with wonder as stars showered them. 'Oh, my beauty,' he whispered. 'Oh, my nymph. All these years. What have we been missing?'

Phoebe smiled, stroking her hand across his temple and feeling the light pulse of him deep inside her. 'If I'd known,' she said to his jawline.

'If you'd known…what?'

'Mm…mm, I don't know. Perhaps it's as well that I didn't. Then this wouldn't have happened, would it? I would not have done this with anyone else. Only Buck Ransome would walk into a woman's garden at night to make violent love to her.'

He stirred, kissed her and pulled away, drawing her close to him with her midnight hair strewed across his arm. 'Unfinished business,' he said.

'You planned it.'

'Spontaneously planned it. That's much the best way with difficult widows.'

'*What* difficult widows?'

'Beautiful wild ones called Phoebe, that a man

doesn't have time to take his boots off for, before he makes love to her. *That* kind of difficult widow.'

She smiled again, sleepily, stealing a hand beneath his shirt to discover a soft fuzz of hair around his navel. 'Oh, I see,' she said.

It was not easy, after that, for Phoebe to return to her room without being noticed and without looking as if something momentous had happened to her, physically and emotionally. After a hard and masterful kiss, Lord Ransome had mounted his black horse and clattered away into the night with no more than a sympathetic 'Tch!' at her rumpled state and a comment that her household might have to start getting used to seeing it. Which was tantamount to saying that *she* might have to, too. Still, she could not complain that he'd left the shed in a mess, for they'd been careful to leave no trace of their activities behind them. The morning packers would find nothing amiss.

But as Phoebe lay soaking in a warm bath early next morning with the scent of myrtle and elder steaming into her hair, she had time to ponder over that amazing day and to agree with Lord Ransome when he'd said that the recent events might be the best thing that had ever happened to her brother Leon, who they hoped would be with them by the afternoon. It might also, she thought, be the best thing that had happened to her, too. So when Claudette came in to share her mama's bath, it was as well that the pretty child had plenty to say about her forthcoming visit to Aunt Mimi at Twickenham, for that way she hardly noticed her mama's drowsiness or the secret smile that would not wash off. Miss Evie Cowling, however, certainly *had* noticed the swollen lips, amongst other things, as she patted her mistress dry. Sensibly keeping her thoughts to herself, she chose a day gown with a pie-frill neckline, a choice that Phoebe accepted without demur.

If she had been in the habit of indulging herself she would no doubt have spent the day in a daze, picking flowers, staring at the flowing river and its cargoes and wondering about the meaning of life. She had, whether she liked it or not, entered a new phase, well…not so much *entered* it as been hauled into it with barely a nod towards her objections. But she could not indulge herself, having things to organise such as the produce orders, Claudette's harp lessons, the preparation of rooms for her guest. Consequently, there was little time for reflection, only for a strange fluttering sensation whenever she recalled how it felt to be stormed and sweetly conquered by the only man ever to disconcert her simply by being in the same room.

There had been no agreed time for Leon's arrival, since no one could be certain how Ransome would find him, or where, or in what state. So when suppertime came and went, then Claudette's bedtime, Phoebe was not unduly disturbed, only anxious for his safety. She had expected to hear the rumble of a carriage and an unloading of trunks, at least, not the single rider on the big black horse whose lone arrival brought instant images of the worst sort where Leon clung to life by a thread.

'Go inside, sweetheart, and I'll tell you about it. Yes…yes, I have him safe.'

'Safe? Where is he, then?'

Ransome smiled at the 'then', placing an arm about her shoulders and pulling her gently to his side as they entered the parlour. Candles had already been lit. Bowls of flowers covered the window sills. 'He's at my house,' he said. 'I couldn't have brought him here, Phoebe. Not until he's more recovered.'

Searching his face, she saw the tiredness in the line of his brow and a longing for her understanding in his eyes, and she knew he would have known better than she how to handle the uprooting of a man in Leon's state. She took a deep breath and led him to a wing chair beside the window where a soft breeze stirred a bowl of sweet williams and cranesbill. 'Is he very ill?' she whispered, watching him sink back with closed eyes until a sigh opened them again.

He shook his head. 'No, not *very* ill, but certainly not in a state to be brought to a lady's house.'

'Not even his sister's?'

'No. He made rather a nasty mess of my carriage. I thought it best to take him straight to Mortlake, sweetheart. Just to recover. Then he can come to you.'

'Oh!' Hands covered her face, stopping the tears on a tide of concern.

He was beside her on the window-seat, drawing her against his chest, his lips to her forehead above the fingertips. 'He'll be all right, I promise.'

She wailed into his shirt-front, 'But it's *not,* is it? Who's there to look after him at Mortlake? He can't stay *there,* can he?' Visions of the mistress came and went.

'He's not going to stay there, nymph. I have two men, my valet and my steward, who know exactly what he needs. They'll tend him, watch over him, bathe him, clean him up, shave him, doctor him…'

'And is there a woman there?'

It was easy, and natural, to mistake the querulous voice. 'No, sweetheart, but a woman is the last thing he needs at the moment. He's feeling very sorry for himself. Men know how to deal with this kind of thing best.'

She sniffed. 'What kind of thing?' she said, adjusting herself in his arms.

'Are you going to offer me some refreshment, Madame Donville?'

'Oh, yes. I'm so sorry. Let me send for some food. I wasn't sure…'

'Burgundy? Claret?'

She blinked, touching the tip of her nose with a knuckle in a gesture that bewitched him. 'This is where this *mistress* business is going to fall apart, my lord. I have only damson, gooseberry, elderflower and—'

'Oh, good lord, woman,' he groaned. 'I can see I shall—'

The door opened before his criticism reached its finale, with a rattle, and a flash of silver, and dear Hetty holding it all together on a lace-covered tray. After her came a maid bearing a plate of sandwiches, garnished with parsley and radishes in one hand and a large fruit cake in the other. Hetty and Lord Ransome had met many years ago in London, so she was pleased to accept Phoebe's invitation to stay with them while the food and tea was consumed and the story of Leon's discovery, between mouthfuls, was told, all spectres of Mortlake mistresses pushed aside for the time being.

Poor Leon, it transpired, having discovered what he had done with his sister's home, had then drunk himself into oblivion in order to forget, since there was no question of regaining it. When Ransome found him, none of his family had called to see him, either to offer support or to discuss the implications, his mother being in the throes of organising a dinner party for her husband at the time. Leon was at home being tended by his valet, who had begun to despair of his master's health, for he had not eaten since last weekend. Physically weakened, he was in no state to protest, therefore, when Ransome took his carriage to Harley Street and, with the help of the valet, proceeded to pack Leon's bags, wrap him in blankets with accompanying bowls and bottles, and carry him off to Mortlake. Without the two men to help him, his lordship told them, the journey might have taken twice as long, but to hand him over to a houseful of women would have been unkind while Leon was so ashamed of himself. After which both Phoebe and Hetty agreed that Leon would need time in which to recover, and their own desires to mother him must wait. Whether the phantom-like Mortlake family would get a chance to mother him before she did, Phoebe could not hope to find out unless, of course, she were to go there herself.

The most astonishing part of this episode, Hetty later volunteered, was Lord Ransome's part in all this, for how many gamesters, having won an estate from a man, would go and rescue that same man from such wretchedness, bring him all that way in his own vehicle, house him in his own house, and tend him like a brother?

Certainly not their other brother, Phoebe agreed, wryly.

So, said Hetty, whether he had a woman at Mortlake or not, Lord Ransome was a most remarkable man who must be inordinately fond of her to wish to win her approval in such a manner. And if she were Phoebe, she would not fret too much about who he did or did not house there, when it was clear that the man had more than a smattering of the Good Samaritan about him.

It was at this point that Phoebe, her lips still tingling from Ransome's parting kiss, felt obliged to tell dear Hetty how things had moved on from intense dislike to something more akin to… well…love, she supposed, if that's what this sick feeling was that churned her insides whenever she thought of him. Nothing like that had happened with Claude Donville, only an awareness of success, a settled future and her mother pleased, for once.

Oh, said Hetty, was that why she'd poured the tea-slops into the sugar basin? She had thought something was not quite right.

'But I don't *want* to be in love with him, Hetty,' Phoebe explained. 'He's not the kind of man I should be involved with, is he? You've seen for yourself what he's like, and he's *still* insisting there's no woman at Mortlake. What am I to believe?'

'We didn't see a woman, love.'

'And what kind of a man can take over a woman's home, just like that, whether she likes it or not? If that's not ruthlessness, then I don't know what is. He says he always knew I was attracted to him, but that's sheer arrogance. I wasn't.'

'Is that why you kept the dance programme he signed when you were sixteen?'

'His is not the only name on it.'

'I think it is, dear.'

'It doesn't prove anything, Hetty.'

'No, dear. Indications and evidence are not proof, that's very true, but…'

'But what?'

Hetty sighed and readjusted her spectacles, taking the tatting-shuttle from her workbasket. 'One can go on looking, and rejecting, and wondering why life flies past at an alarming rate, Phoebe dear, and suddenly one can wake up to the fact that, if *we're* not perfect, why should we expect to find someone who is? Viscount Ransome has offered to marry you, yet you're still looking for reasons why you should not accept him, even though it's the answer to our problems. Isn't it time you thought about the advantages? Does he have to leap into the lion's den to retrieve your handkerchief next?' It had once been a favourite story, ending badly.

'No, Hetty. Don't be cross with me. I can see the advantages for all of us, not just for myself. But I trusted once, and now I'm trying to be careful.'

'But time is not on your side, is it, love? He appears to have fulfilled his side of the bargain.'

'Yes, I know. Perhaps we're a bit further on than you think.'

Looking up sharply from her tatting with fingers poised over a half-made picot, Hetty studied Phoebe's pink face, then continued with her edging. 'Ah,' she murmured, mysteriously. 'That would explain quite a lot.'

As previously arranged, Phoebe was driven over to Mortlake in Lord Ransome's phaeton just after breakfast, dressed in her prettiest white muslin walking-dress sprigged with tiny blue flowers. A pale blue spencer covered most of the bodice, leaving deep white frills all round the neckline and wrists. Blue satin ribbons fluttered from the ruched bonnet, a creation which was rudely disturbed when, after drawing his team to a halt in the middle of Richmond Park, Lord Ransome turned to kiss her with a trace of that ruthlessness she had complained about only last evening. Then, without a word of explanation, he continued the journey.

Phoebe righted her bonnet, tucked a stray curl inside, and held the back of her gloved hand to her mouth with the merest sideways glance at the rather smug expression on her companion's face. 'Is that what a mistress must expect, my lord?'

'Yes. A wife, too. Planned spontaneously again.'

'Tell me about Leon, if you please. Is there any improvement?'

'The transformation is remarkable. He was sitting

up in bed eating breakfast when I left. However,' he warned, 'I think you may see a change in him since you last met. He's lost weight, for one thing. Nothing to worry about. We'll soon fatten him up. He needs exercise, too. And fresh air. Don't be too concerned.'

She was glad of his lordship's warning, as her first impression of her brother was that, if this was looking remarkably better, she was glad not to have seen him yesterday or she might have burst into tears. It was yet another reason, she thought, to be grateful to Lord Ransome for his forethought. Sitting up in bed against the white pillows, Leon might have been invisible but for his unruly shock of black curling hair that corkscrewed damply after a recent bath. His eyes, sunken beneath heavy brown lids, were dark and still bloodshot, fastening on his sister's concerned face and filling with sorry tears even before a word had been exchanged.

'Dearest…ah, dearest one!' Phoebe said, taking him into her arms. 'Hush, love, don't weep. It's all right… really…it's going to be all right. Now we can look after you, and feed you. Shh!'

'Can you forgive me, Pheeb? I'd never have hurt you willingly, you know that. I've been such an idiot.'

'We help each other out, love. That's all there is to it. Where was Mama in all this? Did she not contact you?'

'Under Templeman's thumb, where she usually is, these days.'

'Mama? Under a man's thumb? That's news.'

'Does Ross know?' he said, wiping one eye on the sheet.

'Yes. Mama wrote to tell *him*, not me.'

'That's another Hawkin under a thumb,' he whispered.

Phoebe sat back, puzzled. 'Ross? Under Josephine's thumb? Surely not.'

Leon's single nod was unambiguous. 'Certainly is, Pheeb. Always has been. Social climber. If you stand still long enough, she'll take you for a ladder. She angled for me before Ross, remember, because I'm the eldest. And before that—' he glanced across at his host with a raised eyebrow that spoke volumes '—she had her sights set on that great hulk. But enough about them. What happens to you, Pheeb? That's what bothers me.'

'I have plans, but the main thing is you, Leon. Are you still painting?'

He looked away, unable to meet her questioning. 'Not for ages,' he whispered. 'I want to, but… well…'

'We have a friend who wants to help. Is your hand steady?'

'I dunno, Pheeb. My eyes are not.'

Ransome was more optimistic. 'They will be, my friend. Stretch out your hand and let's see if yesterday's shakes have gone.'

The hand was steady, the wrist slender and graceful, the nails too long.

'Nothing wrong with that. All you need is rest and good food. We'll take you to see this friend of ours in a day or two. He likes your work.'

Leon frowned. 'Where's he seen it? I don't exhibit.'

'My watercolour,' Phoebe said. 'The one you gave me. I took it to show the Earl of Dysart at Ham House. He says you have a rare talent.'

They had not expected a show of excitement, not from a man in his frail condition, but nor had they expected his face to crumple like a child's, and his eyes to fill with tears, for the second time. 'Why?' he croaked. 'Why are you being so kind? I don't deserve it. I've ruined everything for you, Pheeb, and you're rewarding me. Is it some kind of new punishment?'

Phoebe squeezed his hand and, at a signal from Ransome, kissed her brother's forehead and stood up to go. 'Just rest, love, and we'll talk about it later.' She left the Viscount alone with him for a few words before he joined her, but in those brief moments she had time to see that there were many doors all round the spacious landing and that the house was in fact larger than it appeared from the outside. Why would anyone want to enlarge a house with so many rooms already? She had caught a glimpse of the housekeeper on the way in, middle-aged in grey gown and white mob-cap, definitely not a mistress. But no sign of the two young boys.

'He's sleeping again,' Ransome said, closing the

door. 'He needs to catch up. Don't be distressed, sweetheart. He'll be up and about tomorrow. And all my wines and spirits are under lock and key, so he won't get a drop from me, I promise you. Now, come downstairs. I have something interesting to show you.'

The entrance hall was spacious too, with high-ceilinged rooms leading off in all directions, rather sparsely furnished, serviceable rather than elegant, and enough dining chairs to seat a generous dinner party. So, she thought, he intended to entertain, did he? There was so much she ought to know about him before their relationship moved on.

'In here,' he said, 'is my study.'

All men had studies, book-lined offices for the clutter of estate management, correspondence, hobbies, a place to talk to agents and stewards. Ransome's was no different from a hundred others with leather-covered chairs and the aroma of beeswax and snuff. 'I had a letter from your other brother this morning,' he said when she was seated. 'Delivered by hand. Not before time. Perhaps you'd like to take a look?'

'Thank you, I would. But you made no mention of it to Leon just now.'

'Read it.'

It was brief, taking her only a few moments to get the gist of what Ross was proposing and even less for her to react, her eyes blazing with indignation. The letter shook in her hand. 'He wants you to *sell* it? To *him?*

Increase in the family…needs more rooms for nurse…and the large garden? Ferry House? *My* home? Well, he didn't waste much time there, did he?'

Ransome took the letter from her. 'Perhaps he thinks I don't need it,' he said.

Stunned, Phoebe shook her head, trying to understand what lay behind the offer, real need, or the need to get his own way after all the hints and grumbles. 'I could have understood it if he'd wanted it for me, so that I could stay there. You might still have said no, but at least it would have been a charitable thing to do. But to ignore the fact that I need somewhere to live, with my household, is the most selfish thing I've ever heard, Buck. He didn't offer to buy it when it was empty and derelict, did he? Leon might have sold it to him then. But now? How could he do such a thing?'

'I must admit I'm quite puzzled by it. Did they discuss where you might go?'

'Not seriously. But they've been hankering after Ferry House ever since I spent all my money on it. Too big for me. Just right for them. But you won't consider his offer, will you, Buck? It's part of our agreement.'

Leaning down, he took her by the hand and pulled her up against him. 'Stop worrying,' he said, softly. 'Our agreement stands. We shall need Ferry House to live in, shan't we? I'm not selling it to anybody.'

'Oh, Buck! You won't change your mind, will you?' Her arms slid round his back to rest upon the solid warmth of him, and the breath was gently squeezed out of her in a gasp of laughter before their lips met for the second time that morning.

'I cannot get enough of you,' he breathed. 'And, no, I shall not be changing my mind about anything, Madame Donville. You are my responsibility now, and there will be no going back.'

'Thank you again for rescuing Leon. After our first meeting last week, I didn't think you were capable of such kindness. I see I have much to discover about you.'

'I intend that you shall discover all kinds of wonderful things before many more days. And nights,' he added, kissing the tip of her nose.

'I suppose Ross thinks you'll be living here. As you do now.'

'He can think what he likes, sweetheart. But you're partial to the idea of shocking him, are you not? So if you wish to take a little sweet revenge that will do no harm, I could agree to discuss the matter with him. To keep him interested.'

'To raise his hopes, you mean? Oh, that would be *wicked,* wouldn't it?' she laughed. 'He deserves it, Buck. Truly, he deserves to be let down, for a change.'

'I'll send a message to him today.'

'And shall you tell him we have Leon here?'

'I think we might let him find that out for himself, don't you? He's shown very little interest in Leon's plight, and none in yours either.'

'So will you show me round, now that I'm here?'

'No, I'm taking you back home. We have a concert to attend this evening, remember. However, since you have a moment or two to spare…' Untying the ribbons of her bonnet, he removed it and laid it upon his desk. 'There,' he said, pulling her back into his embrace, 'now I can kiss you without poking my eye out.'

'I would like to have looked round, though.'

'When the workmen have finished, you shall. I want you to see it ready for use. Now, can you contain your questions while I use your lips for something else, please?'

For *what* use? she wanteds to ask. Why would a man like Buck Ransome need two houses in the same area unless he had two families to maintain? Without admitting that she'd spied on him, how could she find out the truth?

CHAPTER SIX

HANDING HER MISTRESS the carved ivory fan, Miss Cowling cast a critical eye over Phoebe's deep red gown shot with blue, adjusted the bows on the short sleeves and almost smiled with approval. Miss Cowling never smiled, but one knew by her manner when she was pleased. The silk changed colour as it caught the light, showing up the dressmaker's art in the bias-cut panels, the bands, and the layered bodice cut low across the bosom. 'Thank you, Evie,' Phoebe said. 'Is that my reticule?'

'Handkerchief. Mirror. Lip salve,' said Miss Cowling, passing her the purse. 'And your velvet cloak in case you need it. It might be cool later on.' It had been years since Phoebe had worn the red silk dress, now subtlely altered to suit current fashion but no one would have known it from her demeanour, least of all the one who waited below, almost lost for words at the sight of her beauty.

Lord Ransome, who looked outrageously handsome whatever he wore, never looked better than in the evening dress-coat of dark blue with a collar of black velvet, his long limbs moulded into tight silk-jersey breeches the sight of which would be the envy of most men at the Ham House soirée. It was to be an evening, they both knew, when they would find it difficult to keep their minds on the social event instead of what might happen afterwards.

As it turned out, their evening was not the ordeal Phoebe thought it might be after being out of company for so long, expecting to know only a handful of the other guests. She knew several members of the Vestry in Richmond who were responsible for, amongst other things, the poor people of the parish, but the presence of so many French noblemen and ladies was not at first one of the more pleasant surprises.

'I thought, dear,' said the Countess of Dysart just before they took their seats in the great hall, 'that it would be nice for you to meet them. They know all about you, but they're great respecters of privacy, of course.'

'*All* about me?' Phoebe whispered to Ransome in alarm. 'Does she mean that?'

'From the French guests. Water under the bridge,' he said. 'Forget about it. I told you, they're more thankful to be over here in safety than to hang on to past offences, especially when the offences were not yours.'

'It's all very well for you to say that,' she retorted in a whisper. 'So why did you wave the subject under my nose when you first came to see me?'

'How else could I make sure you'd keep talking to me?'

'That was *most* ungentlemanly, my lord.'

He smiled wickedly and took her hand. 'Come, we'll sit with the Misses Berry, shall we? You know them, don't you?'

'We've met a few times. They live on The Green.'

The hall at Ham House was not vast, but sixty people seated on plush-covered chairs was a comfortable crush of silks and velvets, gauzes and feathers, diamonds, frills and fluttering fans. More guests sat upstairs all round the balcony to look down upon the nodding heads and the group of musicians at the dais end, and to catch the music as it floated upwards. The Earl and his lady were perfect hosts, the Earl in a powdered wig worn only by the older generation these days, with a long embroidered frockcoat of brown velvet over cream satin. His beloved wife could be seen, rather like a church steeple, from any part of the room by the amazing confection of tall feathers and spumes of blonde lace spouting from her head-dress. But perhaps that was the intention, Phoebe thought as she glanced around her.

Her eye was caught by the young lady sitting on the other side of the Misses Berry, shimmering in white silver-threaded lawn, obviously French and classically fashionable. The young lady turned to smile at her with large dark eyes, as if she knew who Phoebe was, and would be her friend.

'The niece of the Princess d'Henin,' Ransome told her. 'She lives on The Green too. I'll introduce you.'

It was obvious, Phoebe thought, returning the smile, that he had been to these events before. She tried to concentrate on the music. 'Jesu, Joy of Man's Desiring' was a favourite of hers. The Royal Firework Music. One of the Bach Brandenburg Concertos, arias by Purcell, and a beautiful Schubert string quartet. All favourites. But her mind and body, which should have been in accord, all senses engaged, were not as in tune with each other as the instruments. Memories pervaded every soaring phrase with the sound of his voice, the scent and touch of him as he sat close, shoulders touching; hands strong and tender, resting only inches away; memories of knees and thighs nudging hers, his mouth savouring her skin, making her quiver, vibrate, and cry out. She *had* cried out, she remembered. And that had only been the beginning. Unclothed, there would be more.

He took her hand and held it on her lap. He knew her thoughts. Too much for a man of such short acquaintance. And she would marry him. Oh, yes, there was no doubt about that. She had allowed him into her life, and had discovered in only a few days what it was like to have a man to take charge of problems, to make decisions, to offer her the peace and safety of his protection. Already she was less fearful about the nagging French issue and all its ramifications. With him beside her here in the Earl and Countess's home, what need was there to carry her fears into the future? He was right. It was time to let them go.

During the interval the guests were led away into the dining room where a beautiful parquet floor made an interesting talking point as they gathered to seek friends, food and drink. Crimson curtains glowed warmly in the candlelight from mahogany stands, silver and crystal winked between salvers of food, flowers and fruit drooping from epergnes. It was time, Phoebe said to herself, that she did some entertaining of her own, for, judging by the number of guests eager to meet her, she had more friends than she had thought possible.

So, between sips of wine and nibbles at tiny delicacies, the magnificent widow Madame Donville, tragic victim of the Revolution and therefore linked to themselves by association, was introduced to the Richmond

French set, the young Marquise de la Tour du Pin who had smiled at her, the Comtesse de Balbi, mistress of the Comte de Provence who lived in Sir Joshua Reynold's house on the Hill, two aged princesses and a duchess, writers and musicians, artists and architects. Speaking to them fluently in their own language, she immediately won their hearts, and by the end of the supper interlude, her sparkling eyes radiated a kind of happiness she had not experienced for many years. It was as if that particular ghost was laid for ever. Not even the thought of her relatives finding out about Claude could mar the sense of relief that overwhelmed her for, if these people could accept the tragedy, then why not her own family?

The Earl of Dysart wanted to know how soon he would be able to meet her brother, the artist. 'Bring him over tomorrow,' he said, patting Phoebe's hand like a father. 'It's my tenants' feast day, you know. We have it outside every summer. You'll love it. Everybody dresses up, and my friend Rowlandson always comes over. It would be good for your brother to meet him. Bring the family with you. Good, that's settled then.'

Phoebe would have liked to talk longer with the Countess, having heard how Ham House had suffered years of neglect, like her own, until the new Earl and his lady had begun a programme of restoration. Many of the rooms had been refurbished in an earlier style which, although not to Phoebe's modern taste, had been carried out lovingly and with consideration. It would have to wait, she thought. The Countess would not have time tomorrow, with a tenants' party to organise straight after a musical evening.

'You have never looked more beautiful, *madame,*' Ransome whispered to her as they returned to the hall. 'Happiness becomes you.'

'You are very kind, my lord.'

'No, I'm not being kind. You know me better than that.'

'Yes, I do. I'm happy because things appear to be falling into place, at last. And I'm happy to be here with you. To be known as your mistress.'

'As my future wife, perhaps?'

'You have certainly removed almost all my reservations about that, my lord. Ah, but see…the musicians are returning.'

'*Almost* all? What's the remaining one, may I ask?'

'Shh! I'll tell you when it's gone,' she said, arranging the red silk over her knees. Then, to comfort him, she laid a hand over his and kept it there as the musicians launched into excerpts from Mozart's *Magic Flute* with a group of enthusiastic soloists. But again, the music became incidental to Phoebe's more private and personal needs, and the hand that held hers conveyed its own message in an occasional squeeze that said as clearly as words that their thoughts were the same.

* * *

The journey back to Richmond was taken in the intimate silence of reflection and anticipation, too short to do more than sit close together, too long to be bearable.

The time for polite conversation and half-understood phrases had passed, and Miss Cowling was dismissed before she'd done more than open the bedroom door without a blink of surprise. She had seen this coming. They would not even hear her 'Goodnight, ma'am.'

No reticence or pretence, no more proprieties to be observed, they came together with only one song between them, their mouths, arms and bodies desperate for the kind of music only they could create, unaccompanied. A duet of love to which only they knew the words.

'Beloved…ah, my delight…thou art like a ripe plum…'

She laughed. 'A plum?'

'Yes, a red, juicy…sweet…plum…for my mouth to…plunder. Take off this…damn skin… and let me get…to the flesh, woman.'

Only Buck Ransome could say it like that, she thought, and make it sound so romantic. Feverishly, with pauses, fingers working frantically to remove all the trappings of the evening, they helped each other out of their clothes, flinging them carelessly aside with laughter and some curses, until Ransome stood before her in his linen drawers and Phoebe reached her chemise, suddenly overcome with modesty, captivated by the first sight of his supremely beautiful candle-lit torso.

She had known the kind of thing to expect, but knowing had not prepared her for the reality, the width of shoulder and powerful chest, the sinewy neck and arms, the smooth slender hips of an athlete, his handsome head with the black hair that rose above the widow's peak in thick waves, with some mutinous exceptions. Since their first wary encounters, he had always been impeccably dressed, and to see him like this reminded her forcibly of how Claude Donville's finery had concealed a boy's body, a deceit as mean as his bedroom manners. If Ransome was high-handed, straightforward and lordly, he had a body to match his lofty ways and a manner of deceptive kindness, rather than the opposite. Whatever he was concealing from her could surely not be bad enough to turn her against him, as she'd been before.

'What is it, sweetheart?' he said, watching her eyes in the dim light.

Like a child in doubt, she bit at her top lip and released it, laying a hand over his arm, aware of the silky covering. 'A thought,' she whispered. 'That's all. Just a thought.'

He took her hand from his arm and drew her forwards until she could feel the warmth of him from knee to shoulder. 'Yes,' he said, 'it's been an evening that stirred up the past, sweetheart, as I knew it would. But it was a moving on too, wasn't it? Like this. We've dealt with the past, yours and mine, and now we're free. And I swear I shall never deceive you. Never. Whatever your reservations are, ask me and I'll tell you. I would not hide anything from you that can affect our relationship, and if I used you badly when I forced you to accept me, that was the only ammunition I had, sweet nymph. Desperate measures.'

She was trembling as he lifted her and carried her in his arms across to the curtained bed, laying her upon the sun-warmed sheets. The scene had begun in haste, but her hesitation had slowed them down to a wonderment of delicious details, overlooked the first time. The gentle unpinning of her hair, the spreading of it, her hands seeking over the sweep of his long back, their lips moving over silky skin, tasting new surfaces. Lingering.

Keeping her hand captive on the pillow, he pulled at the cord of her chemise to open the neckline and to draw the fabric down, inch by inch, following it with lips and hand until she was naked under him, shifting in delight as he explored and discovered hidden valleys, folds, creases and private places that came alive, sending urgent demands for something more. Slowly, deliberately, he answered her demands with a skill previously only hinted at when conditions had been restricted, finding that her responses were as immediate as the first time, her moans becoming cries for consummation. Eagerly, her hands urged him on, positioning herself without his prompting, arching and meeting him, ready for his possession. 'Now,' she whispered. 'Don't hold back, beloved. Love me.'

His reply to her passionate invitation was as tempestuous as her dreams of him and, as her fingers dug into his arms, she felt the answering fierceness she had wanted, needed, yearned for over the past empty years, taking her to heights she could never have imagined. This was the man she had waited for, the only one to break down the wall she'd built around herself, to challenge the so-called peace of her life that was only one step away from isolation. The first time, in the garden, had been limited in scope and tailored to her newness, but now she was new no longer, and the evening had mended some of her broken dreams. It was time to give back, to be as fervently generous as he had been to her.

There was to be no leading or following on this second occasion, but a sharing of pleasures all the more potent for being linked to those fading old memories of discouragement on her part and rejection on his. She felt the mastery in his powerful control, but it was something to be gloried in, not resented or passively accepted, and what might have seemed like a mock-battle was, in fact, a wildness of the kind that had made him want Phoebe in the first place and, but for her interfering mother, would have won. She fought him, but only in love; she made him labour, but paid him handsomely. It was the most exciting and rewarding loving of their lives, rolling them over and over and across the bed in escape and pursuit, possession and submission, sweetness, and the kind of grim determination that takes hold of a man at the end, silent and intent.

Exhausted, exhilarated, Phoebe reached the pinnacle at the same moment and hovered, weightless, as the sky came crashing down on them. They clung, moaning, holding on to the last fading star, their lips sharing the same shallow breath.

The candle had died and the moon shone a white floodlight through the open curtains of the bed when they moved, at last, from one tangle of limbs to another. Drowsily, Phoebe snuggled deeper into her lover and smiled as one large hand smoothed over the roundness of her hip. 'Licence my roving hands,' she murmured, 'and let them go…'

'Before, behind, above, below,' he answered, caressing.

Stretching like a sleepy cat, Phoebe turned to him again, offering him her lips.

The next morning she drove the phaeton over to Mortlake, hoping to persuade Leon to take up residence at Ferry House until his future and health were more settled.

The patient, having benefited from a long rest, careful nursing and the best food that Ransome's cook could devise, had changed beyond recognition from the pathetic creature he had been only a few days ago to the usual nattily dressed beau with trimmed black hair, and eyes that had already begun to show the blue-whites of health. Naturally, there was an apologetic air clouding his more usual confidence, as if he was still unsure what had happened to him, or why, or what he could do about it. 'Whatever you think, Pheeb,' he said. 'I'll stay at Ferry House if you want me to. Though it's all a bit temporary, isn't it?'

'We'll see, love. No need to make decisions all at once.'

To avoid Claudette's curiosity, Ransome had left Ferry House at first light. Agreeing to Leon's change of venue, he had offered to convey his luggage later on in the coach where it would be unremarked by wagging tongues, an arrangement that gave the brother and sister a chance to be alone. Leon could not remember ever visiting Ferry House, and the difference in its appearance did nothing to aid his memory. Not until the gates opened for the phaeton did he realise that this was the lovely house he had lost over a game of chance.

'Oh, *Pheeb*,' he said in a subdued voice. 'Is this it? Your home?'

In theory, there had been an opportunity for her to

explain exactly what the plan was and how it had come about so soon, after her well-known antipathy to Lord Ransome. But sitting side by side over a bumpy road with her attention more on her driving than on affairs of the heart was hardly the best way to do it. She decided to wait until the meeting and greeting was over.

The welcome almost overwhelmed him. Hetty, Claudette and Tabby Maskell had all changed in varying degrees, but Claudette most of all. They had not met for years, but Hetty's later reference to the Prodigal Son was not so far out, except for the fatted calf, and soon he was being shown round the house and garden, Claudette not realising that her enthusiasm for her lovely home was somewhat misplaced, in the circumstances. It was Tabby, her governess, who noticed the despairing expression on Uncle Leon's comely face and who suggested that he needed a rest. With his sister. Alone.

'Listen, Pheeb,' he said, flopping into a chair in her study. 'I've had time to think about all this... well, about you, that is. I've still got the family home on Harley Street. It's not as big as this one and it doesn't have the garden either, but there's enough room for you and—'

'Leon, stop...love. The problem has been solved already.' It was not the kind of news one could blurt out in a rush to someone recovering from the mother of all hangovers. It had to be administered by degrees, like medicine.

'What?' he frowned, accepting the coffee cup she passed him. 'Is there something going on between you and Ransome? What's he been up to? You've never liked him, and now suddenly you're speaking. And why is he doing all this for me, after what he… Oh, it was my own damned fault. Why deny it?'

'Leon, let me explain. We came to an agreement, that's all.' Whichever way she tried it, the words seemed to take on a new ambiguity.

The coffee cup clattered. 'An agreement? That's *not* all, Pheeb, is it? You've sold yourself to him, haven't you? For this place. For me. Is that it?'

'I have not *sold* myself, Leon. Don't over-dramat-ise things so.'

'But you've agreed to become his mistress, and he's letting you stay here. Don't try to pull the wool over my eyes, because I can see clearly now. All that polite ac-cord, after you couldn't stand the sight of him?' He stood up, ramrod straight, alert and, she thought, rather in-sulted.

How could she make him understand? 'Please, will you *listen* to me?'

But it was already too late. Even as she spoke, a man's voice could be heard in the hall, the wail of a child, a woman's high whine.

'Damn!' said Leon. 'That's Ross, isn't it? What does *he* want?'

At once, Phoebe saw her chance of an explanation slip away, Leon being more confused, herself trying to defend him from Ross's accusations and scheming. Grabbing him by the arm, she pulled him to face her. 'Please, Leon, let me handle this, will you? I know what they've come for. Don't look shocked, for pity's sake. Look as if you *know*.'

'Know what?'

'What I'm about to *tell* them, dammit! Ross... Josephine! What a surprise, so *soon*. And Arthur. Hello, young man. Might it be best if we were to sit in the parlour? I don't receive visitors in here.' Taking control of things before *they* did, Phoebe thought, was the best way to deal with this family gathering. Nothing she could have done, or said, however, could have lessened the open-mouthed astonishment on the faces of Ross and his wife.

Ross drew himself up like an army officer about to lecture a new recruit. 'Oh!' he said. 'What are *you* doing here?'

'Taking coffee with my sister, Ross. Good morning, dear Josephine. You're looking as well as ever. Good heavens, how the infant has grown.'

'When did you arrive?' Ross wanted to know, so-licitor-like. Leon's presence had clearly unsettled him, his hard look at his wife seeming to imply that whatever they had come for might have to be approached from a different angle.

Leon's presence did no such thing for Josephine's line of attack, for her cross-examination began even before Ross had an answer to his first question, and no sooner had they trouped across to the parlour than she demanded to be told all the details of what exactly Leon thought he was doing to place poor *dear* Phoebe in such a *dreadful* position, in that *awful* man's dependence. And did he not know that *they* had been the first to offer her their—?

'Your *what,* Josephine?' Phoebe said, politely. 'What was it you and Ross offered me? Do you know, I've quite forgotten.'

'I don't think that's relevant,' Ross said, lifting up the squealing child. 'The thing is, we've found a way round the problem, so it's just as well you're here, Leon, because it involves you.'

'Oh, you *do* surprise me, brother,' said Leon, wincing at the ear-splitting howl emanating from Arthur's huge pink mouth. 'But do you think we could discuss my involvement without the accompaniment?'

It took several minutes for the unhappy child to be taken off to the garden with his cousin, for coffee to be poured and handed round by the ubiquitous Hetty, and for Leon to discover that, if nothing else, his sartorial aptitude exceeded his brother's by a mile. Which boosted his morale enough for him to initiate the next phase of the 'who-has-done-most' discussion, and to bestow a smile of something close to enjoyment upon Hetty. 'Sugar, but no milk, thank you, Het,' he said. 'Now, Ross, what's this solution you have in mind? Does it involve me alone, or all of us?'

Ross cleared his throat, but he was too slow.

Josephine did not intend to cede this moment to anyone. 'It was my idea,' she said, taking a biscuit. 'I wrote to Lady Templeman in reply to her letter. Well, as a daughter-in-law, I had to do what I could to ease her mind, didn't I? Poor lady. And I knew she was in no position to offer dear Phoebe a room at—'

'I should hope not,' said Leon, stoutly, 'when *dear* Pheeb could hardly wait to get away from the place. I've just sugg—'

'Leon!' said Phoebe. 'Allow Josephine to continue, if you please.'

His eyebrows flickered, but the message was understood.

'Thank you, Phoebe. As I was saying, I have proposed to Lady Templeman that Leon should make *his* house available to you as your home. After all, he should be the one to be inconvenienced, and although I realise that—'

'You did *what*?' Phoebe said, sharply, pinning her sister-in-law back into her seat with a dagger-like look. 'Did it occur to you that I might wish to be consulted on the matter, Josephine? Did *you*, Ross?'

Josephine blinked at her biscuit and replaced it on her plate. 'Well, what would have been the point in that, dear? Were you in a position to…?'

'When I am *not* in a position to make my own decisions regarding my future, Josephine, you may carry me off in a coffin. And what about Leon? Is he not to be consulted about who lives with him?'

'Leon has been in no position to be consulted about anything,' said Ross. 'Has he?'

'How d'ye know that?' said Leon, looking across at his younger brother with a sobriety that impressed Phoebe, after what she'd seen yesterday. 'You haven't exactly made it your business to find out *what* my position was, have you, Ross? Ransome was the one to offer me help. He actually came to find me.'

'But we *are* offering you help, Leon,' Josephine whined, glancing at her husband in the hope of support. 'And Phoebe too. We thought it would be best for both of you, now everything has changed. Didn't we, Mr Hawkin, dear?'

Phoebe stepped in before he could say 'yes, dear.' 'So which of you is going to break the news to me that you've made an offer for Ferry House? Which of you two is the most confused between opportunism, greed, help and downright interference?'

'Pheeb,' said Leon, quietly. 'Sit down, love. Let Ross explain. He's used to making out a good case, aren't you, brother?'

Ross's shifty eyes flitted between his siblings like a shuttlecock waiting to fall. When they did, it was upon his hands, thumbs twitching. 'We came to tell you about that, too, Phoebe. It was part of our…er…'

'Plan? Scheme?'

'Part of our rescue. Lord Ransome has agreed to discuss the matter with me tomorrow morning. That's why we thought you should know today. I'm sorry. We understand how disappointed you must be.'

'Oh, don't concern yourself about me, Ross. Not at this late stage. And dear Josephine, wanting rooms for another nurse, and larger gardens, and—'

'You've seen the letter?' Ross said. 'Oh!'

'This is most entertaining,' Leon murmured, looking askance at Hetty.

'Have *you* seen my letter too, then?' Ross snapped at him.

'Not yet. But I can imagine whose grand idea it was.' His darkly studied look switched from Hetty to Josephine in a slow blink that sent a blush of guilty pink into her cheeks. Before she could retaliate, however, Leon had more to say. 'I dare say I'm letting the cat out of the bag somewhat prematurely, my dears, but I think you ought to be appraised of the facts before you go chasing any more fancy ideas about buying Ferry House. Phoebe will not be leaving. The house is not for sale.'

'*Leon!*' Phoebe's wail held every nuance of shock and anger. 'You must not say another *word*.'

'Sorry, love. I'm not going to sit here and let my younger brother think he's taken the cherry off the cake. I am still the eldest, and my head is as clear as a bell-jar in your garden. I realise you'd not meant Ross and Josephine to know before Ransome could tell them—'

'Tell us *what*?' Ross barked, petulantly.

'Oh…sorry, I'm running ahead of myself…that he's Pheeb's lover.'

The high yelp from Josephine went unnoticed.

'What?' Ross squeaked.

'Yes, they'll be living here themselves, you see.'

With her eyes half-closed, Phoebe sat very still, watching a beam of sunlight dance across the blue-and-white coffee cups. She had not for a moment thought that Leon would assess the situation so fast or so accurately when she had not denied his first indignant accusation, which had not, she saw it now, been an accusation at all. Nor had he been insulted, only suddenly comprehending what he thought he'd seen between them. She had intended to break the news herself, but how much better to come from Leon, even if it was a bit of a gamble that he'd get it right.

'She didn't want to shock you, you see,' Leon was saying, unable to keep a gurgle of laughter out of his voice, 'because she knows how you feel about that kind of thing, but the attraction has always *been* there, hasn't it? Even when…well, never mind that. It just *had* to happen one day. I expect that was what Ransome was going to tell you tomorrow, Ross.'

'Oh!' Josephine cried with a hand clasped to her forehead. 'His *mistress?* How *could* you, Phoebe? That's…quite…disgraceful!'

'Is it true, Phoebe?' Ross growled.

'Yes,' she whispered. 'It is. Lord Ransome would have told you about it.'

He stood up, hooking a hand beneath his wife's arm. 'Then I have no more to say, and no more help to offer. We did our best.'

'That will be a severe blow to her,' said Leon, 'but I doubt she'll notice it much. Perhaps you could write another letter to Mama, Josephine, with the good news. Tell her not to change any of her plans, won't you?'

Turning to Phoebe, Josephine's pale red-rimmed eyes were cold with dislike. 'I had not realised how desperate you must be to remain here, Phoebe. I never thought you would go that far, knowing what kind of a man he is. Has he told you about the children he keeps at Greenwater?'

'I know about the children, thank you, Josephine.'

'And you'll allow Claudette to associate with them, will you? Really. Mr Hawkin,' she said, leaning heavily on Ross's arm, 'I think you should call our little Arthur away immediately. We cannot afford to have your reputation…' Her parting shot did not have quite the impact she'd hoped, for she had been wondering whether to throw in the word 'bastards' before she departed. The appearance of Lord Ransome, however, made her glad she had not.

Pausing on the threshhold, he took in the situation with one haughty glance that swept the room and came to rest on Phoebe with the raising of one articulate eyebrow. The corner of his mouth lifted. 'I'm too late,' he said. 'The news is out, I see.'

'Good morning, my lord,' said Ross, being first to recover himself. 'My wife and I were just on our way out, but now there will be no need for us to meet tomorrow after all. I fear I was rather premature with my offer. Please accept my apologies.'

'No harm done, Hawkin. Simply brought things forward, that's all. Felicitations might be more appropriate, don't you think?' Graceful and totally at ease, he sauntered across to Phoebe and stood beside her, close enough to leave no doubt about their relationship. His hand rested on her upper arm where the white frill of her sleeve gave it shelter.

Ross was puzzled. 'Felicitations…on…becoming my sister's…lover?' he whispered. Disapproval clouded his eyes, and his quick glance at his wife's bowed head gave him no hope of encouragement. 'Is that what you meant, my lord?' The look exchanged between the two lovers, one teasingly scolding and the other blameless, irritated Ross, who preferred the facts to be either black or white.

'Ah,' said Ransome, enjoying the expected shock, 'the situation, as they say, is fluid. To be resolved. At the moment, yes, Madame Donville and I have an understanding which will eventually—' he pulled Phoebe gently to him '—become permanent. For the moment we are happy for things to stay as they are until we decide to move forward into matrimony. Which we will, of course, as soon as my Mortlake house is finished and properly staffed.'

Josephine squeaked again. 'Oh, *do* take me home, Mr Hawkin, if you please. Arthur! Where is he?' Calling pitifully, she left the room, followed by Hetty.

Ross was not quite as distressed as his wife. 'Phoebe,' he said, more brotherly now his wife was out of earshot, 'is this what you want?'

'It's not quite what I expected, Ross, but, yes, it is what I want. Perhaps it's what I've always wanted, without knowing it.'

Resigned, he nodded. 'And you, brother? You'll return home, I suppose, and carry on from where you left off, will you, and hope to remember who lives in your property next time?'

'I appreciate your concern,' Leon said without a trace of regret. 'It comes rather late in the day, but we can see where *your* motivation comes from. You go and patter after your wife, and leave me and Pheeb to manage our own affairs. Eh?'

Ross looked away, clearly stung by his brother's

perception of him. 'Yes. I'm sorry I came, Phoebe. Addle-brained thing to do, wasn't it?'

She went to him and, placing a gentle hand on his arm, kissed him lightly on the cheek. 'Yes, love. It *was* an addle-brained thing to do. But we'll send you an invitation to the wedding, and I'll let you know what Leon decides to do.'

'Oh. You'll definitely marry then, will you?'

'Most certainly, love. As soon as I've got used to the idea.' Linking her arm through Ross's, she walked out with him to the sunny courtyard where Josephine was already bundling her recalcitrant child up the steps into the coach as if the devil himself was after them.

CHAPTER SEVEN

LEON HAD ENJOYED his brief moment of superiority in the parlour, but he had noted Phoebe's compassion after the anger, and it was not in his nature to be at odds with anyone for long. Particularly with the successful henpecked brother he'd not seen for some years. Following his sister and brother to the courtyard, he held out a hand, pulling Ross into an embrace which he seemed happy to share. 'I'll probably be staying around for a while,' Leon said to him, quietly. 'I'll come and see you, shall I?'

'You'll always be welcome, brother. What are you going to do?'

'Paint, I think. Not sure yet. I'll tell you when I

know more. And don't worry about Pheeb. She'll not
do anything stupid.'

'Thank heaven there's one of us, then.'

Leon did not ask his brother to explain the doleful
remark, but as the coach rumbled away out of the
courtyard with only Ross's arm waving out of the
window, he took Claudette by the hand and walked
with her and her governess away through the garden
towards the river.

When Hetty made as if to follow them, Phoebe
caught her by the hand to stop her, placing a quick
peck on her cheek. 'Thank you for your help, love.
Come and have a chat with us until lunch is ready.'

Not surprisingly, Viscount Ransome's frequent visits to Ferry House could not be dismissed as the casual calls that Miss Maskell said they were, when
anyone could see that they were not. It was Lord
Ransome himself who suggested to Phoebe that, since
they would all be together for lunch, a general discussion of the situation of the kind that Claudette was used
to would be much the best way to make her feel part
of the plan.

Agreeing, Phoebe was again struck by Ransome's
thoughtfulness and apparent understanding of how
young minds work, and since Claudette was never so
pleased as when she was being treated as a grown-up,
the lunch was a perfect setting for a very natural conversation about the sometimes unplanned, unorthodox

relationships between adults. It was the kind of discourse that would have horrified Aunt Josephine, and probably Uncle Ross too, if they'd heard it, yet it told Claudette what she needed to know about the possible changes to her family, and made her feel that her understanding mattered to them. The addition of an uncle *and* a Viscount at the meal was to Claudette quite an event, but it was felt no less by Phoebe herself, especially when the two men appeared to like each other despite the most extraordinary circumstances.

Just as warmly felt was the regard Leon showed towards Tabby Maskell, and hers to him, noticed even by Claudette, who was most observant of such things. Her saucy grin thrown over her shoulder showed she recognised that she was there to chaperon her governess. Deciding that six in one coach was too many, the two men rode on horseback to Ham House to join the tenants' feast while the ladies, prettily dressed in pale muslins with matching parasols, used the coach that Lord Ransome had brought from Mortlake with Leon's belongings.

There was to be no turning into the north forecourt of Ham House that day, for spread right across the meadow between the road and the gates, dozens of trestles and benches were alive with people, a sea of heads and bodies making a buzz of noise like swarming bees. Beneath the trees, the Earl's tenants were dressed for the occasion, older men in wigs and waist-coats, the women in Sunday best, bonneted and bare-headed, sweethearts, children and babes in arms, men carrying bowls of punch and tapping huge barrels of ale, dogs yapping and begging for scraps. Empty jugs and tubs clustered around the tables, indicating to the new arrivals that the feast had been under way for some time.

Dressed in the uniform of major of his regiment, Lord Dysart strolled along the tables with his Countess, whose plume of feathers indicated her presence as easily as her husband's red coat, both of them stop-ping to talk and to have their health drunk with loud cheers and the clapping of hands. No one could doubt their popularity with the tenants. Spying the Viscount and his party, they came to meet them with smiles and a courteous word for each one, and though they all sus-pected that Leon was the one the Earl most wanted to meet, it was to young Claudette he gave special atten-tion, taking her by the hand in a relationship neither of them had ever enjoyed—grandfather and grand-daughter. The sight of them together, hand in hand, wrung Phoebe's heart. It was no imposition for any of them to join in the Dysart's happy occasion, to drink the punch, to sing glee songs with gusto and to laugh at the teasing tales, the banter and swapping of hats.

But there was another guest present, one they had not noticed as they walked into the feast, their attention all on the scene ahead of them. The Earl and Claudette went off to find him, returning moments later with a middle-aged, balding gentleman carrying a leather bag and a scruffy sketchbook under his arm, his other hand holding Claudette's. She had never felt so important as when she told them that this gentleman was Mr Thomas Rowlandson who exhibited at the Royal Academy.

Unlike the dapper Thomas Lawrence, portraitist of some influence amongst the fashionable set, Rowlandson wore well-worn, workmanlike clothes, his intention being not to be noticed as he sketched scenes of everyday life, as he was doing today. As easy with the Earl's patronage as with any villager, he sat between them to show them his sketch of the tenants' feast, explaining that he would add the light watercolour effects later on.

'Glad to meet you, Mr Hawkin,' he said to Leon, pushing the sketchbook towards Claudette. 'His lordship has mentioned you to me as one of his new discoveries. Now, a word in your ear, my friend.' He leaned forwards with a twinkle in his eye, but speaking loud enough to be heard by them all. 'When his lordship discovers a talent, it ends up on every wall in the house. Even the Duchess's Bathroom. It's better than the Royal Academy in there, sir, believe me.' His smile showed several gaps, his fingers were broad and stubby, stained with ink and paint, his talent for capturing every delicate detail of a scene totally belied by his appearance. It was his honesty and wit that had won him friends, as well as enemies. Rowlandson and Viscount Ransome were already well known to each other, sharing similar traits of character and, as the Earl continued to host his gathering, Ransome, Leon and Rowlandson strolled away to talk about how artists made a living.

It was the Countess herself who suggested a rest in the shade as the party began to break up, the tenants straggling away into the formal gardens or along the riverside. 'We call these the Cloisters,' she said, leading Phoebe to one side of the front door where a room without walls was created by open arches and stone benches, with views of the garden painted on the plasterwork. Its counterpart was on the opposite side where Claudette sat with Hetty and Tabby to look through the sketchbook.

Inevitably, the tête-à-tête turned to Phoebe's enjoyment of the concert on the previous evening and how delighted she had been to meet the French guests who had been, in turn, intrigued to meet the living descendant of the portrait hanging in the gallery. Little by little, for the Countess was a very good and sympathetic listener, Phoebe's concerns emerged regarding her brother, and the kindness that Lord Ransome had shown him recently. 'May I ask, my lady,' Phoebe ventured, 'how you and the Earl first met Lord Ransome?

Was it in London? I find it quite difficult to reconcile your gentle life with the way he lives his.'

The Countess found that amusing. 'Ah, you mean his reputation for hard living, I suppose. But you must have discovered for yourself, my dear, that most men have a side they prefer to keep to themselves. Haven't you? Your brother Ross, for instance, knows little about his elder brother's gift for painting. My kind and sensitive husband kept his love of gardening from most of his comrades in the army. And your late husband too, Phoebe. He must have been a delight to know, or presumably you'd not have been attracted to him?'

'So you know about him, my lady?'

The frail hand came to rest lightly upon Phoebe's clasped hands, and the delicate lines of her face were a map of concern. 'Of course, my dear. As I said, the double-sidedness that men cultivate would not be half so successful or exciting if it was common knowledge. Especially so when it involves charitable work, of which the whole point is not to seek attention or praise. Don't you agree?'

'Yes, indeed. But are you telling me that Lord Ransome is leading a double life, my lady? I thought his life was dangerous enough as it is, without adding more facets.'

'Not a double life exactly, Phoebe, but men such as Buck like to believe that women fall for their dangerous side rather than for their good works. That comes like the icing on top of the cake.'

'Good works? Lord Ransome? Does he assist the Earl, then?'

'Oh, no, we got to know him through the orphanages in London, first of all. He was elected as a governor to the Foundling Hospital, and then to the Vestry Committee at Mortlake. We found we were working towards the same goal, helping to rescue abandoned and ill-treated orphans from the streets. But Buck goes even further, he takes them off the streets and houses them at his own expense. I know he has a home for about twenty boys on the outskirts of North London, but now he's bought this place at Mortlake that he's extending. You've not seen it yet?'

'Er…yes, yes…I have. But he didn't say…any of that. He said he'd show me all the rooms when they were ready, but I didn't know he meant ready for *orphans.*' Phoebe was reeling with shock as the pictures fell into place.

'The overflow from London, my dear,' said the Countess, airily. 'Sometimes he brings a few here for a day out, to let them climb the trees and play by the river. It's a far cry from the terrible conditions they were brought up in, slums, filth, near starvation, made to work for chimney-sweeps and thieves. The money he wins at the clubs in London is all used to rehouse the little fellows, but he never tells anyone about it, of course. I believe his aim is to house some of the little girls too, once he can install a suitable house-mistress as well as a house-master. He's a remarkable man, Phoebe. We never had a son but, if we had, we'd have liked one like him.'

A house-mistress. The new extension was for a *house*-mistress. The two little boys, not his own, but orphans, shrieking with delight at their freedom and a river at the bottom of the garden, the strong arms to catch and spin them round. The laughter. His remarks about people sleeping rough, and about there being enough bastards in the world already. His assurance that he would never deceive her. His total acceptance of the unfortunate women she employed, without references. His unselfish help for Leon, the man he could not bear to see slide further downhill into despair, not only because of her, but because it was not his way to ruin a man, only to relieve him of excess wealth.

'Are you all right, my dear? You're shocked by this?'

'It's a side of him that never occurred to me, my lady. He would have told me of it, I'm sure, but I think he would have made light of it, just the same. But I wonder why he didn't try to win me over with that, to show me his charitable side rather than the frivolous gambler who cares for nothing and nobody. Most women would rather have known about—' She stopped, knowing what the Countess would reply before she spoke.

'But you're *not* most women, Phoebe, are you? You're a Hawkin, and from what I've heard about the Hawkin women, they're drawn to forceful men. Would you have responded to sweet words and love songs and tales of charity and brave deeds after what happened to you?'

They were still laughing about it when Claudette, Hetty and Tabby joined them, asking to be shown the Hawkynne portrait in the gallery, which the Countess used as an excuse, if she needed one, to show them around the house.

The four guests were intrigued and impressed by the high-sounding useage to which the rooms had once been put, the Queen's Bedchamber, the Duke's Dressing Room, the closets and antechambers. But Claudette was most delighted by the doors concealed in the larger rooms that could only be detected by the vertical cuts in the wallpaper, placed there to give the servants access to the service passage. To her mind, this was a perfect way for ghosts to come and go, but since Mama would not appreciate her talking about such matters, she kept her fancies to herself, thinking it a pity that, on the whole, adults were too matter of fact for their own good.

Phoebe's thoughts, however, were only half on the beautifully restored rooms, the other half mulling over the extraordinary information concerning Ransome's use of *his* rooms at Mortlake. It made her realise, more than anything else, how quick she had been to impose on him the irritation she had felt all those years ago when she was first widowed, a natural reaction against her mother's insistent ways. Then, she had not even bothered to find out what he was like behind the public image, never suspecting that there might be more to him than what most people saw. The problem had not been that he'd had mistresses. So many men did, when they married for wealth and heirs, not for love. But for a man to *offer* marriage to a woman while in the process of accommodating a mistress a mere couple of miles away was a situation few women would accept without making a fuss about it. And that, she saw it now, had been dear Josephine's unhelpful contribution, which she herself had been only too ready to believe.

Of course, he had done absolutely nothing to dispel Phoebe's jaundiced picture of him, especially on his first visit, when he had been considerably less than gentlemanly, as if he'd known for certain that, with a threat to hold over her, he could make her think again. And she had. And now, mistress or no mistress, she had agreed to let him into her life, not so much for his kindness to Leon but because part of her had responded to his dangerous side, as the Countess had suggested, and because she had answered his call to her physical longings, her desires, her needs. Wanting him more than anything, she had agreed in principle to be his wife while using the title of mistress to embarrass the family who had embarrassed her. Hardly the behaviour of a rational woman, but rationality had so far played only a minor role in her feelings for this amazing man. And now she could not help questioning whether she would have accepted him sooner if she'd known about his plans for the Mortlake house, or not. The Countess was a very perceptive woman.

'And this is known as the Yellow Satin Bedroom,' she was saying as she led the ladies out of the Queen's Closet, 'where the Duchess of Lauderdale had cages of birds all round the window. Such a pretty room. Lovely view across to the river.' Out and round, they passed through to the gallery, 'Which was once the dining room over the hall, until the ceiling was knocked through. Much better now. And here is Sir Leo and Lady Phoebe. Your ancestors, Miss Claudette. Is she not very like your mama?'

Again, Phoebe experienced the same prickling sensation of kinship that had taken her so much by surprise, this time no less surreal than the first. Drawn to forceful men, the Countess had told her, so perhaps these two had had their ups and downs, like her.

Apart from pointing out the lovely costumes and the pretty enamelled pendant with a moon and pearls, the children and the dog, Phoebe could find little to say and, when the others had moved on round the corner towards the staircase, she stayed behind as if to commune with her namesake in private.

Lady Phoebe looked straight out of the picture, like her husband.

Phoebe waited. The voices on the staircase trailed away, as if into another time.

Lips moved almost imperceptibly as she watched.

No, it was not possible. There was no sound. She must have imagined it.

Yet a voice somewhere had told her to look. Look…look where?

On impulse, without questioning why, she turned to lean on the wooden rail to see down to the hall below where limpid figures moved, forwards, backwards, coming together and separating. Then she saw, mistily, the sharp flash of steel, the cold blue murderous glint of long rapiers, the white shirt of one figure catching the light from the windows of the north front. She could see through him, like smoky crystal.

She shook her head to clear it, to hear what was happening through the tunnels of silence that kept her attention fixed, but it was like a dream where only one sense was engaged. There was nothing to be heard, no shouts, no padding of feet, no squeal of blades, no cries from the figures who huddled into the corners, holding hands to their mouths. There was a large buxom woman with two young ladies standing beside a billiard table. Phoebe could just make out their faces, strangely transparent.

A *billiard* table?

There was a man wearing a long wig. He was large, stout, authoritative, a man from another era. As they all were. But now her attention was all on the two duellists, the more petite one of the two wearing a waistcoat over a shirt, tight breeches and white stockings. No shoes. A head of black curling hair like…like? She put a hand up to her head. Like herself. Phoebe. It was a woman, not a man. A woman. Phoebe Hawkynne. Duelling with…yes, her husband, the broad-shouldered athletic figure of the portrait Did he intend to kill her? Did they allow women to duel in those days? Is this what she was seeing? *Those* days?

Casting a furtive glance to each side of her, sure that she was unobserved, and devoid of any sense of being, she leaned forwards to watch the ghostly scene being enacted in utter silence below her, though she knew there *should* have been something to hear, a clatter, a shriek of blades, the panting as the woman was beaten back by her stronger opponent. She could feel her desperation.

A gold button went flying through the air as the tip of his rapier nicked the top of her waistcoat, and she threw up her arms in anger. The large man waved an arm, mouthing a command. The woman continued, but she was angry, slashing wildly at her opponent's arm, while he called out something to the people on the fireplace side, hidden from Phoebe's view, an arrogant remark that clearly unsettled the woman. At one point, she was given a moment to unbutton her waistcoat and fling it into a corner without waiting to see where it fell. But the watching Phoebe did, saw also how the gold button was picked up and held tight against the skirt of the taller young woman, how she retrieved the waistcoat and passed it to her mother, as if it were hers. Well, it might once have been, Phoebe thought, but not for some years, for the duelling Phoebe was slender and shapely. Few men would be able to keep their mind on the duel with that creature dancing balletically before them.

The duel began again, but already Phoebe could see how her namesake was tiring, her face showing pain and fatigue on every line, her sword arm drooping and unable to withstand Sir Leo's punishing blows. He could, Phoebe thought, have plunged his rapier into her at any time, if he'd wanted to.

But apparently he did not, for instead of making an end to it or disarming her, he made her keep going, on and on, until she could no longer lift the point of her rapier from the floor. Then, backing her against the billiard table, bending her, he held his sword to her throat, barking out a command that failed to break through the silence, not even when her rapier slid across the floor, not even when her open mouth let out a stream of defiance, her face contorted by exhaustion. Only silence and a terrible tension that filled the hall below.

Horrified, entranced, spellbound, Phoebe saw all

that happened after that; the prolonged humiliating victory kiss and the fascinated stare of the girl who had kept the button, the look of moonstruck adulation on her face which, for some strange reason, had become clear enough to show Phoebe the pain there, too. The other filmy figures swayed and stirred with relief, though there was distress in the way they conferred, unable to do more than watch Sir Leo lift the half-fainting woman into his arms and silently glide with her across to the bottom of the staircase.

Phoebe being carried upstairs, to where *she* was, eavesdropping. Imagining.

Except that she could never have imagined this. Never.

Sounds came from a distant place, faint sounds like the beginning of waking, fixing the senses with real substance, one after the other. They were coming up the stairs towards her.

But, no, as she turned to look, the dear familiar figure was not carrying anyone in his arms, nor was he wearing a white shirt with a slash on the sleeve, but a deep blue cutaway tailcoat with buff doeskin breeches and riding boots. Purposely, he strode towards her, his feet making a comforting clack-clack on the floor, his body as solid and real as life. Substantial. Beloved.

Clinging, afraid to let go of the banister rail for fear her trembling legs would give way, Phoebe heard his distant greeting through the loud hammering of her heart and a rushing sound of water. She tried to speak, but could only whisper, 'Look!' indicating with her head to the floor below.

But she knew, even as she spoke, that they had gone. The little figure who waved up to her was Claudette. Hetty was there talking to the Countess. Leon and Tabby Maskell were studying a portrait between the windows. The billiard table had vanished, the furniture slightly readjusted, solid and real.

'Yes,' said Ransome, 'there they are. Waiting for you…why…what is it, sweetheart? You're as white as a sheet. Is it the heat?' Lifting her off the rail and pulling her into his arms, supporting her, he turned her away from the light towards the portrait, which now she was able to search with new eyes.

Lady Hawkynne stared out, as before, though Phoebe had not until this moment noticed the faintest of smiles playing around her mouth. Nor had she noticed something else, that just behind and to one side of her on a polished walnut table was a white linen garment draped over the corner, upon which was a reel of white linen thread and a pin-cushion, heavily beaded. The patch on the sleeve was clearly visible. To Phoebe, after her experience, the message could not have been clearer, though she knew that the symbolism would have been lost since the portrait was painted.

'Nothing,' she whispered, pressing her cheek

against his immaculate neckcloth, 'no, it's nothing, dearest...*dearest* heart. Oh, hold me. Don't let me go. Don't *ever* let me go, Buck. Let me stay with you. Always.'

His arms slackened as he bent to look into her eyes, holding her chin up with his knuckle. 'What's all this, sweet Phoebe? Eh? Of *course* I shall not let you go. I've already told you so. You're mine. I won you. Reservations or not.'

'No reservations,' she whispered. 'Not a single one. I love you, Buck Ransome. I want to be your wife. For all the right reasons, dear one.'

Buck had never been one to waste words when kisses would do but now, uncharacteristically, the full impact of her declaration made him hesitate and search her deep brown eyes as if he would dredge her soul for the last grain of honesty. 'I have waited,' he said, 'all my life to hear you say that to me. I have loved you and wanted you, and thought I'd lost you for ever, and now at last I have all I've ever wanted. The gloriously lovely Phoebe Hawkin telling me she loves me. Am I dreaming?'

'No, my love. You're not dreaming. It's time for us to patch things up now. Let's move on before it's too late for both of us. It's not your house I need, but you. Just you.'

'You've always had me,' he said, moving his lips closer to hers, 'and I have carried you in my heart since you were a girl of sixteen. Can you understand why I took advantage of you so shamelessly? Can you forgive me?'

Phoebe smiled up at him, a bewitching radiant smile of complete understanding. 'You are not the first to take advantage of a woman's vulnerability, dear heart, and I don't suppose you'll be the last. It's all in the name of love, isn't it?'

She did not manage to catch the merry eye of Lady Hawkynne behind Buck's head, for her own eyes were closed, the better to savour his deep kisses and to languish in the strength of his arms. Nevertheless, although there was nothing quite as concrete as a thought between the two Phoebes, the feeling passed to Madame Donville down the generations that men had their own methods of dealing with love and women had another. Yet it was up to the woman to let him think he'd won, and to mend the damage caused in the process, whatever it was. It also occurred to her, vaguely, that one's relatives had a lot to answer for.

CHAPTER EIGHT

IDEALLY, PHOEBE WOULD like to have returned immedidately to Ferry House. With so much to think about, revelations, ghostly phenomena and the exchange of hearts, anything else was too much for one day. But one of the main reasons for being at Ham House was to bring Leon into contact with Lord Dysart and for them to discuss both their requirements.

So, although still deeply disturbed by what she had witnessed, if one could call it that, she sat through another hour after the departure of the Earl's tenants, to talk over tea and Madeira cake about what the benevolent gentleman wanted from the artist as though it was Leon doing *him* a favour rather than the other way round. His commission was all the more important, he said, because he had not expected to inherit, nor did he have an heir to inherit after him.

If Leon wanted it, the work would keep him occupied indefinitely and, in return for that, he was offered a cottage in Ham village, a generous remuneration, stabling for his horses and an extra allowance for his materials. He could eat at Ham House whenever he wished, and the Countess would find him a housekeeper to see to all his needs. A few days previously, Leon would have wept at so much generosity. Now, however, he shook the Earl's hand with just a trace of dewiness around the eyes that turned to laughter as everyone applauded, and Claudette hugged not only her uncle but her newly adopted grandfather too. But after loud complaints from Viscount Ransome and Mr Rowlandson, she was more or less obliged to do the same for them before order was restored. She took her Uncle Leon up to the gallery to see the Hawkynne portrait, and to show him how like Lady Phoebe he and his sister were.

It was agreed that Leon should take up his appointment as soon as he had put his London affairs in order, but tomorrow he could view the cottage and list whatever he needed for it. Although little was said about his amazing good fortune, it became obvious to all of them that both he and Phoebe had acquired a substitute father in Lord Dysart, for no one could have been more paternal. Whether he knew that the commission was exactly what Leon needed to keep him out of bad company he did not say, but perhaps it was his experience of young soldiers that helped to set Leon's feet moving in the right direction.

Phoebe had already decided to keep her experience to herself. Since her own dear ones knew of her scepticism regarding Gothic apparitions, the kind of nonsense found in contemporary novels, she doubted her ability to convince them of what she'd seen. To be sure, it was almost as easy for her to begin doubting as it was to believe it, and even now she didn't know if she could possibly have made it up. And where had Sir Leo carried his wife off to? Which room? And what then? She would love to have known what it was all about.

By the time they reached Richmond, the excitement of the day was beginning to make its effects felt, and although Phoebe was used to filling every moment with activity, this particular day had been an emotional one, for more than one reason. Her unusual quietness was noticed, and as soon as she had changed into an old muslin gown somewhere between dress and undress, Ransome was waiting to lead her out to the lawn overlooking the river where a supper table had been laid. She was given a well-padded day-bed to lounge on, her food was brought to her, her cider was iced, and her head was cushioned and shaded against the glare of the low sun as the day's events were unfolded for review.

But it was Hetty who took them further. 'Mr Leon will need a housekeeper,' she said, 'and I think that position will suit me very well. I know his habits better than anyone else, and—'

'But, Hetty dear, you *can't!*' said Phoebe. 'You belong here.'

'It's only a change within the family, isn't it? And truthfully, Phoebe, you're not going to need a chaperon any more, are you? Besides, the Countess would like me to help her with the renovations. She finds it quite hard work now, and yet she cannot leave things entirely to her staff. If I were at Ham, I could help her. And,' she added plaintively, 'I'd like to.'

'I'd like it too, Het,' said Leon. 'The cottage Lord Dysart is talking about is actually a six-bedroomed Queen Anne house big enough for a whole family.'

'Then perhaps you should start thinking about acquiring one,' said Ransome, laconically.

'I intend to,' replied Leon, swivelling his eyes towards Miss Maskell, 'as soon as I can sort myself out.'

'But,' said Claudette, looking sulkily at her governess, 'if Uncle Leon takes you away from me, what am I going to do for a governess?'

Miss Maskell laid a hand on Claudette's knee. 'Nobody is taking anyone away for quite some time, so stop worrying,' she said, reassuringly.

'Oh. Are you not going to drop your handker-chief, then?'

'Claudette! Where on *earth* did you pick up such a vulgar expression?'

Cups rattled on saucers and discreet splutters became laughter. 'I suppose that's what comes,' Phoebe said, 'of playing with the village children. And,' she continued, responding to Ransome's steady look, 'of allowing you to take part in adult conversation. The two are sure to become confused, now and then.'

'Sorry,' said Claudette. 'I meant no disrespect.'

'So,' said Lord Ransome, 'since I am about to acquire a beautiful stepdaughter who requires some tuition in the exact art of using cant, I shall take it upon myself to instruct her. Report to me tomorrow, Mademoiselle Donville, if you please, and ask your long-suffering Miss Maskell to accompany you.'

Claudette's expression changed from regret to rapture. 'Oh, *yes*! Will you?'

'My duties must begin somewhere,' he said, and although the lines of his face gave little away, his eyes danced with laughter.

'Will you teach me to drive a phaeton too, my lord? And a curricle?'

'No, young lady, I certainly will not. Miss Maskell,

you should be knighted, I think, for your services to education above and beyond the call of duty.'

'Thank you, my lord,' she said, solemnly.

'You're *teasing*!' Claudette cried.

'On the contrary, I'm serious. I will, however, endeavour to teach you how to ride a horse properly.'

'Oh, thank you. But I have no horse, you see.'

'Then we shall have to address that problem first, shan't we?' he said.

The two lovers were still chuckling about Claudette's ecstatic response later that evening as they lay in each other's embrace on top of Phoebe's bed, taking advantage of the light breeze that filled the curtains like sails. They had made love, after a long day of wanting to say more about their passionate feelings than had been said before, about the love Phoebe had discovered, buried, asleep, patiently waiting for summer. Ransome's waiting, on the other hand, had been far less patient.

'But you didn't come to find me, Buck,' she whispered, sprawling across him. 'You didn't even know I was here.'

'I tried to put you out of my mind, sweetheart. You were so set against remarriage, weren't you? And even if you had not been, I was nowhere near the top of your list, was I? But I *couldn't* get you out of my thoughts, and I couldn't find a woman I wanted half as much as you. All I could do was to watch what your brother got up to and to be there at the right time. I knew he had a place somewhere in Surrey, but the rest was pure chance. If he'd won that game instead of lost it, it would have taken me a bit longer to find you, that's all.'

'Could you not have asked Mama, or the Templeman boys?'

'Yes, and let her start interfering again? Not likely, sweetheart. And the Templeman idiots would have it all over town that I was still lusting after Hawkin's sister, after all these years.'

'Which you were, my lord?'

'Which I was, Madame Donville. But I'm careful who I tell my affairs to. And since you are so eager,' he said, sleepily smoothing a hand over her arm, 'to find out what I'm up to at Mortlake, I shall take you over there tomorrow and show you.'

'I am *not* eager to find out what you're up to,' she retorted. 'If you choose to have another house so close to my brother and his wife, I'm sure it's no concern of mine.'

'You are *bursting* with curiosity, *madame*. You cannot deny it.'

She squirmed as his smoothing hand slid down on to her hip. 'Well, just a *little* curious, my lord. I dare say there are plenty of men who require two houses so close together. As long as you have only one wifely mistress, I don't think I shall be making too much fuss about it.'

'Good. So the little outing to Mortlake in your phaeton was simply to take the evening air, was it?' He caught her as she tried to roll away, pulling her back under him. 'Just a *little* curious, were you? Eh?'

'No!' she retorted. 'I was *green* with jealousy, and fury, and *desperate* to know who you kept there. And how did you know, anyway?'

'The workmen,' he said, smiling in the dark. 'They saw you turn round. They were not too impressed by your driving skills, sweetheart.'

'I was trying not to weep,' she whispered. 'The Countess explained to me today, about the orphans. I would never have guessed it.'

'Oh…nymph. Come here. I should have told you. I *could* have.'

She did not ask him why he had not, having been offered a perfectly plausible reason to do with the kind of reticence very few would have associated with the outspoken, devil-may-care Buck Ransome.

'Do you mind…about the orphans?' he asked.

'I think what you're doing is *wonderful,* my love. We'll have one house for them, and this one for our own children. I know several good women who'd want to work there.'

'I like the sound of our own family, my lovely

Phoebe. Like the horse for your daughter, I think we could address that problem immediately, don't you?'

'Mmm,' she said, snuggling closer to him. 'First things first, my lord.'

The second of Phoebe's visits to Greenwater, accompanied this time by Hetty, Tabby, Claudette and Leon, was a much more lively affair that did justice to the homeliness Ransome had tried to create in the warm colours and robust farmhouse-type furnishings. She was now able to understand the multiple dining chairs and benches, and the lack of ostentation that had seemed so strange before. The upstairs rooms held only two beds each, but the new extension had provided more, as well as rooms for 'the mistress' about whom they could laugh and tease, now she was explained.

Outside in the grounds, gardeners had made small plots where the young boys could learn how to grow things. There were ponies for the lads to care for, an aviary for birds, hen coops, goats and their kids. The boys, Ransome told them, had no idea where milk came from, or eggs, and some had never tasted them. Watching him stride about in his shirt sleeves, enthusiastically leading them from wood-workshop to coach-house and then, finding the two first occupants and catching them up like a father with a squealing hug, Phoebe felt again the astonishment of seeing the other side of the man she had once thought to be no more than a well-heeled coxcomb. Ashamed by her blinkered disposition, she knew that, if her sister-in-law's opinion of him had not been accidently disproved, she herself would still be harbouring doubts about his ability to be faithful.

The little lads clung to their hands, dragging them along to show them their favourite hen and her chicks, the tack room, the coachman, grooms and ponies, the part of the river they were allowed to fish. Their emaciated bodies were beginning to fill out, their scars of ill treatment to heal with new pink flesh, their speech so full of London slang that Leon and Ransome had to act as interpreters. Claudette was fascinated by it, challenging some of Ransome's good intentions by her casual references to one's 'bread-basket' and to the 'bum-trap' by whom the boys had once been caught and 'clapped up in the Fleet' until their release was paid for by 'this 'ere High Stickler with rolls of the soft.' Had they not indicated 'milor', she might at first have been no wiser for the information, but in half an hour her vocabulary had improved beyond recognition. The party's removal to Ham to see the Earl and Countess was seen as an interruption to Claudette's education, although the visit to Mortlake had shown her the direction in which her young life was about to change, as well as that of the adults.

About the eventual loss of her dear governess

Claudette was becoming less concerned since Mama had explained to her what it would mean to Miss Maskell and Uncle Leon. Both of them needed security in their lives, someone to love and make a home with, and if an eldest son marrying a governess was rather unconventional, well, that was hardly surprising, coming from their family. One should not be afraid of being unconventional, Claudette's mama told her, when one's happiness was at stake. Besides which, there could be no better woman for Uncle Leon than dear Tabby.

That same morning, the Earl and Countess had been supervising the clearing out of some of the upper rooms and attics at Ham House and had come across spare items of furniture that would be useful to Leon for his 'cottage.' Now they were all spread out in the Great Hall like a house auction, with the usual eclectic mixture of junk, valuable and sentimental items covered with the dust of generations, old-fashioned and moth-eaten hangings, toys, pictures, weapons brought home from the wars with outdated uniforms and strange headgear. Being comparative newcomers to the house and its accoutrements, his lordship could not recognise much of what had been stored away and saw no good reason to keep it.

'We shall throw some of this lot on the bonfire,' he said with a glint in his eye. There was nothing as much fun as a blazing good bonfire. 'Some of the furniture will do for Leon. These pictures too. Those he doesn't want can be sold at auction.'

'I'll have those miniatures up on the wall of my Duchess's Closet,' said the Countess. 'Now why don't you take Leon down to the cottage for a look round, Wilbraham, dear? Then we shall know what's needed. No good giving him rubbish if he doesn't like it.'

Not surprisingly, the two men were accompanied on their short walk by Miss Maskell and Claudette, who were eager to give advice on every aspect of interior decoration which they saw as entirely their province, while wishing to prevent Leon filling his new home with unfashionable cast-offs from the Dysart's attic. The Countess had already seen the problem.

'Some of this stuff,' she said to Hetty, Phoebe and Ransome, 'is absolute rubbish, and if it's not sorted out, Wilbraham will be burning things I could use and keeping things that are quite revolting simply because he likes them. Look at this pair of two turbaned figures, for instance. Did you ever see anything more ridiculous? I expect he'll keep them. But here's something I *know* he'll not want to keep. Buck dear, just pull out that long box, will you? Yes, that one.'

'The sword-box, my lady?'

'Yes, dear, it's a pair of rapiers. He'll not want to keep it. I brought it out of the Duchess's Room hidden just inside the door to the service-passage.'

'The one in the wallpaper?' Phoebe said, craning forwards to look.

'Yes, the concealed one. I believe she used to exercise with rapiers until her gout prevented it. There,' she said, sweeping off the cobwebs and opening the lid, 'still as good as new. Wilbraham's brother John was killed in a duel, you know. Someone made up a song about John's lovely wife, but he was no swordsman. So rapiers will not be wanted here, I think. You take them, Buck. Why, Phoebe dear…are you all right? Does all this bring back a memory? Would you rather…?'

'Oh, no, my lady, thank you. Nothing like that. It's just so…er, strange.' Taking one of the rapiers in her hand, she lifted it out of its box and held it, balancing it lightly, though with nothing like the skill she had seen demonstrated by the Hawkynnes. So, the rapiers had belonged to the Duchess of Lauderdale who had used them for exercise. But what had *she* to do with the quarrel? Had *that* Phoebe Hawkynne suffered from the kind of female interference she herself had fled from?

Ransome took it from her and replaced it. 'You should sit down, sweetheart,' he said. 'See, Hetty has brought you some water. Take a sip.'

'Thank you. The rapiers are beautifully made, are they not? Is there a date somewhere?' She took the glass and sipped, just to please them.

'Inside the lid. Wilkin. Cheapside. London. 1650. That date would be about correct for the Lauderdales, wouldn't it, my lady?'

'The Countess of Dysart remarried in 1672, I believe, by which time she had quite a family. The eldest daughter Elizabeth married Lord Lorne, the young heir to the ninth Earl of Argyll, but I believe it was not a success. Her two sons were born up in the Yellow Satin Bedroom. Which reminds me,' she went on while her hands lifted and moved a pile of papers and pictures spread out on the table, 'there's something here that came from the cabinet in that room, which will almost certainly find its way to the bonfire if I don't rescue it first. A little mystery…ah! Here it is!' Her hands emerged, holding a small linen package with a piece of faded red ribbon hanging from it, as if it had been undone and put aside. Laying it on Phoebe's lap, she invited her to unwrap it. 'There you are. Take a look.'

'It's…a button,' Phoebe whispered. 'A *gold* button.'

'Looks rather like a waistcoat button,' Ransome said. 'What does the little note say? Look, there's writing on it.'

It was faded and brown with age, written in the most beautiful copperplate hand. Phoebe read, *'The button cut off my waistcoat by Sir Leo Hawkynne, Secretary to his Grace the Duke of Lauderdale, here at Ham House, being the only man I ever loved, though he will never know of it. Written on this 23rd*

day of June, AD 1676. Oh, that is *so* sad,' she said.
'So…*so* sad.'

The memory returned. The young woman's expression of adoration. The pain as she watched him kiss his wife. The furtive concealment of the button. And exactly *whose* waistcoat was it? Perhaps she would never know, but if Elizabeth had told a little comforting fib, she could surely be excused? For she had written as if Sir Leo had cut it off the waistcoat while *she* was wearing it, which put a different connotation on the facts, connotations which were more like what she *wanted* to believe than the truth. Poor Elizabeth, made to marry, no doubt, a man she could never love, by whom she was obliged to bear children. Was there something about the Yellow Satin Bedroom then, where birds in cages had been placed all round the windows at some stage?

Phoebe knuckled a teardrop away from her cheek before it dropped on to the note, but Ransome had seen it. 'Why, sweetheart…is it so sad? A little keepsake, that's all. Don't weep.' Tenderly, he removed the linen and its contents and passed them to Hetty.

'It's nothing,' she whispered, mentally sending an apology to the desolate young woman for whom it had meant everything and all she could ever hope for. A button. Cut off by his sword. 'She meant it to be a keepsake, so it should be kept, my lady.'

'You're right, of course,' said the Countess, sympathetically. 'Keepsakes are meant for keeping, so you take it, Phoebe dear, since it refers to your ancestor. I've no idea who could have been so in love with Sir Leo without him knowing of it. Obviously it was not his wife. If I come across the waistcoat, my dear, I'll keep it for you, shall I?'

'Thank you. I would like to have that too. In memory.'

'In memory of what, sweetheart?' Ransome said, smiling at her whimsy.

She smiled back at him, her heart overflowing with emotion. 'Oh, I'm being sentimental,' she said. 'Love is such a fragile thing, isn't it?'

'It is indeed, dear,' said Hetty. 'It is indeed.'

Having shown signs of fragility herself, Phoebe returned to Richmond after a day in which the last remaining pieces of her life fell neatly into place, as if the whole saga of events had been shaped to fit a previously ordained plan. She knew such things happened, but to others, not to oneself.

They sat together in the little topiary garden at the side of Ferry House, talking about plans for the future as they had not done before. 'I think we might do some entertaining of our own,' Ransome said, resting a hand on her shoulder and twisting a black curl round his thumb. 'How does her ladyship feel about holding a dinner party for all the helpful and unhelpful relatives and friends?

The French Set, too? We could hold a betrothal ball, if you prefer. Then a wedding breakfast? Whatever?'

'Then am I betrothed, dear heart?'

'Er…I think so. Aren't you?'

'Well, don't intended husbands get down on one knee and offer their intended wives some kind of token, my lord? A ring of sorts?'

'A *ring*! Oh…er…yes. That's right. Here—' he said, digging into his waistcoat pocket '—is something I had made in case I should ever find you. I'd have given it to you some years ago, but you seemed rather against the idea, I remember. Now, I wonder if it fits. Give me your hand. No, the other one. There!'

Like the very last piece of the picture, the exquisite golden ring slipped on to her finger as if it had been waiting only for her to submit to Fate. 'A white pearl moon surrounded by diamonds,' she said. 'Oh, it's perfect! Thank you.'

'The most perfect I could find, sweetheart. For a perfect woman.'

'And it's almost like the pendant in the portrait, Buck. Was that intentional?'

'Partly. But Lady Hawkynne's enamel moon would not have been suitable for my Phoebe. I wanted something more brilliant. More appropriate.'

She had teased him, not in the least expecting he would have given a moment's thought to the purchase of a ring, let alone the ceremony that went with it. Nor did she think he would have given much thought to whether she was betrothed, or still his mistress, as long as she was his. The process had been fluid, as he'd said to Ross, with his tongue firmly in his cheek.

But now she enclosed his head within her arms, drawing his face to hers, offering herself, her love and her life for as long as he wanted them. 'Let's go up,' she said. 'It's getting late, and we have a lot to celebrate, dear heart. We'll talk about dinner parties tomorrow, shall we?'

She had not been prepared for him to lift her in his arms and to carry her through the house and up the stairs as if she was too exhausted to walk, but she had time, between kisses, to recall something similar that had happened to the other Phoebe. But then, of course, they had been quarrelling, and *her* quarrels with Viscount Ransome were well and truly over.

Epilogue

The Yellow Satin Bedroom and its adjoining dressing room on the first floor, now closed to the public, was created by the sixth Earl of Dysart after he inherited in 1799. There was, however, a Yellow Bedchamber on the ground floor when the Duchess of Lauderdale lived there at the time of my story in 1676. This became known as The Volury Room after 1683, from the bird theme used to decorate it. All rather confusing, I thought. So I have brought the use of the Yellow Satin Bedroom on the first floor into Part I because it suits my story better, and I have made mention of the birds for the same reason, hoping that those informed people who know Ham House well will accept my fusing of the two rooms into one. All other rooms are as they should be, though it is not easy to find one's way around the alterations to the grounds outside, the old walks, walls and pathways. I hope any discrepancies will not spoil the story.

It is a fact that the Duchess's eldest daughter, known as Betty, gave birth to her two sons in the Yellow Bedchamber in 1680 and 1682 and that her marriage to the eldest son of the Earl of Argyll was not a happy one. They lived apart after 1696. She was seventeen years old at the time of the story, her sister Katherine about two years younger. The second-eldest son of the Duchess, Thomas, born in 1651, became a famous soldier. Although in my story he comes across as rather immature, I am sure he became the charming man much commended for his bravery.

Portraits exist of the Duke and Duchess of Lauderdale, together and separate, as does the bronze bust of the Duchess's mother. The portrait of Sir Leo and Lady Phoebe Hawkynne is, of course, quite fictitious. A childhood portrait of the sixth Earl, Wilbraham, hangs in the Great Hall near that of his beloved wife, Anna Maria, who died in 1804, the year after the story. The 1803 pen-and-watercolour painting by Thomas Rowlandson (1756–1827) of 'Lord Dysart Treating his Tenantry' is in the possession of the Tollemache family. This event would probably have taken place each year at harvest-time, but I have brought it forward to June to fit my story.

The quotation on page 250 is from John Donne, the seventeenth-century English poet and one-time Dean of St Paul's Cathedral in London.

The little gold moon pendant made by the first Phoebe's brother, Timothy Laker, was passed down through the Hawkynne (later Hawkin) family until it reached Sir Leon, the second Phoebe's father. His wife inherited it but did not appreciate its significance so, when she became Lady Templeman, she kept it in her jewel-box because it was unfashionable. It was only after she died that it came, with a few other trinkets, to Claudette, Lady Ransome's eldest daughter. But by this time the Hawkynne portrait was in the possession of her Uncle Leon at his Harley Street house, and Claudette was able to relate the two.

The black velvet waistcoat was never found, but this is not surprising at a time when clothes were passed down through the family, then to servants, until they literally dropped to pieces. The remaining gold buttons would have been removed and re-used, time and again.

Leon Hawkin and Tabitha Maskell were married later in 1803, but his commission to paint the Ham House renovations came to an abrupt end with the death of the Countess the following year, after which the Earl left Ham House for many years. So they closed 'the cottage' at Ham and went to live as housemaster and housemistress at Greenwater, Mortlake, to look after the orphans, by which time Leon was able to sell everything he produced, like his friend Thomas Rowlandson. He exhibited at the Royal Academy almost every year after that, still keeping Hetty as his housekeeper and still maintaining his London house on Harley Street. Some of the orphans became artists too.

The Viscount and Viscountess Ransome continued to live at Ferry House, with its productive gardens, and at their London home, where they entertained and raised a large family of sisters and a brother for Claudette. It was not until many years later, when Phoebe looked into the records of the Hawkynne family, that she discovered the date of Sir Leo and Phoebe's wedding to be one year *after* the date on the note found with the button. Which told her what we knew, that the scene in the Great Hall was enacted before the two were married. Weddings were not allowed to interrupt the Duke's plans; Phoebe and Sir Leo had to wait upon His Grace's generosity.

MORE ABOUT THIS BOOK

MORE ABOUT THE AUTHOR

ABOUT THE NATIONAL TRUST

INSPIRATION FOR WRITING
Scandalous Innocent

In most of my previous novels I have included real places, and sometimes real people too, to give an extra flavour of authenticity to the story. It seems a pity not to use those parts of our history that are still there to be seen – large houses, castles, palaces and natural features, some of which have changed little over the centuries. One of the closest great houses to me is Ham House at Richmond in Surrey: a National Trust property that celebrates its four-hundredth anniversary in 2010. What better reason could there be for using it in a story?

"…Ham House celebrates its four-hundredth anniversary in 2010…"

Visiting it, reading about it, about the occupants of the vast rooms throughout its history, their disappointments and hopes, their dysfunctional families and political intrigues, would provide any writer with a wealth of material. Reading the guidebook alone is enough to set ideas in motion: the Civil War dangers, the periods of excess, neglect, and the changes made to the house and gardens, the sad marriages, bankruptcies, premature deaths, and the influence of the French Revolution on the local population. There is no shortage of ideas, the only question being which era to choose for its most interesting characters, the amount of information available, the outside events that might contribute to the storyline and, not least, the kind of lifestyle people lived. The more colourful this is, literally and metaphorically, the more fun one can have with the characters.

I decided not to have my hero and heroine live at Ham House but instead to associate them closely with the owners at the time – to give them the independence and freedom to come and go. With *Scandalous Innocent* I took the unusual step of using two periods, the first in 1676, only ten years after the Great Fire of London, when many households were in a state of flux (always a good device), and the second in 1803, at the time of the French Revolution. This must, I thought, tie up somehow with the noble fraternity of French émigrés then living in Richmond. The one constant feature would be the house itself, reflecting not only two very different periods but also the changes, structural and decorative, that affected the lives of the main characters. It's surprising how the changes to a house of that importance can affect the tone of the story and the kind of behaviour in which the occupants indulge. To me, the main point of writing *historical* fiction is that social mores and the behaviour of the participants belong securely to certain historical periods and do not transplant well into the modern world. So it makes sense to use all the quirks of the chosen period – except, of course, the language, which would make reading unbearable.

The Ham House owners in my two stories needed no extra embellishments to make them interesting. They fitted in as if they knew the plot already, warts and all, particularly the larger-than-life Lauderdales, who were actually more fascinating than I have made them. Powerful women in history are not hard to find, nor are they all entirely under the domination of men, and to find ways in which women can 'kick over the traces' and still retain their dignity is one of the aims of the romantic fiction writer. There are, naturally, things a heroine could not and *would* not do. Living entirely alone is one of them, so she has to be placed somewhere on the edge of society, making her reasonably independent yet rather vulnerable, which is why the idea of marriage to the right man must be made to sound more attractive than the alternative. Staying single was never a happy prospect, yet my heroines have usually had some kind of experience that has made them resistant to the idea of marriage. This is where I had to persuade them both, either by a set of inescapable circumstances, as in the second Phoebe's story, or by a love rekindled, as with the first Phoebe. Having strong, opinionated women also acts as a link between the stories, as 'strength of character' is what Mills & Boon® readers expect. We like to see ourselves putting up a fight. From the safety of our armchairs, of course.

"...the seventeenth century was a time of extravagant gestures, quick tempers and overreaction..."

The position of secretary to the powerful Duke in the first story seemed like a useful place for my hero to be – he's influential, socially adept, intelligent, wealthy, experienced and peripatetic – which explains why he and Phoebe had not sorted out their differences before. This also gave her time to gain a 'reputation'. As Samuel Pepys's Diaries show, the seventeenth century was a time of extravagant gestures, quick tempers and overreaction, and the sword-contest between Phoebe and Leo would not have seemed as absurd to them as it would in a later era. Even so, coming early on in the story, I could not allow it to settle the quarrel as it was meant to: I had to make it do the opposite, as in life. It made things worse for a while, until the hero tackled the problem head-on – although there had to be some question left unanswered to take the first story on into the next one. I liked the idea of this 'something' being as small as a button, but the truth is that I didn't know what it was going to be until the seventeen-year-old Elizabeth Tollemache picked it up in the ghost scene. Honestly, she did it without any instruction from me. Nor did I even know there was going to be a ghost scene. It appeared quite without warning. When it happens like that, I just let it.

Things moved around a little with the second Phoebe and her brother Leon, who are direct descendants of the first Leo and Phoebe. I had to draw a family tree to make sure the generations coincided with the sixth Earl at Ham House, but it was coincidental that the lovely Wilbraham and his Countess were there doing wonderful things when Phoebe and her Buck were at Ferry House in Richmond. Another family tree, more ground-plans, dates and maps were needed for this, as discrepancies are picked up immediately by sharp-eyed readers. Naturally, I needed my second hero to be quite different from the first, both in character and lifestyle, but the similarities are that Buck, like Leo, is already known to Phoebe, disliked but attractive. He also has the upper hand from the start, and has a powerful ally at Ham House, who this time helps rather than hinders. I would rather have liked the Countess to live longer, but she didn't, and that is a fact an author may not change.

The sad truth that dissolute young men sometimes lost their entire inheritances was the start of my second story, and one can read of many occasions when families suffered terribly from out-of-control gambling. And, since Mortlake featured in the first story as Phoebe's home, I wanted to continue the link in the second by having Buck Ransome live there, and Phoebe's other brother too. Living so close, there had to be some serious interference and wrong conclusions between them to throw things off course.

There is a danger, though, of presenting a set of problems that could so easily be solved if only the characters would act a little more rationally.

6

So the main problem of 'the other mistress' had to be made water-tight – not only by hearsay, which is hardly enough to go on, but by taking a look at first hand, which is what Phoebe did. Interestingly, what she actually witnessed was the opposite of the construction she put on it, which is so often the case. This is why I like to look at both sides of the picture to avoid the obvious. I am not naturally a devious person, but I believe some deviousness may have developed in me as a writer of fiction. I have to admit to becoming dreadfully tangled at times.

HOW CLOSE IS THE HAM HOUSE OF TODAY TO THE HAM HOUSE SEEN IN *Scandalous Innocent*?

I made several visits to Ham House, first to get the general feel of the place, and then to fill in some details I knew I could use – such as the routes my characters would have taken, which way the hall doors opened, and where exactly was the fountain in the little orchard. Visits also gave me a more accurate sense of scale than photographs did, and I found that the great hall with the chequered floor was not as large as it appears in the guidebook.

"…Visits also gave me a more accurate sense of scale…"

But inevitably there are differences that one must accept – like the room now used for displaying artefacts, the upper storey and some of the second-floor rooms closed to visitors, the servants' access passage that is hidden until one asks the reason for those doors in the wallpaper, and the old kitchen garden and orangery, which have changed beyond recognition. Here, one must impose a fertile imagination on what *is* there and what *was* there. To their credit, the National Trust has tried to recreate the interior as closely as possible, using some of the seventeenth-century furniture that could have been used by Phoebe and Leo, but not the billiard table, and sourcing similar items on loan from the Victoria and Albert Museum in London. And although the house looks massive from the outside, on the inside it is really quite compact. One particular bonus was the painting by Thomas Rowlandson that appeared in an earlier Ham House guidebook, showing our dear sixth Earl of Dysart with his missus at a garden party for the workers. That was a piece of history I had to include – though the space they used has changed over the years, as has the other side of the house where the great Wilderness

8

was. Thankfully, the River Thames is still there, although I believe even that has changed shape a little in four hundred years.

BIBLIOGRAPHY

My first essential reading was the guidebook
to Ham House that gave me the exact layout
of the rooms and all they contained, both past
and present. Each generation made alterations,
which had to be pinpointed exactly for each of
my two periods – right down to the colour of
the staircase. This helped to set the scene in my
mind for what might conceivably happen there:
the furniture and décor, light sources and views
from windows, hidden passages and the way
rooms connect (which determines how characters move about the house), the amenities in the
gardens, hedges and seats, secluded places and
pathways, access to the river, and so on. Ground
plans are enlarged and simplified, altered to suit
the period, notes and sketches added.

The second essential reading was *Ham House
and Its Owners Through Five Centuries, 1610-
2006* by Evelyn Pritchard, published by the
Richmond Local History Society. This told me
everything about the families, so anything I
invented had to fit into this framework. This is
not as inhibiting as it sounds; rather it provides
a useful scaffolding for the story, and often
makes the writer more inventive in an attempt
to avoid logistical problems.

As I had never written about the 1700s before,
I found Liza Picard's *Restoration London*
immensely useful for information on daily life
and customs, and I consulted *Richmond Past* by
John Cloake for details about what was there
during the times of my stories. Old maps and
prints are very informative too.

JULIET LANDON – BIOGRAPHY

Juliet Landon is the pseudonym I use for my historical fiction. Jan Messent is my real name, to which my life as a professional textile artist and author of embroidery books belongs. After teaching art, English and history in secondary schools (which I enjoyed but never saw as a lifelong career), I gave all my attention to my family while working on embroidery at home. This led me to write and illustrate books on embroidery design (my own and other people's), adding lecturing and teaching to the list as the children grew older. For various publishers I produced about twenty books, large and small, including one to accompany 'The Bayeux Tapestry Finale', which is an eight-foot hanging reconstructing the missing end of the ancient embroidery belonging to Bayeux in France, made in eleventh-century England.

It was my abiding interest in history (which also permeates my embroidery) that made me wonder if I could also write historical fiction, and when I sent my first attempt, set in the 1340s, to Mills & Boon, they accepted it. Because they are such a delight to work with I carried on, and am now working on my twentieth novel – under the name of Juliet Landon, to avoid confusion. So began a writing career parallel with my work in embroidery, one taking precedence over the other as time and circumstance allow. I no longer lecture or teach, but continue to work full-time at my peaceful home, spanning historical periods from Roman Britain to Regency England. A new Jan Messent embroidery book will appear early in 2010 on Celtic, Viking and Anglo-Saxon themes, just before *Scandalous Innocent* is published, while Juliet Landon beavers away on a story set in Roman Bath. Do the two writers ever get mixed up? No. Women are multi-taskers, aren't they?

However, we both live in Fleet in Hampshire, next door to my daughter and her family. I also have two married sons and a grandson, and am President of the Basingstoke branch of the Embroiderers' Guild.

JULIET LANDON ON WRITING

What do you love about being a writer?

Everything – except perhaps the revisions.
These are essential, of course, and make for a
better book, but I am usually well into the next
one when I have to go back and tweak the one
before. But I love being able to give pleasure
and romantic escapism to readers just as much
as I enjoy being each character, playing out their
roles, thinking their thoughts, imagining their
lives and emotions. (Wearing their clothes, too.)
It's extremely good therapy to drag them into
some emotional tangle and then to walk away
until you've decided how to get them out of it.

Where do you go for inspiration?

As I have a large library of history and art
books, and write history, that is where I find
my ideas and themes, with each story generat-
ing fresh situations. I love reading social history,
but one cannot exclude the politics, as the two
depend upon each other. The adage that truth
is stranger than fiction is so often demonstrated
through historical events, particularly at times
of social unrest – deprivation and unfair laws,
women's struggles against convention, family
feuds and delinquency, for instance. There is
never a time when I'm stuck for inspiration;
the usual problem is how to make the current
idea totally different from the last. I usually
get round this by changing periods frequently.
This keeps me on my toes and demands more
research. I also tried writing in the first person
recently and, despite thinking that it might
inhibit me, I found that I thoroughly enjoyed
it. (*Marrying the Mistress*: Juliet Landon)

"...I enjoy
being each
character,
playing
out their
roles..."

How important to you is historical accuracy in romantic fiction?

The short answer is *very*. A writer can make historical events up, just as she can invent characters, but if she is thinking to change politics, religion, the monarchy or the laws of the land, then readers (not to mention editors) would have a problem with that. Accuracy comes down to a more personal level with writers who sometimes impose twenty-first-century perceptions and behaviour on people of earlier centuries, which is tricky because the earlier you go back in time the less likely it is that people *think* the way we do now. Time and relationships were perceived differently, for instance, as were people's attitudes to birth, marriage, death and religion, ownership and work. The best historical writers are those who understand these differences and use them, yet still produce a believable story that rings true to our modern ears. Early writers of historical fiction used 'ancient speak' that was accepted at the time but which now sounds ridiculous. Our records are mainly of what people wrote, not how they spoke to each other. Authors usually get round this by avoiding modern slang and words that are glaringly before their time, or inappropriately old-fashioned. Other areas are easy to spot – costume errors, building regula-tions, that kind of thing – but I find it hard to excuse a character who is found doing some-thing incorrectly when he is supposed to be proficient at it. Rather like a story I read about the nuns making the Bayeux Tapestry licking the ends of the wool before threading it into the needles. There is no substitute for in-depth research, and the last thing you want a reader to say is, 'She wouldn't have done that.'

How much research do you do, and how do you know when to start writing?

One of the snares in researching a historical period is that, because it's less demanding than writing, you're tempted to go on for ever and never start your story. I like to do a lot of reading beforehand, so that I know my period as if I lived in it – from every angle. I keep information on record cards in file boxes, because they're easier to access that way, but only the *sources* of my references – not the notes themselves, as this might involve whole chapters. This tells me which book to look at for, say, medicines, the page numbers and the cross-references. However, for all my characters and their backgrounds I write every detail down on a file card, and sometimes I draw them too: date of birth, relatives, colouring, temperament, early life, etc. Only when I feel I know my characters and the story in enough detail for at least the first twenty thousand words (i.e. about three chapters) do I begin to write. I work from a page of notes giving me the chapter outline and the main events in order, and this usually overflows into the next chapter, because my characters sometimes do things I didn't know about or because something has to be explained before the chance is lost. If this ties in with the story as I originally saw it I let it stay, but if a character threatens to divert my plot I either revise my plan or bring it back on course. Controlled fluidity, it could be called.

"…I like to do a lot of reading beforehand…"

What one piece of advice would you give to a writer wanting to start a career?

Do what I didn't have the chance to do: attend a course in creative writing. This will show you how to structure a story, beginning, middle and end, how to find your 'voice' and your style.

You may have the most original story in the world, but unless you are a naturally gifted writer you'll need to learn how to string it together. If you can't do a course read books about writing fiction, and read other authors whose work you admire – not with a view to emulate but to see how they handle words, sentence structure, ideas and events, conversation and emotions.

Which book do you wish you had written?

Several, actually. But if I had to choose it would be *King Hereafter* by Dorothy Dunnett, my favourite historical author of all time. Scholarly, clever, witty, erudite, deep, brilliantly researched – the kind of book you can read over and over again, finding new things each time. It's about the eleventh-century Macbeth. A gem of a book.

Do your characters ever surprise you as you write?

Yes, constantly. I begin by thinking I know them quite well, but as soon as they get onto the page they take on a life of their own that amuses and delights me – saying things I had not planned, adopting mannerisms, showing frailties. People-watching is essential for writers, but more than anything else I believe that people are complex beings, contradictory, wayward, often inconsistent, and very much affected by circumstances. I like my characters to reflect something of the situation in which they find themselves and to respond to it – either appropriately or not.

How do you successfully and seamlessly merge fact with fiction?

This is part of the excitement of writing in this genre. First one has to decide which historical facts are needed to set the scene, and second how important this will be to the story of two people: the hero and heroine. In romantic fiction particularly, the attention must centre around these two characters more than anything else, so the idea is to use the facts as props only – to move the story on but not to take it over. Events like the Great Fire and the Plague, for instance, left their marks on the first Phoebe, but it was unnecessary to load her story with extraneous detail. The merging of facts was not difficult in that instance, when one recalls how many people were directly affected by these tragedies one way or another. In other words it was not specific to Phoebe; its effects were widespread and open to various interpretations.

I find that it helps me to 'see' my characters *in situ* and to watch them move through the scene I have set for them, doing what they would have done but always in the light of who *they* are, not who *I* am, how they are feeling, what they're wearing, standing on, being with, using, hearing, seeing. The historical props are a part of this scene, so the lighting is not good, the streets are filthy and smelly, there is very limited privacy and arguments tend to become public rather quickly, relatives interfere, communication takes days, transport is uncomfortable and maids are hard to find. This is why I usually set my stories within wealthy households. There's more to go wrong, more colourfully.

"...the merging of facts was not difficult..."

JULIET LANDON - A Writer's Life

Paper and pen, or straight onto the computer?

Paper and pen for the first two drafts. I like to hold a pen in my hand, to see all my alterations, and to sit in comfort when I'm creating. I put the third draft onto my laptop and tidy it up, print it off, make corrections, then write the next chapter.

Music or silence?

I dislike noise of any kind when I'm working, even music.

Morning or night?

I have been known to work morning, noon and night, but not any more. Morning is by far the best, the earlier the better – particularly in summer.

Do you have a writing schedule?

I try to write every day, if I can. When I'm not writing I'm working out the next scene in my head, or a resolution to an impasse, but to leave it for days is not helpful as I then have to think myself back into the characters and their situation.

Coffee or tea?

Strong coffee in the morning; Earl Grey in the afternoon. Cups, not beakers.

The first book you loved?

Black Beauty by Anna Sewell. I was crazy about horses, and still am.

The last book you read?

Wolf Hall by Hilary Mantel, the 2009 Man Booker Prize Winner. Utterly brilliant. Highly recommended. This is creative writing at its very best.

National Trust

ABOUT THE NATIONAL TRUST

The National Trust was founded in 1895 by three Victorian philanthropists – Miss Octavia Hill, Sir Robert Hunter and Canon Hardwicke Rawnsley.

"The need of quiet, the need of air, the need of exercise, and…the sight of sky and of things growing seem human needs, common to all men.'"

Octavia Hill (1838-1912)

Concerned about the impact of uncontrolled development and industrialisation, they set up the Trust to act as a guardian for the nation. For more than a hundred years the National Trust has looked after places which connect the present and the future to the past. It works to preserve and protect the coastline, countryside and buildings of England, Wales and Northern Ireland.

The Trust does this in a range of ways: through practical caring and conservation, through learning and discovery, and through encouraging millions of people to visit and enjoy their national heritage.

Without its many members, visitors and volunteers it would be unable to carry on with its work. However, it is not just through visiting properties that people help out. The Trust's many commercial activities include National Trust tearooms and shops, and also holiday cottages – an increasingly popular choice for places to stay.

The Trust protects over seven hundred miles of coastline and in total it looks after 626,051 acres (253,349 hectares) of countryside, moorland, beaches and coastline.

Among the historic properties in the Trust's care

are two hundred and fifteen houses and gardens, forty castles, seventy-six nature reserves, six World Heritage Sites, twelve lighthouses, and forty-three pubs and inns.

The millions of objects in the care of the National Trust reflect its diversity. Conservation staff and volunteers care for an astonishing range of structures and contents – from over twenty-six sets of samurai armour and nineteen magnificent paintings by Turner, to the Oscar awarded to George Bernard Shaw, the national collection of lawnmowers, fifty-seven meat strainers and a photograph album the size of a postage stamp.

An estimated fifty million people visited the National Trust's open-air properties in 2007.

Visit www.nationaltrust.org.uk to find out more.

HAM HOUSE HISTORY

Ham House was built in 1610 for Sir Thomas Vavasour, Knight Marshal to James I. On Sir Thomas's death in 1620 the house passed briefly to the Earl of Holdernesse, before becoming the home of William Murray, a childhood friend of Charles I, in 1626. Between 1637 and 1639 he remodelled the interior of Ham. When the English Civil War broke out in 1642 Murray naturally joined the Royalist cause, and was created first Earl of Dysart in 1643 (although not officially until 1651). He spent the rest of his life in exile, making only brief visits to England, before dying in Edinburgh in 1655.

© NTPL/Derek Croucher

Murray had no male heir, and Ham passed to his eldest daughter, Elizabeth. Her father's titles were conferred upon her in 1670, when she became Countess of Dysart. Her first marriage in 1648 was to Sir Lionel Tollemache, third Baronet of Helmingham Hall in Suffolk, a wealthy and cultivated squire. Even before her husband's death in 1669, Lady Dysart was rumoured to have formed an attachment to the ambitious John Maitland, first Duke of Lauderdale, Secretary of State for Scotland. Following their

marriage in 1672, they extended and refur-
nished Ham as a palatial villa for one of the
most powerful ministers of Charles II. Much
of this luxurious interior decoration survives,
together with pictures, furniture and textiles.
After the Duke's death in 1682 the Duchess had
to curb her extravagance, and was eventually
reduced to pawning her favourite pictures and
jewellery. Crippled by gout, and embittered by
years of legal wrangling with the Duke's
relatives, Elizabeth died at Ham in 1698.

*"...the Duchess
had to
curb her
extravagance..."*

Ham House and the Dysart title then passed
to her eldest son from her first marriage: Lionel
Tollemache, third Earl of Dysart (1649-1727).
Lionel had inherited the Tollemache estates
nearly thirty years before, and took little interest
in the house that had been so much his mother's
creation. By contrast, the third Earl's grandson
and heir – another Lionel, the fourth Earl –
carried out major structural repairs in the 1740s
(which included the rebuilding of the bays on
the north and south fronts), and filled many of
the rooms with new furniture and paintings.
Most notably, the Queen's Bedchamber, built by
the Lauderdales, was converted into a first-floor
drawing-room, with the mahogany chairs, gilt
pier-glasses and tables, and tapestries after
Watteau which survive *in situ*. The fifth Earl
was renowned for his rigid economy, and his
only changes at Ham appear to have been a
partial landscaping of the garden.

He was succeeded in 1799 by his brother,
Wilbraham, who immediately made improvements inside and outside the house. The
sixth Earl was a generous patron of Reynolds
and Gainsborough, but most of his changes
were antiquarian in spirit, enhancing Ham's
seventeenth-century character. Little changed
at Ham between the sixth Earl's death in 1821

and 1884, when William, ninth Earl of Dysart, came of age.

Sixty years of benign neglect had left the house and its contents in urgent need of repair, and Lord Dysart embarked on a thorough restoration campaign: the roof was renewed, electricity and heating installed, and much of the seventeenth-century furniture repaired. The ninth Earl died in 1935, when Ham passed to his second cousin, Sir Lyonel Tollemache. Sir Lyonel and his son, Cecil, gave Ham to the National Trust in 1948.

© National Trust 2009

FILMS AT HAM

Being close to London has made Ham ideal for being used as a filming location. While TV and film make up much of Ham's film credits, it is also frequently used for fashion shoots, TV commercials and comedy shows. Recent projects are:

44 Inch Chest (2009)
John Hurt, Ray Winstone, Ian McShane

Brideshead Revisited (2007)
Emma Thompson, Matthew Goode, Ben Whishaw

Never Let Me Go (2009/10)
Keira Knightley, Charlotte Rampling, Sally Hawkins

Spiceworld the Movie (1997)
Spice Girls, Richard E Grant

The Young Victoria (2009)
Rupert Friend, Miranda Richardson, Mark Strong, Emily Blunt

Amazing Mrs Pritchard (2006) BBC
Jane Horrocks, Janet McTeer

Ballet Shoes (2007) BBC
Victoria Wood, Emma Watson

Little Dorritt (2008) BBC
Andy Serkis, Matthew Macfadyen

Sense and Sensibility (2007) BBC
David Morrissey, Claire Skinner

As listed above, Ham House was home to one of 2009's most popular films – *The Young Victoria*.

The film chronicles Queen Victoria's ascension to the throne, focusing on the early and turbulent years of her reign and her legendary romance and marriage to Prince Albert.

Both the interiors and exteriors of Ham House were used in the film to represent Kensington Palace, where Victoria was born and spent her early years.

With a cast including Emily Blunt as Victoria, Jim Broadbent as King William and Miranda Richardson as the Duchess of Kent, producers including Martin Scorsese and Sarah Ferguson, Duchess of York, and with sumptuously shot scenes featuring stunning costumes and set designs, it was the period blockbuster for spring 2009.

Jorge Ferreira, Visitor Services Manager at Ham House, describes what it was like to be involved in the filming:

"The cast and crew were with us for just under a month in 2007, and returned for a few days last year. They seemed to enjoy their time at Ham and were everywhere – from the gardens to the Great Hall. These two areas, as well as the Long Gallery and Great Stairs, were used for scenes in the movie."

Little of Ham's interior was altered for the film, as Jorge explains:

"Many rooms and spaces within the House were barely touched, which is testimony to the grandeur of Ham House. Props aided some scenes, but the majority was shot *in situ*."

Visitors to Ham were shown snippets of the filming, although some work and scenes were hidden from view in anticipation of the final product.

Jane Austen's *Sense and Sensibility* is the story of two young sisters on a voyage of burgeoning sexual and romantic discovery. The death of Elinor and Marianne Dashwood's father throws their privileged world into chaos, and with no entitlement to his estate they are forced to live in poverty. For its three-part adaptation of the story in 2007 the BBC chose Ham House as the location for the interior of Norland, the Dashwood family home.

Harvey Edgington, Broadcast & Media Liaison Officer at the National Trust, recalls the filming:

"The BBC alighted on Ham as the ideal location for the tense scene involving the fate of the Dashwoods. The shoot involved building a lighting rig across the entrance hall, effectively as a suspended ceiling, and using one hundred and forty-four candles. Naturally rules were contractually put in to reduce fire risk, as well as the usual safeguards when shooting in a historical house."

GHOSTS AT HAM

Ham House is reputed to be one of the National
Trust's most haunted properties. A paranormal
investigation by the Ghost Club reckons that, in
total, there are around fifteen ghosts in residence,
with a large proportion being canine. In the
second part of *Scandalous Innocent*, Phoebe expe-
riences echoes from the past – echoes which still
appear today, particularly concerning
Elizabeth, Duchess of Lauderdale (1626-1698).

The Duchess's ghost is supposed to roam the
house still. Disquieted by the death of her
second husband, John Maitland (first Duke of
Lauderdale) in 1682, who had fallen out of
favour at court, she tried to sue his brother for
her husband's funeral expenses. The case lasted
ten years and, as costs mounted, Elizabeth
became penniless and gout-ridden, and was
forced to sell much of her valued collection
from the house. She died in 1698, after having
written: "I am a prisoner in my beloved Ham
House, and I will never leave…"

*"…Footsteps
have been
heard
overnight…"*

Footsteps and a rose scent often appear in her
ground-floor Bedchamber, pets refuse to enter,
and visitors often remark on being rather
terrified by her portrait, hanging over the fireplace. In the nearby Dining Room, wafts
of tobacco can be often smelt. It was Elizabeth's
husband, the first Duke, who enjoyed smoking
Virginia tobacco.

Footsteps have been heard overnight, and
occasionally footprints are found on the stairs
and in the Bedchamber, which appear to have
lifted the varnish from the floorboards. At times,
a lady clothed in a long black dress is spotted
going downstairs and into the Chapel. After her
husband's death, the Duchess of Lauderdale is

known to have spent much of the week preceding his funeral in the Chapel, praying alongside his coffin. During conservation cleaning one morning, a handprint was found among the dust on the rail of the Duchess's pew. The Chapel had been closed and alarmed since the previous clean.

Indeed, Sir Horace Walpole (1717-1797) commented:

"Every minute I expected to see ghosts sweeping by; ghosts I would not give sixpence to see, Lauderdales, Tallemaches (sic) and Maitlands…"

Many other ghosts too numerous to mention also frequent Ham House and other National Trust properties.

(Based on a chapter from: *Ghosts: Mysterious Tales from the National Trust* by Siân Evans, National Trust Books 2006)

THE QUEEN'S ANTECHAMBER WALL HANGINGS

"3 pieces of blew Damusk inpain'd and bordered wth. blew velvet embroidered wth. gould & fringed."

Ham House 1679 inventory

Textiles were a crucial part of creating an impressive interior in the Restoration period. Tapestries, made of wool, had been used for many years as decoration and draught-proofing, but by the Restoration period silk wall hangings were becoming fashionable. These textiles were the most expensive and luxurious part of the interior décor.

Due to its fragile and fine nature, silk is not durable. It is also extremely sensitive to light damage. Therefore, unlike tapestries and furniture from this period, these wall hangings seldom survive. At Ham there are silk wall hangings in the Queen's Antechamber and the Queen's Closet. They are renowned as rare survivals in furniture-history circles and offer an almost unique opportunity for the public to view a complete interior from the late seventeenth century.

Textile conservator May Berkouwer has won the contract to conserve the west wall section of the hangings in the Queen's Antechamber. The hanging needs to be transported to her studio in Sudbury, Suffolk. Purpose-built equipment has been employed to take the hanging down from the wall. The conservation work will take several years in total.

Fifty pence from the sale of every copy of *Scandalous Innocent* sold through National Trust shops will go to aid this conservation project.

NATIONAL TRUST MEMBERSHIP

Join today and you'll enjoy:

- **FREE** entry and parking at more than three hundred historic houses and gardens.

- **FREE** parking at our countryside and coastline locations.

- Your Members' Handbook – a complete guide to all the places you can visit.

- Regional Newsletters packed with details of special events at locations near you.

- Three editions of the National Trust magazine, featuring news, views, gardening and letters, exclusively for members.

Plus…

- Your membership will get you **FREE** admission to properties cared for by the National Trust for Scotland.

- There are also agreements with a number of other countries. If you're visiting any of these places and have a valid membership card, you can visit their National Trust facilities **FREE** or at a concessionary rate.

Join online today, and you will be e-mailed a temporary admission card, so you can make the most of your membership and start visiting National Trust properties straight away.

Visit **www.nationaltrust.org.uk** for more details or phone 0844 800 1895.

Best of all, you'll know that you are helping to protect the places you enjoy for ever, for everyone.

FROM THE USA

More than forty thousand Americans belong to the Royal Oak Foundation, the National Trust's US membership affiliate.

A not-for-profit organisation, the Royal Oak helps the Trust through the generous tax-deductible support of members and friends by making grants towards its work.

Royal Oak member benefits include:

- Free admission to properties of the National Trust and National Trust for Scotland.

- The National Trust Handbook.

- Three editions of the National Trust members' magazine.

- The quarterly Royal Oak newsletter.

Royal Oak also awards scholarships to US residents to study in Britain and sponsors lectures, tours and events in both the US and UK, designed to inform Americans of the Trust's work.

Visit **www.royal-oak.org**

REGENCY
Silk & Scandal

A season of secrets, scandal and seduction in high society!

Volume 1 – 4th June 2010
The Lord and the Wayward Lady
by Louise Allen

Volume 2 – 2nd July 2010
Paying the Virgin's Price
by Christine Merrill

Volume 3 – 6th August 2010
The Smuggler and the Society Bride
by Julia Justiss

Volume 4 – 3rd September 2010
Claiming the Forbidden Bride
by Gayle Wilson

8 VOLUMES IN ALL TO COLLECT!

www.millsandboon.co.uk
M&B

REGENCY
Silk & Scandal

*A season of secrets, scandal and
seduction in high society!*

Volume 5 – 1st October 2010
The Viscount and the Virgin
by Annie Burrows

Volume 6 – 5th November 2010
Unlacing the Innocent Miss
by Margaret McPhee

Volume 7 – 3rd December 2010
The Officer and the Proper Lady
by Louise Allen

Volume 8 – 7th January 2011
Taken by the Wicked Rake
by Christine Merrill

8 VOLUMES IN ALL TO COLLECT!

M&B

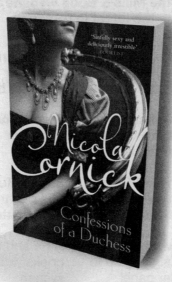

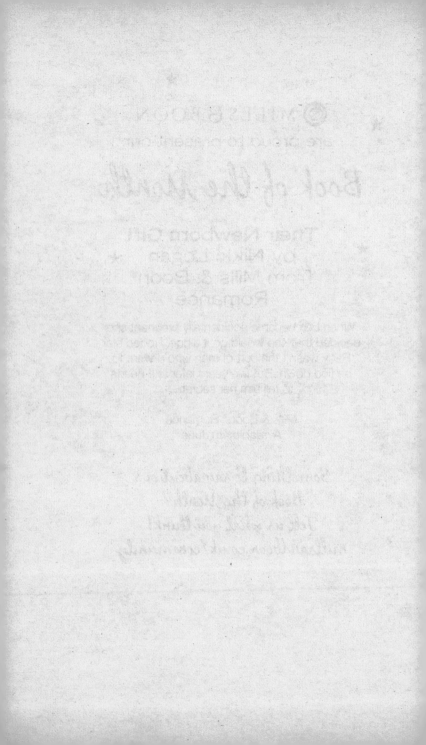